GLENANAAR

CANON SHEEHAN

Introduction
CON HOULIHAN

THE O'BRIEN PRESS
DUBLIN

This edition first published 1989
by The O'Brien Press Ltd.
20 Victoria Road Dublin 6 Ireland.
First published London 1905.

British Library Cataloguing in Publication Data
Sheehan, Patrick, *1852-1913*
Glenanaar. - 3rd ed
I.Title
823'.8 [F]
ISBN 0-86278-195-7

Cover illustration: Woman in Hilly Landscape,
Mildred Anne Butler. With permission from
Christies, Scotland.
Cover design: The Graphiconies

A classical romantic historical novel re-issued by popular demand

GLENANAAR

CANON PATRICK SHEEHAN

During his lifetime, Canon Sheehan's novels were read all over the English-speaking world, and translated into many languages including German, French, Italian, Spanish, Dutch, Hungarian. His outspokenness led to a slower rise to popularity in Ireland, but in the first half of the twentieth century he was a favourite all over the country.

He was born near Mallow, County Cork, in 1852. Poverty and landlord pressure forced the family to move into the town and when he was twelve he lost both parents. From such difficult circumstances he went on to study at St Colman's College, Fermoy, and later at Maynooth Seminary. He was ordained a priest in 1875. As a child and student he was known as a quiet, brooding type with little to say.

As a priest, Sheehan went to work in England, first in Plymouth then in Exeter, where his duties included saying Mass in Dartmoor Prison. He returned to serve as a curate in Mallow and Cobh, and in 1895 he was appointed parish priest of Doneraile, not far from Mallow. He spent the rest of his life there, doing parish work and writing.

He loved the people of Doneraile and was loved in return. Ann Teresa Murphy says:

> The people of Doneraile were not slow to appreciate that they had a talented man in their new parish priest. He had an enormous amount of reading behind him, a superb memory, great powers of observation, and a deep understanding of human nature, especially its weaknesses ... His two major goals in life were to serve God and country.

Canon Sheehan's thoughts and aspirations sprang

from the highest possible levels of idealism and integrity. One decision he made was not to keep a single penny of his income for himself. Most of his earnings from writing went to the bishop for works of charity in the diocese. Some were held back and distributed by the parish priest to cases of need in the area. He could not bear to know that there was anyone in Doneraile suffering for the want of food, clothing or footwear. Ways and means of keeping the donor's name a secret were constantly being devised by him.

He was prolific, and produced a book a year while living in Doneraile, as well as essays, pamphlets, stories and poems. Yet he never neglected his parish and became very involved in the efforts made there to achieve land reform — these efferts resulted in the passing of the Wyndham Act in 1903 giving every Irish farmer the right to his own holding. Canon Sheehan also saw to it that the mud cabins on the outskirts of Doneraile were demolished and replaced with stone cottages, and he played no small part in ensuring that Doneraile was the first town of its size in Ireland to have electricity.

Canon Sheehan's published works include: *My New Curate* (1900), *Luke Delmege* (1901), *Under the Cedars and the Stars* (essays) (1903), *Glenanaar* (1905), *Lisheen* (1907), *A Spoiled Priest and Other Stories* (1905), *The Queen's Fillet* (1911), *Miriam Lucas* (1912), *The Graves at Kilmorna* (1915), *Poems* (1921), *Tristram Lloyd* (completed by Rev. Henry Gaffney) (1929).

CON HOULIHAN

Born in Kerry, Con Houlihan took his masters degree in arts at University College Cork. He has worked for seventeen years as a fulltime journalist, winning many national awards – for sports journalism with the *Evening Press* and political journalism with *The Kerryman*. He has made thirty-one documentaries, with RTE and ITN. He has had a longterm interest in the work of Canon Sheehan.

INTRODUCTION

Canon Sheehan was fortunate in his birthplace: Mallow is a gracious town, blessed by that dark-brown river curiously called the Blackwater and surrounded by countryside which abounds in what D.H. Lawrence called 'the messages that come from out of the earth.'

A little to the west is the moveable feast known as Sliabh Luachra, the hill country where the old language survived until late in the last century and where today you can hear indigenous song and music at its purest.

To the east is the most fertile stretch of the Blackwater valley, a land almost Germanic in its lush acres and woods and orchards.

To the south are the stark Boggeragh mountains crowned by Nead an Fhiolair, the Eagle's Nest.

And to the north are the Ballyhoura hills; they seem unknowable and haunt the imagination — and they are the setting for a great passage in James Joyce's *A Portrait of the Artist as a Young Man*. Up there lived a hardy race who play a big part in Sheehan's novel *Glenanaar*, people whom in his words 'even the savage effects of Elizabethan and Cromwellian freebooters failed to destroy.' Edmund Spenser, 'a rabid exterminator', wrote to Queen Elizabeth that they were hopeless, so fearless of death and so contemptuous of fatigue and wounds that they couldn't be rooted out. Sheehan said: 'No Wordsworth has yet sung the praises of these Irish Dalesmen' — *Glenanaar* was his tribute.

Mallow was a good matrix for a writer; Sheehan was also profoundly influenced by his times. He was a student at the diocesan college in Fermoy when the Fenians went out in their hopeless rising, ill-organised and betrayed but therefore all the more appealing to a young man of romantic spirit. The students knew that a rebel band from East Cork was encamped in the hills of Ballyhoura and for days waited feverishly for news of them. At last, word came down that their leader, Peter O'Neill Crowley, had been mortally wounded in a skirmish in Kilclooney Wood, a resonant name that is now deeply embedded in patriot lore.

A huge crowd attended the funeral — and his coffin was shouldered all the way down from the village of Ballyorgan to the family graveyard in Ballymacoda, close to the Atlantic. The authorities in St Colman's exhibited no sympathy for the Fenians; the students were forbidden to pay their respects to O'Neill Crowley; they had to watch from inside the gates as the cortege went by.

On that bitter evening in the spring of '67 young Sheehan wept with grief and rage; it was a seminal moment in his life — and the origin of his finest novel, *The Graves at Kilmorna*.

Here and there in his work you will find passages which suggest that he opposed armed revolution — but there can be little doubt about where his heart resided.

Sheehan knew that the proliferation of informers made a successful rising almost impossible in the Ireland of his day; he knew too that a rising would almost inevitably entail excesses; his religious faith

VI

was profound — and yet the spirit of the Fenians ran deep in him. The constrictions of his profession prevented him from speaking out. Sheehan was a tormented man; as he awaited death in a Cork hospital, he summoned a kinsman and requested him to destroy his secret papers. What they contained we will never know; the evidence of his novels suggests that the gist was political.

Glenanaar is Sheehan's best-known novel — or at least some passages from it, such as the account of the hurling match and the epic journey of Daniel O'Connell from Derrynane to Cork City and the finding of Nodlag in the blizzard — are familiar because reproduced in school readers.

For a framework it has a typically Victorian plot but essentially it is a political novel; its central theme is the plight of the tenant farmers in those days when security of tenure seemed no more than an impossible dream.

Some of the events it depicts take place in the first half of the nineteenth century; it was a particularly trying time for the peasantry — the Act of Union had abolished the Dublin parliament; many of the landlords were absentees; their affairs were managed by agents, some of whom were more tyrannical than their masters.

The obsession with the land drove decent God-fearing men to kill; the Doneraile Conspiracy (central to the plot in *Glenanaar*) belongs to real life; it was one of the many inchoate attempts at protest that proliferated until the movement led by Davitt and Parnell brought the farmers their freedom.

In *Glenanaar* there is a passage which depicts with

seemingly artless simplicity the relationship between the tenant farmers and the landlords. One evening after a day's fowling a member of the latter class calls into the home of Edmond Connors, one of Sheehan's unsung Dalesmen but nevertheless vulnerable. Of course he is greeted hospitably; the conversation is courteous but guarded and almost tense. Incidentally, the guest is treated to the peasants' favourite tipple — milk liberally laced with poteen (shades of Bailey's Irish Cream).

A sub-theme in *Glenanaar* is the Irish obsession with heredity. Nodlag, the foundling who was discovered in Edmond Connors's cowhouse and later almost lost in the great snow, was the daughter of Cloumper Daly, the notorious informer — and therein hangs a tale. She is a sweet child and the son of the house dotes on her — until he discovers her origin; then he wants her banished. Nodlag grows up and eventually marries Redmond Casey, a local blacksmith. One of her sons, Terence, becomes a famous hurler and in his own words he is also a furious rebel, never done quoting from such patriots as Emmet and Mitchel and Meagher and determined to take his place when 'the day' comes.

He falls in love; his passion is reciprocated but the father of his sweetheart is furious when he asks for her hand and he says that he would rather see her married to the devil; young Terence believes it is because he is only a blacksmith and she is a farmer's daughter — then one catalytic day he discovers the truth.

The occasion is a hurling match between the parishes of Glenroe and Ardpatrick. "It was a glorious evening; the whole countryside was there; our blood was up and we fought like demons for victory." Terence Casey goes on: "So intense was the feeling ... that a big faction fight was expected — and we were near it and I was the innocent cause." In shooting for a goal the blacksmith injures an opponent; he is accused of having done it deliberately. A crowd gathers around Casey; one 'ill-disposed' fellow strikes him and says: "I saw you hit him, you bloody son of an informer." Casey goes on: "It was a sudden flash that lit up all my past and darkened all the future of my life." He leaves the field but returns in the hope that his assailant's slur was unfounded. He confronts him and forces him to blurt out: "You know as well as I do that your mother is the daughter of Cloumper Daly, the informer."

Next day in the forge young Casey uttered words to his father that he would forever regret: "What the devil possessed you to marry the daughter of an informer?" Terence's account of how he left home is the most moving passage in all of Sheehan's work.

Technically *Glenanaar* is a flawed novel but it abounds in great things; Sheehan rather like Charles Kickham uses his books as baskets into which he puts ideas, intuitions, observations, stories and whatever else comes into his fertile mind. And he resembles another contemporary, Thomas Hardy, in that you feel he is going down a road which nobody travelled before. This pioneering journey produces a certain awkwardness but, as with Hardy, it is redeemed by total honesty. And there is another palpable resemblance between Sheehan and Hardy: both were unsure of their raw material — they were not confident that it was the stuff of great literature.

And hence came the recourse to heightening: in Hardy it generally takes the form of similes and metaphors based on the classics; Sheehan's ploy was geographical — he tended to jump from the familiar to the faraway, especially so in *My New Curate* and to a minor extent in *Glenanaar*.

Where is Canon Sheehan's place in the gallery of Irish writing? The most sensible answer probably lies in one of his favourite quotations from Dante — 'He stands like a solid tower.'

Daniel Corkery believed that the best writers rarely achieved international fame — and you won't find many thesis-hunters in or around Mallow or Doneraile or Knockanevin or Ballyorgan or Twopothouse. There are no mysteries to unravel in Sheehan's work — but there is no mistaking 'the echo of a noble soul'.

Con Houlihan   1989

Glossary

Note: In local Irish speech many phrases are derived from Gaelic words. Canon Sheehan rendered them in his own phonetic spelling. Here we give the original word and an explanation.

achorra: (*a chara*) friend
aglanna: (*an ghleanna*) of the glen
alannov: (from *a leanbh*) child (used as endearment)
bouchal: (*buachaill*) boy
Cailin deas Crúidhte nam-bó: (*Cailin Deas Crúite na mBó*) song
    title, 'the lovely milking girl'
Céad míle fáilte: a hundred thousand welcomes
creacht: (*creach*) booty from cattle raid
dhoc-a-dhurrus: (*deoch an dorais*) a parting drink
Droleen: (*dreoilín*) the wren
fairin: (*féirín*) gift
galore: (*go leor*) plenty
girsha: (from *girseach*) girl
gorlach: (*garlach*) foundling
grauver: (*grámhar*) loving
inagh: (*an ea*) is that so?
Keol: (*ceol*) music
kinats: derogatory term commonly used in north Cork and
    Tipperary (origin not clear)
m'ainim: (*m'anam*) endearment, 'my soul'
mo chree: (from *croí*, 'heart') endearment, 'my heart'
mo shtig: (from *istigh*, 'inside') endearment, literally 'my inside'
raimeis: (*ráiméis*) nonsense

seanchus: (*seanchas*) chat, gossip

shaugh: (*seach*) turn

sugan: (*súgán*) hay rope

T'ainim an diaoul: (*t'anam don diabhal*) exclamation, 'your soul to the devil'

thescaun: (*taoscán*) a bundle (here referring to a small child)

Thiggin-thu: (*tuigeann tú*) you understand

thraneen: (*tráithnín*) stalk of grass (suggesting uselessness)

thucka: (*toice*) forward girl, wench

vanithee: (*bean an tí*) the 'woman of the house'

CHAPTER I

"THE YANK"

HE suddenly appeared in our village street, gorgeous, and caparisoned from head to heel in all kinds of sartorial splendour. He took away our breath with his grandeur; and people looked at him sideways, partly because of his dazzling equipment, and partly because he had a curious habit of looking one straight in the face, which is sometimes disconcerting. We did not like him at all, at all. By "we" I mean the villagers and myself. They did not like him, because he was stiff and standoffish; and they heard that he was critical and censorious about our ancient and amiable customs; and he steadily declined all advances toward that friendly familiarity which we like so dearly. He was also an impenetrable mystery to a very inquisitive people; and what greater crime could there be? They had gallantly attempted to get at the secret of his life. It was an interesting, and even exciting pastime to a people who, having no particular business of their own to mind, are charitably desirous to mind that of every one else. But no! He declined all familiarity. He would walk with one of those amateur detectives for

1

an hour; speak on all possible subjects but one; and
leave the poor man as much as ever in the dark as to
his own personality and antecedents. Nay, he was
such a "naygur," he would not ask the companion
who had lent him his society for the hour, "whether
he had a mout' on him." So he was decidedly unpop-
ular. It was given out, after a long search, and many
kindly insinuations, that his name was "Fijaral" (our
local interpretation of "Fitzgerald"), but that was soon
discarded as apocryphal and untenable. And so, at
last, he came to be known as "The Yank." Once he
was seen haunting an ancient moss-grown field, in
which were two Danish barrows or forts; and the
report immediately went abroad that he had dreamt
three times running that a crock of gold was buried
there; and he had come home to dig for the treasure.
And more than once he was seen, some miles from
the village, leaning sadly against an old, withered, leaf-
less and gnarled white thorn, or smoking leisurely and
contemplating the little square of grass-grown, nettle-
covered field where were faintly outlined the last traces
of what was once a human habitation.

I cannot say that I liked him much more than the
villagers. He answered my salutation, "A fine day,"
rather gruffly, and once when I ventured a little further,
and said cheerily:

"Coming back to settle down in the old land, I
hope?" he looked me all over, and said, deep down in his
chest, and without any attempt to disguise his irritation:

"Great Scott!"

Besides, it was not conducive to the peace of mind of our young villagers to see him, in languid ease, standing at the door of the hotel, morning, noon, and night. He was there at early dawn, when the mill-hands went to work. He was there at noon, when they returned to dinner. He was there when the six-o'clock bell tolled out for cessation of work in the evening, and the convent and church bells rang out melodiously the *Angelus*. And I knew well, that when the old men, with reverent, uncovered heads, as they repeated the prayer of the Incarnation, passed by that hotel door, and saw "the Yank," so well dressed, with such heavy gold chains and seals, and such shining square-top boots, they said sorrowfully to themselves:

"Ah, if I had only crossed the wather whin I was a boy!"

And I knew that the young men, seeing the same never-to-be-envied-enough spectacle, made frantic resolutions, that as soon as they "gethered" the passage money, they, too, would seek the El Dorado of the West. So in a little while I ceased to notice him, and set him down as a conceited, purse-proud fellow, who had little love left for his faith and motherland. It was not the only occasion when I was mistaken in judging appearances; and in not seeing that there is a human heart beating in every breast, even though we cannot witness or count its pulsations.

* * * *

It was a Sunday afternoon in the late summer. There was a tournament in the Park. In past times

it used to be called a hurling-match, but we are going
ahead in Ireland, and we call things now by their
proper names.   It was a big affair, — the culmination
and critical finish of all the many local trials of strength
that had taken place in the past year.   It was the final
"try" for the County championship between the Cork
"Shandons," and our own brave "Skirmishers." There
was a mighty crowd assembled.   Sidecars, waggonettes,
traps of every shape and hue and form, from the
farmer's cart with the heavy quilt to the smart buggy
of the merchant, brought in all the afternoon a great
concourse of people, who were anxious to put down
the Sunday evening in the best possible manner by
witnessing this great joust of Irish athletes.   We are
no Sabbatarians in Ireland.   Neither are we quite
depleted yet.   It would surprise any one familiar with
all the modern, doleful jeremiads about the depopula-
tion of Ireland to see such a smartly dressed, bright,
intelligent crowd in a country village.   And if he had
any misgivings or doubts about the physique and pluck
of "the fighting race," he had only to stand still, when
the athletes stripped for the contest, and see in those
clean-cut, well-built figures the nerve and muscle that
go to build up an energetic and pushing race.

The sun was shaded under banks of great clouds,
and shed a pale, clear light on the landscape, without
the inconvenience of much heat.   The great belt of
trees to the west was just being dappled from its russet
green by the first tints of approaching autumn.   A
light warm wind stirred their leaves.   The cattle

browsed calmly away upon the forest slopes. And there was a deep hush of expectancy over all these assembled thousands. It was to be a great trial of strength between two nearly matched clubs, in which grit, and wind, and pluck, and muscle, and science were to be put to their final test.

At three o'clock the teams were called to their places by their respective captains. There was a brief consultation with the referee, a coin was flung into the air, sides were taken, the winners turning their backs to the wind, and in a moment, one could only see that ball tossed hither and thither in the struggle, and a confused mass of men and camans, as they fought fiercely for victory and the tide of the battle rolled uncertain here and there across the field. And the combatants were curiously silent. This, too, is a modern characteristic, and a wholesome one. Instead of the whoops and yells of olden times, the words of fierce encouragement or expostulation, the cry of victory, and the curse of defeat, one only saw the set faces and the flying figures, the victory snatched out of the hands of one, the defeat of the other retrieved, and the swift, tumultuous passion that swayed these young athletes as they strained every nerve in the all-important struggle for victory.

Not a word broke from that whirling mass, as the heavy ball leaped hither and thither, tossed by the camans from hand to hand, or rolled swiftly over the level grass, as some young athlete, with the fleetness of a deer, tapped it on before him, until he brought

it within reach of the coveted goal. You heard only
the patter of feet, the light or heavy tap-tap-tap on
the ball, the crack of the camans as they crossed in
the air above or on the grass beneath; and now and
again the screams of women and girls, who stampeded
wildly when the ball was driven into their midst, and
the fierce flying combatants, with heaving breasts and
starting eyes, forgot their chivalry and carried the
tumult of battle right in amongst their excited sisters.
Indeed, the whole excitement seemed to be limited
to the spectators, who cheered and lamented, encouraged or rebuked the silent athletes on whom the honour of the flag depended. One alone amidst the din
and tumult of the field maintained a stoical composure,
and that was "the Yank." He stood apart and
watched the strife, as impassive as an Indian chief,
apparently regardless as to which side victory swayed;
and altogether taking but an academic and far-off
interest in the entire affair.

At half-past four the teams were almost on a tie,
the "Skirmishers" having two goals to their credit,
and the "Shandons" one goal and some points. The
final tussle was just about to come off, when it was
annnounced that the local captain had been taken suddenly ill, and had been ordered off the field. There
was consternation in the ranks of the "Skirmishers."
Just on the point of victory, their hopes were dashed
to the ground. They held a long and eager consultation; and finally decided to enlist one or other of
the spectators, who had been members of the Club,

but not picked men. These shook their heads. The issue was too important. They would not take the responsibility. Five o'clock was near; and the referee was about to give his final decision in favor of the strangers, when, to the astonishment of everyone, "the Yank," throwing away a half-burned cigar, and calmly divesting himself of coat and waistcoat, which he carefully rolled up and placed in the hands of a spectator, came forward, took up a caman, tested it, as if it were a Toledo blade, by leaning all his weight upon it, and said in an accent of cool indifference:

"Let me take a hand: I guess I can manage it."

There was a general laugh. The "Shandons" were delighted. They noticed the grey hairs in his head and beard. The "Skirmishers" demurred; but one wise fellow, who had been studying the splendid build of "the Yank," winked and said:

"Yes, we'll take him. Put him right inside the goal."

The excitement rose rapidly with this new event. The disabled Captain heard of it, and insisted upon being taken back to see the issue. No matter if he died on the field of battle! "Where can man die better?" etc., etc. The ball was once more tossed high, the victory swayed from one side to the other; the cheers rose wildly and voluminously from the adherents of both teams; until, at last, the "Shandons," pressing home for victory, drove the ball right under "the Yank's" legs. The foremost champion, rushing forward to get it through the goal, found himself, he knew not how, about twenty feet away from the ball; and then it seemed as if a cyclone had struck the field. At least, a straight path was cut through the swaying, confused mass of the combatants, who in some mysterious way yielded right and left. Disregarding all modern rules and regulations, "the Yank" had struck straight before him; and with his powerful arms and shoulders had cut his way as clean as a swathe of ripe corn is levelled by the teeth of the mowing-machine in the early harvest time. He swept along quite close to where I was standing, and once I heard him panting: *T'ainim an diaoul.* Then I knew he was Irish; and my heart went out to him. A few cries of "A foul! a foul!" were raised; but they were hushed into ignominious silence by the plaudits of the crowd, whose feelings of respectful aversion were suddenly converted into a paroxysm of unstinted admiration. "Go it, Yank!" "Cheers for the 'Stars and Stripes'!" "Give them 'Hail Columbia,' old fellow!" echoed on every side, until the whole mad tumult culminated in a wild Irish cheer, as the ball flew swiftly over the heads of the rival combatants, and, despite the frantic efforts of the goal-keeper on the "Shandons'" side, passed out gaily through the gates of the goal. Just as the "Yank" struck the ball the blow that gained the victory, there was a wild, mad rush toward him; and under its weight he was flung down, whilst the whole human mass squirmed over him. There was a wild shout of indignation from the field, for he had suddenly become their hero; and it seemed like revenge for defeat. When they were raised, one by one, "the Yank" was unable to lift himself. A hundred willing hands offered to help him; and there were some angry threats toward those who had felled him. A few distinctively Gaelic questions were also put:

"You're not dead, are you?"

"Wal, no," he said, leisurely, but with a gesture of pain, "but I guess there are broken bones somewhere, anyhow."

He was gently raised on a stretcher, and carried in triumph from the field. As the bearers were passing out the front gate, the captain of the local team came forward and proffered his thanks for the assistance given. He looked wretchedly ill, but he thought he had this duty to perform.

"Wal," said the Yank, in his own cool way, "I guess we did lick them. But, young man, you go home, and liquor up as fast as you can."

Half-way down the street, an old man, looking sideways at the hero, said aloud:

"Begobs, there was nothin' seen like it since Casey the Hurler's time."

The Yank raised himself with difficulty, and fixing his eyes on the old man, he said:

"Say that agin, Mister!"

"I say," repeated the old man, somewhat embarrassed now, "that there was nothin' seen like that since Terence Casey single-handed bate the parishes of Ardpatrick and Glenroe."

"That was a long time ago, I guess," said the Yank, leaning back helplessly again.

CHAPTER II

CONFIDENCES

IF for no other reason but because he had so gallantly saved the honour of our parish, I was bound to call on him. That little expression, too, *T'ainim an diaoul*, that escaped from him in the heat of the contest, was eloquent of much. It showed that there was a deep, volcanic fire of Irish feeling under that cold crust of his American manner. Nature will break out and show itself in spite of every kind of artificial envelopment. But I felt, too, that there was something in the man above the common average. I have a decided partiality for those silent fellows, who never talk, but somehow cut in at decidedly critical moments, and by quick, emphatic action, solve difficulties and end suspense, or compel that fickle dame, Fortune, to change her mind, and that, too, without delay.

I called at the hotel. He was in bed, badly bruised, but he looked as calm and imperturbable as ever. He received me with his usual coldness, answered in brief interjections my solicitous inquiries, chilled me, in fact, to the very marrow of my bones, until I was glad of the chance of getting away with the consciousness that I had done my duty. Then, just as I was turning away, he said:

"I'm much obliged for your visit, Father. I do hope you will soon come again!"

That upset all my calculations. What a country America must be, I thought, when a poor fellow has to wear such a coat of mail of cold polished steel around him to cover his natural warmth and sincerity! I came again and again. We became fast friends.

Now, I had become much fascinated by what that old man had said, on the day of our great triumph, about Casey the Hurler, because amongst my reminiscences of a thrice beloved curacy two refrains of popular ballads were continually recurring to lip and memory. The one was the chorus of a famous election ballad in those days when we had borough elections in Ireland; and when fun, fighting and whiskey were the order of the day. The other was a more recent Homeric effusion, chanted outside my windows in later years when I had a more appreciative sense of the value of ballad literature as enshrining the local history of the country. It was generally sung in strophes, and by two voices, male and female alternately, both combining in the fourth and final line. It ran thus:

> Then here's to bould young Casey,
> Like a lion did he chase ye,
> From the Galtees to the Funcheon,
> From the Funcheon to the say;
> Sure nayther Mars nor Hecthor
> Would ever prove the victhor,
> When bould young Casey's hurley,
> It went dancing through the fray.

"Bould young Casey" became a dim demigod in my imagination, because, being somewhat enthusiastic about Gaelic pastimes, I felt that this athlete was great, excelling, unrivalled in his own department, and that he was, in fact, a hero.

It was with no vulgar sense of a prurient and un-chastened curiosity, therefore, that I introduced the subject to the invalid in one of our numerous friendly conferences by his bedside. I think that the man that picks secrets is a hundred times worse than the fellow who picks pockets; and, indeed, it was with a certain kind of alarm I ascertained that "the Yank" was none other than the redoubtable Casey himself. I had a certain awe of him, as you feel before a great personage who has hitherto been to you but a name; and I had also a dim presentiment that there was a story, perhaps a tragedy, behind this *incognito*. The secret leaked out in this wise.

He was complaining of the attendance at the hotel, — that it was not all a sick man had a right to expect, etc.

"Well," I said, "the waiter is a good fellow, except when he takes 'liminade, which does not agree with him, because he says he has a 'wake' stomach; and the doctor told him to avoid anything sweet. But it seems to me, if you will pardon the suggestion, that you need a woman's hand around you here, to tidy up things a little, to get your drinks, etc."

"Wal, I was thinking so, too, myself," he said. "But you see I don't like to offend those good people" (which showed that he was a gentleman in heart and feeling); "they have been very kind in their own way. And then, well, your people, my good Father, are not quite — shall I say, methodical enough —"

I guessed what he meant; and I flared up a little.

"As for that," I said, "I can get you as neat-handed and as tidy a little woman as you'd get in Chicago or Boston. She is a poor little widow with two of the sweetest children you'd see in a day's walk; and I guarantee that you'll like her."

"Widows are dangerous, Father," he said, smiling. "We've old Tony Weller's authority for that. But where is she from? From this parish?"

"No," I said, "not from here. I think she has come down from the hills over there near Glen-an-aar ——"

I thought he looked frightened, because his eyes widened, and he got quite white beneath them. He said nothing for a while, but only shook his head. Then: —

"Let it drop, Father! It wouldn't do, nohow."

Now, I marvelled much at this. I knew that Glen-anaar was the Valley of Slaughter, and that a terrific battle had been fought there several centuries before the Christian era between the Tuatha-de-Danaans and, I think, the Firbolgs. Is not the mountain stream, amber, or wine-coloured, or tawny, called the Own-an-aar, the River of Slaughter, to this day? But what could that have to do with a returned American in the very last decade of the nineteenth century? But I let it drop. He wished it so; and there was an end of the matter. But we did manage to tidy things up somehow, even without the help of the artistic waiter.

One day when he was nearly convalescent, I said to him:

"You'll be prepared for an ovation, my dear sir, when you are setting out for America. The people are so enthusiastic about your great feat that they will insist on inflicting on you some kind of popular demonstration to show their gratitude."

"I hope not," he replied. "I came over just to see things for myself and to remain quiet, and to return safe."

"That won't do, my dear fellow," I replied. "They're already chanting your praises by reviving an ancient ballad, styled *The Life and Adventures of Terence Casey, the famous Hurler*."

Again he was much disturbed, and looked in a pleading way at me. Then, he got suddenly angry:

"Why the d—l," he cried, "cannot they leave a fellow alone when he comes amongst them? I suppose now, some inquisitive fellow has been searching and raking up all my past; and *it* will be flung in my face again."

I marvelled much at this sudden explosion of fury from such a tranquil fellow. I marvelled much more at the allusion. He saw my perplexity, and dissolved it.

"Look here, Father," he said. "'Tis your business to keep secrets, is it not?"

"Yes," I said, "some."

"All," he cried passionately. "If I thought a priest could blab about anything, I'd not trust him even in confession."

"'Tis quite true," I replied. "Whatever you entrust to us as a secret will be inviolably preserved a secret, wherever it is spoken."

"So I thought," he replied. "Now, I want none of these folks to know who I am, or what I came here for. They have been ferreting around here the last couple of months to find out who I am. I can't see what the d—l it is to them. They have bribed even the unfortunate waiter to tell them the name on my trunk and linen."

"That's going rather far," I replied. "I always gave them credit for drawing the line at a man's letters and his own revelations. Inside that, of course, curiosity is almost a virtue. It really springs from benevolence."

"I can't understand that, nohow," he replied. "It seems to me that you folks would do better, if you would try mind your own business."

"Now, that's all your American prejudice," I replied. "Or rather your Anglo-Saxon tradition; for you Americans, unknown to yourselves, are Anglo-Saxons. Why, I'm told that over there a man might be your next-door neighbour for twenty years, and you mightn't know his name, or what he has for breakfast. Now, I call that downright selfishness. You must be awfully afraid of each other, when you lock up every secret in that way. Now, look at us! If my

mare casts a shoe, or develops a splint, every man,
woman, and child in the parish knows it in twenty-
four hours. If I go up to Cork, everyone is asking
where I am gone, and how long I shall remain away.
And if I confess the least ignorance of what is going
on in the parish, from Glenanaar to Twopothouse,
they won't scruple to tell me I am a hermit; and that
I ought to be a Trappist monk. So, too, if a baby is
born, we all want to know whether it is a boy or a
girl, whether it is like the father or mother, when it
will be baptized, what will be its name. And when
a man dies, we all go to his funeral, and while away
the time between our prayers by asking how much he
left behind him, and who was to get it. Before he is
settled in his coffin, every old woman in the parish
must have a look at him, and a pull at his habit to see
is the hood straight; and when the coffin is lowered to
its last resting-place, there is generally a hot dispute
as to whether it is geometrically arranged. Then all
take a last look at the breastplate to see how old he
is; some shake their heads, as if even in his grave he
was not quite candid about his age; then with a final
valediction, 'He was an hones' man; God rest him!'
all depart satisfied with their own benevolence. Now,
I call that Christian charity and kindliness, not like
your pagan exclusiveness."

"Wal," he said, lifting up his hands wearily after
this homily, "I can't make it out. You are queer
folks over here."

"Maybe we are," I said, a little nettled, for nothing

angers me so much as this affectation of superiority
on the part of people whom we could teach for the
next thousand years. "But I tell you, you have a lot
to learn from us yet."

"Wal, to cut matters short," he said, "*I'm Terence
Casey!*"

"Casey, the Hurler?" I cried, amazed at this sudden
impersonation of my ideal hero.

"Yes," he replied, "but you mustn't mention it even
after I'm gone."

"Certainly," I replied, "your secret will be relig-
iously respected. But — would you allow me to
touch your hand?"

"For what?" he said, starting back.

"Only to satisfy my hero-worship," I said. "You
must know, my dear fellow, that for over twenty years
you have been associated in my mind with the gods
of Grecian fable, with Ajax and Achilles, not to speak
of the Mars or Hector of the ballad. Why, if it were
known that you were Casey, I don't know what honours
would be heaped on you. The band would be out
every night to serenade you; you'd have had deputa-
tions from every Gaelic club in the country; and I'm
quite sure you'd be presented with an illuminated
address on your return to the 'Stars and Stripes.'"

He laughed.

"It is a good escape," he said. "But, Father, I
bind you to your promise of secrecy. No one must
know who I am, and why I am here."

"As to the first part," I said, "'tis all right. No

one knows who you are, or ever shall know, so far as
I am concerned.   As to the second clause of the secret,
every man, woman, and child in the village knows
what you came for!"

"No?" he interrogated with alarm.   "What is it?"

"Why, what could it be," I said, "but to take back
an Irish wife to the States?   Why, every little colleen
in the parish thinks that she will be your choice."

"The Irish are the devils painted," he said, sinking
into the pillows.

"That's a matter of opinion," I said.   "My own
impression is, that they're angels without the paint.
At any rate, I can guarantee you a score of young
colleens here, any one of whom would do credit to the
finest brownstone mansion on the banks of the Hudson
or Mississippi.   I'll go farther and declare that you
might pick out one or two who would grace the par-
quetted floor of the White House itself."

"I've heard you saying these things, or something
like them, off the altar, since I came home," he said.
"But, of course, you exaggerate.   You good Irish
priests think Ireland the 'hub' of the universe.   But
these good people have guessed rightly, but not in the
way they think.   I came to Ireland not to lose my
heart, but to get rid of an image that's there these
twenty years."

"The only way," I replied, "to manage that, is to
paint another over it."

He shook his head.

"Many and many a fair picture has been painted

over it," he said, "but 'tis of no use. That face will come up through all. 'Twill haunt me to my dying day. Unless ——"

He stopped.

"Unless I can see it again, but that's not likely. I was hoping that she had changed, and that I might see the change, and be freed from the ghost of that face. Or, if there were no change, to make it mine own forever."

"Twenty years is a long time," I said. "Few are unchanged in so long a period."

"True," he replied. "That's why I despair."

CHAPTER III

JUST around the corner, as you turn toward Butte-
vant, lived the little woman whom I had so confidently
recommended to the Yank as an amateur nurse. She
was small of stature, and somewhat faded in beauty,
both by reason of the transforming power of Time and
the more destructive agencies of trouble and want.
Yet there was a strange, pensive look in her face, as
of one who lived altogether in the past; and a tone of
quiet resignation, as of one who had parted with the
interests of life and was looking habitually toward
eternity. This feature, however, did not prevent her
from being cheerful, and even happy; and no one
could suspect from the bright way in which she spoke
that there was a deeper and holier feeling in her heart.
You should come on her unawares to know that that
steady gazing into the fire, or that abstracted look
through her little shop-window, was that of one who
saw all earthly things rounded in the circle of eternity.
She was never seen on the street, except in the early
morning, when she was the first to take her place in
an obscure corner of the church to hear early Mass.
Even then no one noticed her, as she glided through
the street with her black shawl folded tightly around

her and covering her head. She studiously avoided all village gossipers, and therefore was never implicated in a quarrel. At first this was resented as a sign of exclusiveness and pride. Then it was unnoticed, or noticed only to be respected. She had two children, — Teresa, or Tessie, the eldest, just breaking into womanhood; and so perfect a picture of her mother, as she had been in her youth, that friends who had not seen them for a long time used to address her as "Norah," — her mother's name. Her younger sister, Kathleen, was of a different type. For whereas Tessie was grave, even to solemnity, and seemed to have inherited her mother's pensiveness with her beautiful features, Kathleen was so vivacious, so fond of being out of doors, and romping and playing, that her mother always spoke of her as "that Tomboy." Several times I was requisitioned to lecture her severely on these little indiscretions of youth, but somehow I always broke down in the attempt. Her look of demure gravity would disarm a more unrelenting Mentor; and besides, I knew she could quote against me several little lectures that I imprudently gave in school, to the effect that they should cram into their childhood years all the sunshine and happiness they could find; for that the skies would become grayer as they advanced in life and walked under shadows not of their own seeking. But they were both sweet children, as I told the Yank; and Tessie, who had passed through the usual curriculum of studies, was now learning such accomplishments as music, painting on glass and plaques, fancy needle-work, etc. I have some specimens on my own walls of her beautiful handiwork.

They were extremely poor. The wretched little shop, with its window blocked with packages of Col-man's Mustard, Cadbury's Cocoa, etc., did not realize in its stock these splendid advertisements. A few red herrings hung from the ceiling, and a few strings of onions. There was a make-believe of two or three gorgeous canisters, on which "Tea" was printed in crimson and gold letters. A few clay pipes and a dozen or two of candles completed its equipment. But they were never hungry. He who feeds the ravens had concern also for His children; and He who clothes the lilies wrapped these little ones from the cold. But it was pathetic to see how they strove to be always neatly clad. The efforts of the poor to conceal pov-erty are always pathetic. And it was only when you saw beneath the spotless pinafores the carefully in-serted patch on the blue serge, or the darn on the sleeve, or the slightly broken shoe, that you knew how gal-lantly these brave, simple souls were fighting to keep up appearances under the perpetual friction and dis-integration of great poverty. And when sometimes I expressed my wonder that under such attenuated circumstances they were able to survive, one word always solved the puzzle to that good mother's mind, and that was — God!

I am sure it was out of pure sympathy that I pro-posed Norah Leonard as nurse to the wealthy American. I broached the matter also to herself, rather in a tentative way, and in the hope that the Yank might change his mind.

"I was hoping to see my way lately to get something for you to do," I said to her, a day or two after my interview with the invalid.

"Well, then, Father," she said, "I would be very glad. The nuns wouldn't mind Tessie staying at home a few days to mind the shop."

"Oh," I said, "Tessie is getting such a grand young lady now, with her long dress and her hair turned up, that we can't stand her at all."

Tessie was poring over a book on a desk near the window. She was bent down over it, so that the coils of her rich, auburn hair, so like her mother's — but there were silver threads among the gold in the latter's — were plainly visible. She blushed scarlet, for girls are very sensitive just then when they are leaving behind them the irresponsibilities of childhood and assuming the duties of the larger life.

"I'd just as soon," said her mother, "that she knew nothing of business. I hope God has something better for her in store."

"Business," I thought, as I looked around the bare and desolate shop. "'Tis a big sacrifice, indeed!"

"I tell you now," I said, "as I often told you before, that Kathleen will be the nun."

"Yerra, is it that Tomboy, your reverence?" said Mrs. Leonard, raising herself from the counter. "I promise you she has something in her head besides a convent. But you're spoiling that child, your reverence, out and out. You're taking such notice of her that we'll never get any good out of her."

"She's worth the whole box-and-dice of ye put together," I said. "Mark me, she'll have the veil on her yet."

"Wisha, thin," said Mrs. Leonard, "I'd make a present of her to any one of these nuns that do be coming here from Texas, or South Africa, or California. They're welcome to her, with my blessing."

I did not like this disparagement of my little favourite at all, and I told the mother so roundly.

"She won't go to South Africa, nor to Texas, nor to California," I said, angrily. "We want our best little girls at home. And leave it to me! You may call me Davy, if I haven't that young lady, snug and safe, in one of our best Irish convents before many years."

"Well, God bless your reverence," said the grateful woman. "I'll leave her to you and God, and she'll be in good hands, I warrant. But what was the situation your reverence was going to get for me?"

"I wanted you to go to the hotel and nurse the strange American gentleman that's sick there."

She started back in surprise and alarm.

"Yerra, is it me to be a nurse, Father? What do I know about nursing?" she said.

"You know quite as much about it as any other woman," I said. "Every woman is, or ought to be, a nurse."

"'Twould be well in me way, indeed," she said, with a little toss of her head, "to go fixing and bindin' and sootherin' a sick man. Maybe," she said, with a little stifled laugh, "he'd want to marry me in the end."

"He might do worse," I said, gravely.

"Well, thin," said she, "I'm not the woman for him. I got enough of that before."

And as the old, pensive look came into her face, the melancholy retrospect of the unhappy past, the spirit of humour and bantering died away, and left her but a woman of sorrow.

"In any case, 'tis all over," I replied. "He is on the way to recovery now, and will soon be off to America again."

"I hope he'll take a good wife with him," she said. "Sure the people say that's what he kem for."

"And you won't go?" I said at parting.

She shook her head sadly.

No wonder, poor thing! She had had some bitter experiences of life. If any one had told the young belle of the country-side, Norah Curtin, that she would wind up her days as a little shop-keeper or huckster on the side of the street in Doneraile, she would have deemed it an insult. And if any one had told her, on the morning of her marriage, that Hugh Leonard would lead her such a life that she would gladly pray for her own death, not his, she would have called them ravens of evil and prophets of misfortune. Alas! it so turned out. Hugh Leonard was one of those worthless, heartless fellows that should be whipped at the cart tail as

women of Marblehead flogged the scuttling Captain.
It was pretty well known that Norah Curtin did not
care for him. It was whispered that her heart was
elsewhere. But she married to please her father; and
her young husband was so proud of his prize, that he
vowed by all that was sacred in heaven or on earth to
be kind to her beyond the hopes of woman. Alas!
A few years and he tired of her, and all was wreck and
ruin. He spent his days on the mountains coursing,
and his nights on the river poaching. He would be a
gentleman. Were not all the Leonards gentlemen?
He was told that he had "demaned" himself by marrying a small farmer's daughter. He could not give
up his gentlemanly habits. He was caught and fined
heavily again and again. He laughed it off; and to
show his independence, he appeared at every fair and
market in the neighbourhood in shooting-jacket and
yellow gaiters. Then, their little boy, their only son,
died; and what more cared Hugh, when he could not
leave his farm to a "Leonard"? He became reckless,
bet heavily on race horses, and lost. And, at last, he
sank down to the level of a sot, spending his days in
the tap-room of a rural public house, pipe in mouth, the
bottle by his side, and the blackened cards in his hands.
He speedily won the reputation of being the best hand
at "Forty-five" in the country, and he was proud of the
distinction. Meanwhile, the inevitable dissolution was
proceeding at home. Broken fences, repaired with a
furze bush, gates hanging from the hinges, cart wheels
minus their tires here and there in the yard, thatch

rotting on the roof, great rents in the slated roof of the
out-offices, — all told their tale. Meanwhile, in came
demand after demand for rents overdue. Leonard
became indignant.

"How dared they? Evict a Leonard? Never, so
long as powder and shot were sold," etc., etc.

"Bad — to you, you spalpeen," said a candid friend,
"you couldn't hit a haystack with thim hands of yours
shaking l'ke collywobbles. Give over the farm to your
wife, you fool, as you can't manage it yourself."

Then, one day the end came. They were flung out
into the world; and with their wrecked furniture had to
seek shelter in a half-ruined labourer's cottage. Some
months of misery elapsed, during which the snug old
farm ran rapidly to ruin. And then Hugh Leonard
was on his death-bed. At the last moment he consented to forego his pride and sell the farm. But even
in these moments his pride came uppermost and forced
him into an injustice from which his family were yet
suffering. For a "friend" was allowed to his bedside, who dinned into the ear of the dying man, that
he should forget his devoted wife even in that solemn
crisis.

"She's young and flighty, ye know," he said, "and
you won't be cowld in your grave whin she'll pick up
with the first gallivanter that comes acrass her. Tie
up the money for your childhre, Hugh, so that she
can't tetch it."

And so he did. Tied it up with all the red-tape
and sealed it with all the sealing-wax the law would

allow. Then Hugh, "Gentleman Hugh," as he was
called in scorn by his neighbours, died. And it was
pitiable to see that poor woman divesting herself of
every comfort to have Masses said for his soul. It
was years before the truth dawned on her. It was
only the pinch of poverty that revealed it; as she found
that the very interest on her children's money was
unavailable for their support. Then the sadness of
all her married life broke over her soul, like a torrent.

"Well, thin," she said to Tessie, when I had gone,
"that was a quare thing intirely to come into the
priest's head. He knew enough of me and me sorrow
to wish me dead, sooner than married agin."

"'Twas his anxiety about us, mother," said the
saintly girl. "We must keep on praying, he says.
Sooner or later the clouds will lift."

And so this futile attempt to tie together the threads
of these two lives that had fallen into my hands was
doomed to failure. But in the attempt I pulled open
the cabinets of history, so long locked that their hinges
were rusty; and saw there the parchment-scrolls of
records that are now almost forgotten, and yet are
worthy to be revealed. And if here and there, there
are gouts of blood upon them, I shall make them as
pale as possible; and I shall try to smooth out the
blisters left by human tears.

CHAPTER IV

GLOOM, deep, sepulchral gloom, as of Phlegethon,
hung down on the city of Cork, the evening of October
21, 1829. It was not only that skies were dark and
weeping, anticipating the rain and sombre aspects of
the approaching November; but a heavy shadow was
over the city, as of some great event transpiring, or
some dread horror being enacted in its midst. And
such was the case. In the dingy courthouse, dimly
lighted with tallow candles in tin sconces, and heavy
with the damp air and the heated breath of hundreds
of human beings, an advocate of the Crown was putting forth all his powers of eloquence; and satisfying
his employers, the greater part of his audience, and his
own professional conscience, by driving into the jaws
of death his first batch of victims, the four unhappy
prisoners who stared out despairingly from behind the
iron spikes of the dock. The voice of this man, clear,
modulated, precise, emphatic, was the only sound
heard in that chamber of death. It rose and fell in
waves of sound that seemed to the doomed men like
the undulations of the bell that was tolling for their
execution. And there was a tone of triumph in it,
that said plainly: "Death for you, my prisoners: and

your corpses the stepping-stones to the Bench for me!"
It had all the fatal assurance of success in its ringing
tones.   There was no pause, no waver, no trembling,
— only the deep tone of the prison bell, marking the
inevitable hour.

Those who heard it said: "No use in sending that
case before a jury! It is a waste of time! These
men are already convicted!"

And what was it all about? Well, it was the old,
old story, with which we are all so familiar in Ireland,
— the story of injustice and revenge; cruelty and
rapine, and consequent hate and reprisals. Men will
never learn that wrong begets wrong; but then you
have statesmen, jurists, philosophers, political econo-
mists, conjecturing in Parliamentary speeches and
learned folios the answer to the eternal riddle:

> Whether is worst,
> The child accurst,
> Or else the cruel mother?
> The mother worst!
> The child accurst!
> As bad the one as th' other!

It was the lesson of every Greek drama; but we have
not yet learned it.   But how easy the transition! How
swift and close the cause and consequence!

It was the time of the Whiteboy or Rockite agitation. We, who barely remember hearing our fathers
speak of it, retain but one dim, troubled memory of
that fearful time — a sudden thunder of tramping
horses at midnight, a flash of white-shirted riders

against the dark, the sudden halt at some doomed
house, the awful summons to the sleepers, the flash
and report of pistols, the sudden order to close up;
and again the tread and trample of the ghostly horse-
men, as they flashed by on their errand of destruction
through the night.   When the morning dawned, a few
peasants and labourers, here and there, leaned lazily
on their spades, and stared innocently and wonder-
ingly at the yeomanry as they rattled by.   Their deeds
were atrocious, it is said; and the terrible *vendetta* was
held in fear and horror by the people.[1]   And yet these
latter rather seek to excuse them.   The tradition is,
that the people were wrought to a pitch of madness
by the brutality exercised toward them.   The English
King had come; and the excitable people, in a paroxysm of loyalty and hope, had rushed waist-deep into
the sea at Kingstown to embrace his feet.   The English King had gone; and sworn a solemn oath that he
would lay down his crown and vacate his throne,
sooner than grant them emancipation.   In every farm-
yard in Ireland the tithe-proctor was busy, distraining
from the poor for the support of an alien and hostile
clergy.   Martial law obtained throughout the land,
and men were hung by the wayside without trial by
roving bands of mercenaries and yeomanry.   Here, in
this parish, is shown the field where a poor woman
hid a hunted rebel beneath a flock of sheep; and here

---

[1] One of my teachers had in his possession until quite recently, a kettle, in which
were placed smouldering sods of turf, — the " seed of fire," — which the farmers were
compelled to place outside their doors at night for the Whiteboys.   Doors and windows had to be locked and shuttered, and no one dared look out, under pain of
death.   The kettle was to be found under a hedge in the morning when it had done
its deadly work.

the tree where an innocent man was swung up by the
troopers; and here, pointed out still in whispers, is
the grave of an informer.[1]   Very old people, on their
deathbeds, speak of that disastrous period as the "bad
times."   It remains for some impartial historian to
apportion the blame equally between gentry and rebel,
landlord and tithe-proctor and Whiteboy; yeomanry,
who, under the protection of the law, wrought murder
and havoc amongst the innocent; and outlaws, who,
against the law, took a fearful and an appalling revenge.
Between the two were the innocent, and law-abiding,
and inoffensive population, who were victimized by
both.   These were the respectable, well-to-do farmers,
who tried to suffer injustice in silence, and who, as in
the case we are going to mention, were marked for
vengeance by landlords and Whiteboys alike.

If ever you come to Doneraile, and your journey
should be from east to west, you will pass a white
house on the left-hand side of the road, just beyond
the ancient graveyard of Temple-Ruadhan, and just
above the ancient castle of Ballinamona.

Here, Edmund Burke came to school when he resided with his relatives over there at Castletownroche;
and here lived, at the time of which we write, a landlord and a magistrate, named George Bond Lowe.
We know little of him, except that he was thoroughly

---

[1] Quite close to this village, at the Cross of Brough, in the bed of Skehanagh
river, two bailiffs, or tithe-proctors, were killed.   The perpetrators of the evil deed
fled to America, disguised as women; but two respectable girls of the farming class,
one of them, tradition says, a noble type of Irish womanhood, were arrested and
hanged in Cork.   The only evidence against them was that of two children, a boy
and a girl, aged seven and eight years, who swore they saw these girls closing their
doors, as the crowd swept by.

hated by the peasantry around; and his life was sought more than once. He has left amongst the people the memory of a wanton libertine and a detested tyrant; amongst the gentry, that of an intrepid and fearless magistrate. So history is written; and so it remains, and will ever remain, a rather dubious and discredited art. You can hardly believe a Guelph about a Ghibelline; and take not the verdict of the Bianchi against the Neri. But about the fearlessness of George Bond Lowe there is no question. He was never fired at, but he pursued his enemies; and in nearly every case captured some would-be assassin, and had him promptly executed. Once his horse was shot beneath him. He arose, leaped the hedge, was again fired at, fired in return, and shot one antagonist, pursued the other, and grappled with him and arrested him single-handed, and had him promptly hanged in Cork gaol. Not long after, the carriage of a Dr. Norcott was fired into at the bridge of Ballinamona, and his footman and groom severely wounded. His carriage was mistaken for that of another obnoxious landlord, Admiral Evans of Oldtown. Clearly then something was wrong in this parish of Doneraile. It would never do that in the nineteenth century gentlemen cannot go out to dine without a supper of musket balls and slugs from blunderbusses. Some action must be taken, prompt and decisive. But how? We cannot go round in coats of mail and chain armour, or with a *posse* of special constables behind our carriages. Something more expeditious must be sought; and it must be final and decisive, but above all, judicial. We are representatives of law and order; and our actions must bear the test of a strictly legal investigation. Nay, would it not be better to throw over the responsibility on Astraea herself? She hath the scales and the sword. Let her weigh in the balance, and execute judgment. But on whom? These masked and white-clothed assassins elude our vigilance. We cannot see them by night. Somebody must mark the victims, and then —?

That "somebody" is never long wanting in Ireland; and he was promptly forthcoming in this case. A certain Patrick Daly, with "me cousin" Owen, and some others, is quite ready to swear (for a consideration) to the existence of a foul conspiracy, having for its remote object the extermination of all Cromwellian landlords; and for its immediate and pressing purpose, the removal of three marked men, — Admiral Evans, George Bond Lowe, and Michael Creagh. And how many might be implicated in this plot of Hecate? No less than twenty-one, of whom the Catiline is one Leary, an old man of seventy years, and hitherto of unblemished reputation. It is solemnly sworn before a senate of magistrates held in this very room where I am now writing, that "Leary was the captain, the leading conspirator; that in a tent, at the Fair of Rathclare, he produced a paper, or agreement, for signature by all who consented to murder Admiral Evans, Mr. Lowe, and Mr. Creagh. Several signed the paper, and consented to shoot the three."

Here then was the whole affair in a nutshell. The conspirators are unearthed, twenty-one in all. The sleuth-hounds of the law are put on their track. It will be a Maccabean holocaust. Twenty-one corpses, dangling in the frosty air of a November morning, will assuredly strike terror into the whole army of the disaffected. It is quite true that these Dalys are utterly disreputable ruffians, whose word or oath no man would believe. It is also true that Leary, with his burden of seventy years, paying £230 a year by sheer, honest labour to the landlord whose murder he was sworn to be compassing, was a man of the highest rectitude. And so of the others. What matter? Astraea is blindfolded, if not blind. And is there not a beautiful old Cromwellian doctrine, handed down from generation to generation from that sainted soldier of fortune: "If you can kill the nits you are safe from lice?" This, of course, only applied to babies — the spawn of rebels. But why may we, too, not extend it to parents and grandparents? Surely the converse is equally true: "If we exterminate the lice, there is little to fear from nits!" *Allons*, then!

And so, on this dull October afternoon, Doherty, Solicitor General, "a man of fine physique and gentlemanly presence," is bearing down on his quarries with all the tact and determination of a sleuth-hound of the law. This is a *cause célèbre*, to be tried by a Special Commission, sent down by Dublin Castle. The panic-stricken gentry cannot wait for the ordinary Assizes. The case came before Judge Grady at the

last sittings in the summer; but his Lordship clearly
did not believe in the prisoners' guilt, for he said, with
much solemnity an significance, "that he perceived
that seventeen persons were charged with having par-
ticipated in this conspiracy.   If bills in this case should
go before the grand jury, *and he was not certain they
would*, he besought that they should not be found
*without their having received the weightiest considera-
tion.*"   And out of an immense jury panel of one
hundred and tnirty, altogether those of the county
gentry, but thirty answered their names.   And so,
Judge Torrens and Judge Pennefather, duly commissioned, and clad in red silk, as a symbol of terror, and
white ermine, symbolical of legal purity, are bending
over their note-books, and jotting down the excellent
points the eloquent and most gentlemanly advocate is
making.   Stenography was not then the fine art it
is to-day; but there exist reports of that famous speech,
from which a few sentences are worthy of being culled:
"Gentlemen, I am highly gratified at seeing such an
array of the rank, property, and influence of your
great county, assembled together upon this occasion,
rallying around those laws which, no doubt, it is their
bounden duty to support . . . With respect to the
finding of two grand inquests, even their decision will
fail, unless the petty jury coincide; and when I see
before me such a selection of the grand yeomanry of
this county, I feel confident the subject will undergo
the strictest scrutiny . . . I would call your special
attention to the case of Leary, who, removed from the

temptation of poverty, remains aloof in comparative security, sending out his less guilty emissaries to execute his bloody edicts. If the jury believe these facts, his is not a case that will excite the greatest sympathy. It is likely he will find many to speak for him as to character; but if the facts against him be proved, what will character avail? Of what avail is it, that he be industrious in his pursuits, faithful in his contracts, and sober in his habits, if foul conspiracy and midnight murder can be laid to his charge, and traced to his suggestions? There is a reign of terror that coerces character. I do not anticipate that any such will display itself here, — that the high-minded gentry, the impartial magistrates, or independent yeomanry of the county will stoop to such a mode of conciliating a disgraceful and paltry popularity."

"High-minded gentry!" "Impartial magistrates!" "Independent yeomanry!" Where then were the prisoners' peers? Where, but set aside, and rejected, as they always have been? The very walls of that courthouse, could they speak, would echo as their first articulate sound: "Stand by!"

Nay, in the whole vicinity, not a peasant or a labourer was to be seen. The gentry filled the jury-room, overflowed into the benches of the court and out into the avenues. They thronged the steps, and stretched along the streets, where cavalry and yeomanry patrolled in rank and file, sentinels of justice, and symbols of power. But the frieze-coat of the peasant was nowhere to be seen; nor the long, deep-hooded cloaks

that wrapped the mothers, or sisters, or wives of the
men already doomed to death.   Fear kept them apart
from those they loved.   It was the Red Terror again,
transplanted from the Seine to the Lee.   A look or a
nod of recognition, and they, too, might be looking
from between the spikes of that dreadful dock.   And
this terror originated in the panic of the landlord class,
whose dread drove them hither in crowds as if to seek
mutual support.   Fear is more fatal than hate.   And
hence they thirsted for this banquet of blood.   It is
all well here, for here are the cavalry and yeomanry,
and here are our lusty selves, side by side.   But what
shall it be, if the accused go free, and we have to return to our isolated chateaux, — to barred windows
and loaded pistols there by the black mountain or the
lonely river amongst the nests of Whiteboys and rapparees?   No, there's but one thing clear, — to secure
a judgment that shall make the country white with
terror from the Glen of Aherloe to the sea!

And so, all day long on that eventful Wednesday
and Thursday, approver after approver came upon
the witness-table and swore coherently and categori-
cally to the guilt of these four men behind them.   Why
should they not?   Were not seven hundred and twenty
pounds worth grasping even at the price of awful perjury?   Are there not desert places away in unsur-
veyed America or in aboriginal Australia where their
names shall never be heard, and Nemesis, the ever-
pursuing, the all-seeing, cannot find them?

Two counsel were set apart by the judges for the

prisoners. They were able men enough to argue out a breach of promise case, or get probate of a will refused in the Four Courts. Here, they were powerless as infants to deal with those rascals, hardened in iniquity and trained in their devilish vocation. A practised lawyer would have seen through them at once. Chief Justice Grady at the last Assizes warned the Grand Jury not to bring in bills against these prisoners on the mere evidence of the informers. But this is a *Special* Commission — and its specialty is to try — no, to convict these unhappy men. McCarthy, leading counsel for the prisoners, was a well-meaning but weak man. The Solicitor General awed him; he had to address a jury of gentlemen, and there was a general conviction in the air all around that something must be done. Clearly, he must do his duty and no more, which generally means it is not done at all. For, why did he not produce the prisoners' witnesses? They flung it in his face from the dock, and told him plainly he had betrayed them. The junior counsel, Pigot, was a learned man, an elocutionist, more or less of a *dilettante;* but attitudinizing before a cheval-glass in your library is not the best way to prepare for the arena. No man, not even the poet, needs to be dowered with the "scorn of scorn, the hate of hate," so much as an advocate pleading between life and death.

On Thursday night the case for the Crown closed; the case for the prisoners was never opened. But on Friday morning, as the Solicitor General had anticipated. witnesses were called as to character, — the

weakest defence that can be made in a court of justice.
Dr. O'Brien, parish priest of Doneraile, who built the
parish church and convent yonder, testified to the
good conduct of the four prisoners, — to the special
respectability of Leary.   Mr. Harold-Barry, a Catholic
magnate and a sturdy, masculine character, gave
similar evidence, was examined and cross-examined by
Doherty.   Evidence invulnerable and positive, — such a
man could not be guilty of such a crime.   You appear
sympathetic, friend.   May it not be that you are in
the conspiracy yourself?   What if we should discover
that you, Deputy Lieutenant of his Majesty, hold
another commission as Captain of the Whiteboys?
Harold-Barry turns scornfully on his heel, and leaves
Doherty, "a gentlemanly man, of fine appearance,"
somewhat disconcerted.   Others, witnesses as to character and conduct and general good repute, come on
the witness-table, — some, let it be said to their infinite
honour, landlords and magistrates, who broke through
the iron regulations of caste and creed to testify against
judicial murder.   Lastly, an old man stepped on the
table, — Leary's landlord, and father of the Michael
Creagh whose life, it was said, had been conspired
against.   He was about the same age as the prisoner,
Leary; and, as he mounted the steps, their eyes met.
What shall it be?   We, landlord and tenant, have
stood side by side for fifty years, met our obligations
nobly (witness these two hundred and thirty pounds
annually paid by that man in the dock), coursed these
mountains together, fished that river side by side,

broke bread and ate salt in that whitewashed cottage
above the Awbeg. Are we now to part? The traditions of his class, his love for his son, his own safety,
pull one way. Honour and loyalty, the other. "I
swear," he cried, lifting his hand to heaven, "that I
believe these men guiltless of the charge against them.
No evidence shall ever convince me that Leary had
hand, act, or part in any attempt on the life of my
son." Noble words! and noble old man! If there had
been a few more of your type the tragic history of
Ireland would never have been written. What a ray
of sunshine these words shot across the gloom of that
wretched courthouse! How the prisoners must have
felt — Death now is easy after such a noble vindica-
tion!

And it was death! Judge Torrens, a dark, sullen
frown on his face, charged home against the prisoners.
The jury did not even retire. After five minutes' consultation they returned their verdict, *Guilty*. Torrens
assumed the black cap, and sentenced the four prisoners, Leary, Shine, Roche, Magrath, to be executed
on November 14th, following. As they left the dock,
Leary cried: "We are murdered! There is no justice
here! There is nothing for us but revenge!" Quite
so! Judicial murder! Revenge! Our corpses swinging here in the air of a wintry morning, and your
brains blown out there under the black mountains of
Limerick. A pretty cycle of events, is it not? Cause
and effect; effect and cause, *ad infinitum!* So runs
the whole ghastly genealogy of Irish history: —

Cromwell begat massacres and burning; and massacres and burning begat reprisals; and reprisals begat Penal Laws; and Penal Laws begat insurrection; and insurrection begat the Union; and the Union begat outlawry; and outlawry begat Whiteboyism; and Whiteboyism begat informers and judicial murders; and judicial murders begat revenge, *et da capo*. Surely Astraea hath left the earth. Not yet! She is called back peremptorily for just a little while; and by a voice she cannot disobey.

CHAPTER V

A NIGHT RIDE

IT would be difficult to put in language an adequate description of the consternation that fell upon the whole city, when at six o'clock on that fatal Friday evening, the court broke up, and the alarming tidings spread from mouth to mouth. The charge of Chief Justice Grady at the former Assizes, the difficulty in empanelling a jury, the tradition that no conviction could be obtained on the evidence of approvers, unsupported by direct or circumstantial evidence, had made the acquittal of the prisoners a foregone conclusion in the minds of the people. The friends of the accused had not even taken the trouble to secure the services of counsel. Now all was changed. The convicted prisoners were warned to expect no mercy; and, as the same evidence was forthcoming in the subsequent trials, for the informers had boasted they would "swear up to the mark," that is, to secure convictions for the Crown, it was clear there was no hope for the remaining seventeen prisoners whose trials were to follow. Despair, deep despair was upon the souls of many who had come up from the country to stand by father, or husband, or brother, in this supreme crisis of their lives. There was just one faint gleam of hope. The

43

Solicitor General had announced that the trial of the
next batch would be deferred to Monday morning.
It would never do to lock up a loyal jury for forty-
eight hours. In the afternoon of Saturday, a hurried
conclave was held of all the prisoners' friends. No
one knew who were to form the next batch of prisoners to be placed on trial. But no matter! All were
friends and neighbours here. All should stand or fall
together. Yes! but what hope? The same judges,
the same approvers, the same prosecutor, and a similar
jury. Given these factors you must necessarily have
the same result. Certainly, if no one can be found to
knock that process to bits, and by breaking up one
factor, break up the whole result. But where can he
be found? There is but one man in Ireland — in
the world — that can do it; and he is ninety miles
away in his home by the Atlantic. Nay, he is engaged
for a great meeting in Tralee to-morrow about the
everlasting question of Tenant-right. There is no
train, no telegraph, no postal service. It is impossible!

Nay, not impossible to such love as brother has for
brother. They speak of a certain horse in the city
here, broad-chested, sinewy, deep-winded. He'll do
the journey to Macroom if put to it, and there we get
a relay of horses for the west. And you? Yes, I,
William Burke, whose brother is over yonder awaiting
trial, — I will ride to Derrynane Abbey, I will see the
Counsellor, I will offer him your behests, and bring
him hither if I can. But his fee? That's easily
settled. In one hour, a hundred guineas are collected,

the horse is duly fed and caparisoned, a little group, outside the city, bid the young night-rider God-speed! pat his gallant horse on the neck, grip his hands in a farewell; and the lights of Cork sink behind him, swallowed in utter darkness as he plunges into the night.

It is a wet, warm night, dark as Erebus; and the twain, steed and rider, knew nothing of the road. All they knew was, that they should follow for some time the course of the river, which they could hear murmuring on the left, as it tore over stones and pebbles on its mad rush to the sea. They were soon splashed with mud from head to heel, and the soft, warm rain had penetrated under and through the light garments the rider wore, that his weight might lie easy on the gallant animal, on whose endurance and swiftness so many lives were now depending. But neither animal nor rider felt aught but the stimulus of some mighty force that summoned all their energies, and would make their success a triumph beyond description, and their failure, — well, as the thought of its possibility flashed across the young man's mind, a great lump came into his throat, and he had to gulp down his emotion. His brother — the lad who was endeared to him by a thousand associations, of childhood, boyhood and manhood, was within possible distance of the hangman's grasp, — and oh! it was too terrible to think of it! He freed his bridle hand, and dashed it, wet with the rain of that winter's night, across his eyes, and urged the brave animal more swiftly onwards

on their great mission. He saw but the pale glimmer
of the road before him, and now and again the ghostly
trees that loomed up against the sky and disappeared.
He heard only the swish of the rain, that streamed on
his face and hands, and the hollow murmur of the
river on his left. Now and again he dashed past some
labourer's cottage, saw the glimmer of light against the
tiny window-pane, or perhaps, if the half-door were
open, the humble family sitting around their frugal
supper, and thought of their happiness, and his own,
— O God! so great a trial. And it spurred him onwards into the night. People passed him, and leaped
aside into ditches from the furious horseman, who
tore through mud and slush along the road. "Life
or death!" they cried to one another; "'tis a ride for
life or death." Children cowered over the half smouldering embers in their cabins when the swift, heavy
tread of the gallop smote their ears, and they whispered: "The headless horseman!" Once or twice, a
word of warning was shouted after him, but he heeded
it not. There was one fearful object behind him, the
phantom of a horrible dread; and one objective before
him, — the man who could exorcise that phantom,
and he knew naught else. A few times he had to rein
up before a blazing forge, or a labourer's dwelling, to
ask the way, whilst the villagers, frightened at his
appearance, and his panting horse, would ask:

"What is it, boy? A sick-call?"

"A death-call," he would answer. "Which road?
quick, quick."

And they would point it out, with a muttered ejaculation, as the phantom horseman disappeared in the darkness: "God save us all, this blessed and holy night!"

At last, without stumble or accident, the horse and rider burst into the streets of Macroom about nine o'clock, and drew up at the principal inn. It was a strange apparition and presently attracted a crowd. A great cloud of steam arose from the chestnut coat of the horse, as he stood there panting and covered with sweat; and a similar cloud arose round the rain-soaken garments of the rider. And whither is thy night-ride? was the cry. Rest here! Horse and man both need it!

"Rest?" cried the young man. "I have done but a fraction of my journey. Good friends, food and a drink for this poor animal, and a morsel of food for myself. Then, a fresh horse, if he is to be had for love or money, and I'm off again!"

"But whither, boy? No man ever rode like that before, except to flee death, or win a wife!"

And he explained.

"Derrynane? O'Connell? Sixty-five miles as the crow flies! Nonsense, man, the thing is impossible. Somebody arrest that boy! He's gone clean mad!"

But he only listened, and ate and drank, and said nothing.

The ostler came forward.

"Not a horse to be had in Macroom. All gone up to the Assizes. Big business there! and all the lawyers and gentry are gone up."

The boy's heart sank. He looked at the weary, foam-flecked horse, thought of the seventy miles of road, declared it in his judgment an impossible feat. But then the face of his brother, John, staring out from the dock, rose before him.

"Look here, men of Muskerry, I am riding to-night as no man ever rode before. We are all on the same side. The halter is around my brother's neck to-day. To-morrow it may be around yours, or your sons'. Is there no horse to be had? I was told I could get a change of horses here!"

They greatly pitied him. But no! not a horse was to be had. If McWilliams could not give one, there was nowhere else to look, unless he would take some farmer's *garron*, that would pitch him before he was half a mile on the road. But to-morrow, Sunday, the farmers would be in town, and they would search Muskerry for him.

"To-morrow! Alas! to-morrow would be too late! Seventy miles to go and ninety to return ——."

A gleam of hope shot up.

"Can you, good people, let me have a relay of horses here for the Counsellor and myself to-morrow night?"

"Yes, lad, if they are to be had in Muskerry. Twenty, if you like, and stout men to lead them."

"Can you send forward — say twenty miles or so — a horse or two? The Counsellor will probably drive."

"Ay, ay, lad, it shall be so. They'll meet him at Keim-a-neigh, or beyond Inchigeela, so surely as I hold the Muskerry Hotel."

"A thousand thanks! Now, give him his head," and forward again into the night!

And the women said "God-speed! Surely God and His Mother will help him! The brother of such a cradle must be well worth saving!"

This time he missed the companionship of the river. He had now to plunge into a wild, savage country, across moorlands black with bog and turf, through deep valleys and horrid crevasses between mountains, where the dark night was even blacker than in the open, and he had to trust entirely to the instincts of his horse. He leaned forward and patted the neck of the noble animal and said: "So far, so good! But the worst of our journey is before us. Can you do it?"

And the faithful beast, as if he understood, threw back his ears, as if to say:

"Yes! barring accidents — the casting of a shoe, a stone on the road, a mountain torrent, or a broken bridge, — I shall carry you to your destination!" For who shall say that some secret instinct does not awaken in the minds of these poor dumb beasts, faithful servitors of man; or that some subtle, electric influence does not pass from rider to horse and make them for the moment one? At least this brave animal breasted the night and faced the struggle before it, as if he knew that some great trust was reposed in him, as he strode along through the darkness. For now no light in the cottages by the wayside cast a cheerful gleam across the rider's path. All was hushed into darkness and a silence broken only by the hollow hoofs that echoed

through the blackness, and the far-off bark of some
farmer's collie, awake in the watches of the night.
It was midnight as they passed Inchigeela, leaving
Lough Lua on the left, and the horse's hoofs began to
thunder and wake dreadful echoes from cliff to cliff
amongst the passes that guard the Kingdom of Kerry.
He guessed from the descriptions he had already heard
that they were now beyond the frontier; but the whole
width of Kerry was before them, afar to the very head-
lands that have breasted the Atlantic since Creation.
Will the brave animal do it? Well, who knows?
And surely God is with us. A little after six o'clock
in the morning a faint pearly light behind him foretold
the dawn; and soon the mists cleared away, and he
saw beyond the cloud of steam that rose from his
horse's neck and haunches that they were passing
through glens and valleys of great loveliness, though
the winter was upon them, and the shadow of the night.
Cattle browsed peacefully along the meadows that
skirted the wayside; and here and there, on knolls and
between rocks, hidden in moss and lichens, sheep lay
quietly awaiting the fuller dawn to go to their pastur-
age again. Signs of life, too, became soon visible
amongst this early-rising and industrious people; and
the weary rider was able to dismount and get food
and drink for his horse and himself. And everywhere
the same sympathetic inquiries were met by the same
replies; and great pity was lavished on the boy who
had undertaken so tremendous a task for a brother's
life. But there was no staying nor stopping. The

goal was not yet reached, and there were difficulties yet to be surmounted. The last hours of the weary ride were the worst.

"Go straight on," he was directed, "till you see the say. Then turn sharp to the right, and down in the valley you'll see the Abbey. And may God grant you'll find the Counsellor before you this blessed and holy Sunday morning."

And on he went, his hopes rising as the physical faculties were giving way; on, on, in a kind of dream, for the brain was weary after a night of anxiety. He saw, as in a vision, houses, farms, trees, speeding past; he returned the salute, "God save you! God save you kindly!" as if he were talking in his sleep. He nodded in his saddle, and even the mighty errand on which he was sent was fading away into a thing of insignificance, when a stumble suddenly brought back his senses; and pulling up the animal tightly, and as if by instinct, to save the fall, he looked up and saw the steel-blue sea, shivering in the dawn wind, and he knew his journey was at an end. He turned swiftly to the right, and in a few moments, saw deep down in the valley, at the foot of a purple mountain, and embowered in forest trees, the Abbey of Derrynane, the home of the Liberator, and the goal of all his desires. He stumbled into the courtyard, and dismounted, or rather fell from the fagged and froth-flecked beast.

CHAPTER VI

On that momentous Sabbath morning O'Connell was at breakfast, after having heard Mass in his private oratory, when it was announced that a man, quite exhausted after a night-ride of ninety miles, wished to see him on urgent business. The great tribune was then more than fifty years old. He had won his greatest triumph, when in the April of that year he had wrung the measure of Catholic Emancipation from an unwilling King, Commons, and Lords. He was now resting from professional and parliamentary labours, away from the bustle and noise of cities, and far from the treachery and hostility of men, here in his quiet home by the seaside. He was decidedly unwilling to be dragged from his peaceful retreat into the arena of courts and camps. The Parliamentary session of 1830 was looming up before him; and he foresaw how tumultuous it would be. Yet the moment he heard of this midnight ride, he ordered the young man to be brought into his library. Here, young Burke, face to face with the man whose image was before him all night, blurted out:

"I left Cork last evening at nightfall, and I rode ninety miles to see you, Counsellor. There are four

men already under sentence of death in Cork, on
account of the Doneraile Conspiracy. There are seventeen more to be tried, amongst them my brother,
John. If you don't come, Doherty will hang every
mother's son of them. Here are a hundred guineas!
If you come our men are saved, and you'll have the
blessings of their mothers and wives for ever!"

Briefly, O'Connell, touched with this signal proof
of public confidence, signified his assent. Burke
turned, with light in his eyes, to remount his jaded
horse, and ride back with the glorious news. But
this O'Connell would not allow.

"There's plenty of time. Rest here for the day;
and in the evening we leave together."

Monday morning, October 26th, dawned gloomy
and foreboding for the groups that were gathered here
and there around the corners of the city. The judges
had spent the Sunday at Fota, where they were entertained by Mr. Smith-Barry. The people, the prisoners' friends, spent the same Sabbath in the churches,
hearing Mass and praying the Lord God of Justice to
show justice, which was also mercy, to the accused.
By order of the Bishop, the churches were kept open
all night, and were more or less filled with men and
women, who, leaning on forms and benches, besought
the Invisible Powers to interpose, and stop the iniquity
of men. At nine o'clock the Court assembled, the
Judges took their seats on the bench, and four prisoners — Edmond Connors, Barrett, Wallis, and Lynch

— were put on trial.   Edmond Connors was a respectable farmer, remarkable for his great strength, a frame
of massive proportions, a face of innocence, and the
heart of a child.   Perfectly conscious of his freedom
from all guilt, he looked around at judges, barristers,
and jury with a calm, unembarrassed gaze.   He was
innocent; and God was over him.   If acquitted, well
and good!   If convicted, welcome be the will of God!
You cannot hurt Christian stoicism of this kind.

Just as the proceedings were about to commence,
there was a faint cheeer outside the courthouse, and
young Burke, after his return ride of ninety miles,
pushed his way through the throng and spoke to counsel for defendants.   Scouts had been out all the morning watching for his arrival, and as he rode in triumph
into the city, he had been greeted by a hundred voices:

"What news, William?   Is he coming?"

"He'll be here in an hour!" said the boy with
triumph and exultation in his suppressed tones.

Mr. McCarthy at once applied to the Bench for an
adjournment.   Quite impossible!   The business of the
Court has already been delayed over much.   Proceed!
But there are little stratagems knows to men of the
law by which they can throw little barriers and ob-
structions athwart the course cf business, and these
McCarthy freely used.   It was seen through, however,
and Judge Torrens, raising his head from his papers,
said sullenly, but definitely:

"The Court should make it its business to prevent
delay and defeat artifice."

So the jury (this time partly Catholic, partly Protestant) were sworn, and the Solicitor General was
glibly and gaily unrolling his long arguments against
the unhappy prisoners, when a mighty shout was heard
outside the courthouse. It was taken up and, in increased volume, reverberated around the walls, and
penetrated into the sacred precints of the Court itself.
Even there, men could not control their enthusiasm,
and they cheered in the face of judges and counsel,
as O'Connell, clad in his great frieze-coat, travel-
stained and wet after his night's drive, strode into the
courthouse, surrounded by a wild, exultant crowd,
and escorted to his place by the friends of the prisoners, no longer cowed and frightened, but triumphant
and daring. A new light shone on the faces of the
prisoners in the dock, and the Angel of Resurrection
visited the condemned prisoners behind the bolts and
barriers of their convict cells. It was the *Ave, Liberator!*
put in their own rough way by the people, the people
who worshipped him and would have died for him.

Whilst writing these words, my eyes fell on an open
page, where a certain poet, an idolator of Napoleon,
describes the entry of that world-destroyer into the
streets of Düsseldorf. It was a triumphal march, surrounded by all the pomp and splendour of military
display. Yet it was calm and serene as the face,
coloured and chiselled like that of a Greek statue, or
the little hand that toyed with the bridle of his richly
caparisoned horse. But, beneath that serenity, one
could easily hear "the drums and tramplings of three

conquests," — the crash of artillery, the thunder of
cavalry, the destruction of cities, the death-cries of
two millions of men, the rumble of ammunition-tum-
brils as they tore over the dead and wounded, and you
could hear their mutilated carcases crack beneath the
wagon-wheels that bore the thunderbolts of the little
god. Yes! all was here serene on the calm streets of
the German city; but every one, even to the boy-
bugler, or the drunken dragoon who shouted his *Ave,
Imperator!* knew that this little god was Apollyon, the
Destroyer. How different the enthusiasm and accla-
mation that hailed the Liberator in this city by the
Lee! He comes to save, and not to destroy; to rescue,
not to capture; to open the prisons, not to fill them;
nay, to bring back the already dead from the grave,
and to restore them to their friends. And his very
presence, apart from his ministrations of mercy, is an
assurance that all will be right. The might of England
is against them; the Judges are plainly prejudiced;
most of the juries are packed; the Crown Advocate,
with his gentlemanly presence and aristocratic airs,
is bent on driving that large batch of peasant-farmers
into the hollows of premature graves. But, no matter!
Here is the Deliverer! It shows the genius, as well as
the sufferings of the race, when this people struck on
the only title that was commensurate with O'Connell's
great services to them; and in a far-off echo of that
name which haunted the brains of king and prophets
for four thousand years, saluted their champion with
the ever memorable title, *Ave, Liberator!*

O'Connell bows to the Bench, salutes in a particular manner Baron Pennefather, an old comrade on the circuit, apologizes for his unprofessional appearance (no time for toilettes on that night-journey), and asks permission to breakfast in Court. Certainly! It is unprecedented, but —— A formidable breakfast is supplied, a pile of sandwiches, and a huge bowl of milk. A meal for a giant; but then this *is* a giant. Meanwhile the Solicitor General goes on airily spinning his viscous webs around these men in the dock — finely rounded sentences, for he is a gentleman and an elocutionist, each sentence loaded with its fatal innuendo and appeal to prejudices already keen enough — when suddenly the beautiful sentences are rudely broken by a voice: —

"*That is not law!*"

The Solicitor General is surprised at such audacity. He has not heard anything like it before, — leastways from the gentlemanly advocates who had been playing tierce and quart with him for the last two days. He appeals to the Bench. The Bench decides against him. And on he goes in his spinning minuet, the web now rudely broken, and he trying ineffectually to repair it, when again, the same deep thunder echoes from a mouth filled with meat: —

"*And* THAT *is not law!*"

Hello, there! This is intolerable. The strands of the web hang piteously broken in his hands, as he appeals again to the Bench. Again the Bench decides against him. With somewhat less assurance he proceeds, again to have the airy fabric rudely torn: —

"That statute has been repealed!"

There is no gainsaying the fact. The Bench up-
holds the interruption. Doherty, now quite angry,
forgets himself utterly, and unfairly twisting and
misinterpreting certain evidence given the day before,
asserts that John Harold-Barry had taken the Whiteboy oath, and was privy to the intended murder of
George Bond Lowe. O'Connell springs to his feet,
and regretting that he is not permitted to rebut the
hideous calumny, requests the Solicitor General to
observe the rules of forensic debate, and not to refer
to evidence given in another trial. The Solicitor
General sits down. Clearly this is no gymnasium
exercise; but a duel to the death.

The approvers mount the witness-table. In five
minutes O'Connell elicits the important fact that two
of them had been kept for the last few months in
Dublin in a police-office; also, that Daly's brother had
been tempted by the gentle Owen to join the gang,
and secure a subsistence for life at the simple cost of
perjury and murder of the innocent.

"I never saw such well-drilled witnesses in my
life," said O'Connell.

Solicitor General protests. O'Connell threatens to
have him impeached before the House of Commons.

"The allegation is made on *false facts*," saith Solicitor.

"How can facts be false?" asks O'Connell.

"I have known false facts, and false men, too,"
says Doherty, perturbed and illogical. The cross-

examination proceeds. Patrick Daly, the glib perjurer, is somewhat embarrassed.

"Wisha, thin, Mr. O'Connell, 'tis little I thought I'd have *you* before me this morning."

Yet, so well was the fellow drilled, that O'Connell failed to shake his evidence.

Late at night another approver, named Nowlan, touched by remorse, or irritated at the evident superiority of Patrick Daly, shouted out, as he went down from the witness-table:

"An' if the thruth wor known, there are the innicent there as well as the guilty."

An admission that didn't seem to create any qualms of conscience in the prosecutors or judges.

Jury retires late. Promptly returns to declare there is not the slightest chance of agreement. Ordered into retirement again. Doors thrown open at 10.30 at night. Tumultuous crowd rushes in. "Well, gentlemen, have you agreed to your verdict?" No chance of agreement whatever! Go back and ruminate. No fire, no food. That may bring you to your senses. At two o'clock in the morning, judges summoned from their lodgings. Jury agree to acquit one prisoner, Barrett, who instantly vanishes in the darkness. Jury also acquaint judges with their conviction that they do not believe one single word sworn by three of the informers. Defiant, almost treasonable; but they are cold and very hungry, and these two factors do away with a great deal of caution. Next day it is the same story. One juror, Edward Morrogh, is for acquitting

all the prisoners. Nine for acquitting two. At six
o'clock a certain juror, Atkins, complains of gout, —
a strange experience after an enforced fast. Dr.
Townsend, promptly summoned, is put on oath, and
after some demurring is duly commissioned to briefly
examine the patient, make his diagnosis, speak to this
subject and to other jurors not one word on any other
topic whatsoever, report to Court if life is in danger,
etc., etc. Dr. Townsend is introduced amongst these
weary and doleful gentlemen, examines foot of Atkins,
finds it much swollen (patient has touched no food
since he ate a crust of bread the foregoing morning),
returns to Court, reports juror's life in danger. Judges
wish to discharge jury. Prisoners' counsel, McCarthy,
probably instructed by the wily O'Connell, strenuously
objects. It is quite illegal. They cannot be discharged
until they find a verdict one way or the other. He is
merciful, however. He will allow the jury any food
or refreshments they may require. Court rules this
to be strictly illegal. They must be discharged, or
consent to be starved into a verdict. At last, and after
many a weary legal argument, the jury, after their
forty hours' session, are discharged, and the prisoners
put back for a second trial. But the watchful and
wary O'Connell, who had purposely absented himself
from this discussion between his junior counsel and
the Court, instantly seized on this illegal proceeding
to demand the liberation of the prisoners. During the
whole day, October 28th, there raged a triangular
crossfire between him, the Solicitor General, and Judge

Pennefather, O'Connell strenuously contending against the Court and Crown Counsel that, according to the law, the jury could not be legally discharged; that if discharged, the prisoners should have the benefit of acquittal, and that the presence of the physician constituted a breach of the principle of *non-access*, and therefore vitiated the entire proceedings. As a mere forensic debate it is extremely interesting, as found in the *Southern Reporter* and *Commercial Courier* of that date. One can easily read that O'Connell was no mere platform orator or Parliamentary debater, bearing down all before him in the torrent of his vituperative eloquence, but as close and skilful a reasoner as ever took a knotty point of law, and tried to disentangle it, or use it against his antagonists. He succeeded so far that he compelled the Crown to postpone to next Assizes the trial of those three men, who would otherwise have been arraigned the following morning.

Just before this great debate arose a characteristic episode took place. A poor fellow, named O'Keeffe, forgetting his frieze-coat, had the presumption to show himself on the courthouse steps the previous evening, and was promptly arrested. The other vermin were run to earth; but here was a new quarry. Stunned and bewildered, the unfortunate man bleated pitifully:

"Why am I brought here? I have been tried on this charge before at Doneraile, before Colonel Hill, Major Vokes, and other magistrates, and acquitted. I am as innocent as the judges on the Bench, and am brought here wrongfully. I met Daly the day of the

Fair, and he was so stupidly drunk he was turned out of the tent. This was the plain truth. If there was anything against me, why was I not arrested before?"

Then it transpired that a most important witness for this prisoner, and for John Leary and the other prisoners, named Heireen, had been taken away from the office of the prisoners' solicitor, Mr. Daltera, by the chief constable, Keily, under a distinct engagement that he would be forthcoming at the trial; but he had been spirited away, no one knew where, and was not to be found. It also appeared that one Daniel Keeffe, another material witness for the prisoners, had been seduced away by a man named John Shinnor, connected with Crown affairs, and had not been seen since. Other little things are coming to light, for Astraea is not altogether blind; and Pennefather, apparently a just man, is becoming somewhat scrupulous and concerned. He animadverts bitterly on this system of tactics; men's lives are concerned; already one man, lying now under sentence of death, might have been saved; what were counsel for the prisoners doing, that not a word was said about the spiriting-away of witnesses during Leary's trial? Mr. McCarthy is put on his defence, and pleads that it was Leary's own wish to proceed without this witness. Yes, but Leary was too sure of his innocence. He did not know the subtleties of the law. One witness, more or less, he thought, could make no material difference. But you knew the law, friend McCarthy, its pitfalls and dangers; and these were ignorant peasants. No wonder, they cried.

in the fatal dock: "We are betrayed!" Baron Pennefather is evidently angry. There is some foul play
here, or gross neglect; and he orders the humbled and
penitent McCarthy to sit down. Then he relents a
little and excuses the crest-fallen counsel. But he has
his own ideas clearly on the whole matter. Suddenly
Daltera declares that he had submitted the affidavit
to Leary's counsel, and they had declined using it.
This puts a new complexion on the affair. The
Judge's indignation is rising again. Mr. Pigot admits
that they had read the affidavit, but declined using it
because Heireen could not be got at, and they were
strengthened in that belief by the manner in which
this most important witness had been spirited away
from Daltera's office. So the matter drops. Baron
Pennefather leans back in his seat and thinks a good
deal, — thinks especially of these four men, who are
to swing in the frosty air in two weeks' time. Keeffe
is put back; and the hounds are drawn off. The great
forensic debate commences; and so ends the second
act in the little drama. But somehow the judges seem
a little abstracted; the Crown counsel are a little disconcerted. This little episode has introduced the first
element of panic, which is to end in absolute rout.

CHAPTER VII

ASTRAEA REDUX

"THIS will never do!" So said a famous critic when guillotining a certain poet. So said Solicitor General Doherty, when this mixed jury disagreed, and three of his victims ran the chance of escaping. It was quite clear that mixed juries, like everything else that is mixed and mongrel, are bad. This time we shall take care to have the *sang pur*. There shall be no mistake. Hence, on Thursday morning, young Burke (brother of our midnight rider), Shine (whose brother is already sentenced to death), Connor, and Murphy are in the dock. The panel is called. Gentlemen of the highest respectability, land-owners and agents, are ruthlessly set aside on account of their religion, and an exclusively Protestant jury is carefully empanelled. There shall be no loophole of escape this time. There will be the additional gratification of d feating this Boanerges from Kerry, who, most assuredly, cannot be described as of "very gentlemanly appearance and decidedly aristocratic address."

Patrick Daly improves as he goes along. He wishes to earn his portion of that £720 honestly, and to give good value to his employers. In his own choice language he wants to "swear up to the mark," a pretty simile taken, I believe, from a certain measure of porter. It has transpired already that Patrick Daly was so drunk at that Fair of Rathclare that he couldn't stand. Nevertheless, he testifies glibly as to what took place there; how the famous assassination paper was produced for signature; how Burke, the prisoner, was present as a member of the committee; and how he, Patrick Daly, told it all to Colonel Hill, immediately after the Fair.

This was very satisfactory. But here a dramatic incident occurred. Judge Pennefather beckons to O'Connell to approach the Bench. O'Connell approaches; the Judge shows a paper, and both heads — Judge's and advocate's — are bent in consultation for a few minutes. There is a hush in court. Patrick Daly is melodiously silent, and somewhat perturbed. Doherty cannot make it out. At last, O'Connell returns to his place, the paper in his hand; and, after Daly's direct examination had concluded, O'Connell arose.

"The day after the Fair you described to the magistrates in detail all that had occurred in the tent?"

"Yes!"

"You mentioned the assassination order?"

"Yes!"

"And the names of the committeemen?"

"Yes!"

"This is your signature, I presume?"

"'Tis like it!"

"Then you have told the jury all that happened in the tent?"

"Well, thin, since you want the whole information, Murphy here said that there was as bad min in the counthry as the three gintlemin that wor to be killed; that Major Maxwell and Misther Batwell ought to be killed too; Mr. Daniel Clanchy of Charleville, he said, will give £100 to the man that kills Maxwell, and £200 to the man that 'ull kill the two."

O'Connell read over Daly's deposition (the paper handed him by Baron Pennefather). There was not one word about the assassination order, nor of the other details just sworn to by the accomplished witness.

"Me cousin Owen" appears on the witness table Patrick has sworn that Owen was not with him in the tent. Owen swears that he was. It would never do that Patrick should pocket the whole bribe. He must "swear up to the mark." Of course he was there, and can tell everything just as glibly, and even more picturesquely than "cousin Pat." His zeal and eloquence are wonderful. But, like many in other spheres of life, zeal and eloquence lead him astray. He contradicts "cousin Pat" in a dozen particulars, and is ordered peremptorily from the witness box.

This time Baron Pennefather addresses the jury in a solemn, lengthened speech, daintily balancing the scales of Astraea, instead of flinging in the sword of justice, with a "Væ victis!" against the prisoners. Jury this time, exclusively Protestant as they are, do not leave the box, but promptly acquit the prisoners with their verdict: "not guilty." There is a sense of relief visible in the entire court; and Judge Pennefather leans over the Bench, and whispers to Mr. Bennett, one of the junior counsel for the prosecution:

"George, let me not see you here again!"

The following day, the defeated Solicitor General announces that "his learned friends and himself have decided not to proceed with any further trials at present, and that the remaining untried prisoners might be let out on bail."

Soon after, the sentence of death on the first batch of prisoners was commuted to penal servitude for life, although they were convicted on exactly the same testimony that was so promptly rejected by the third jury. However, that sentence, too, was relaxed after they had been transported; and their children and children's children are here in Doneraile to-day.

The duel, however, between the Solicitor General and O'Connell did not end here. In the next session of Parliament O'Connell moved for the depositions of Patrick Daly, and also for the notes taken by the Judges during the trials. It was unusual to demand the production of the Judges' notes; but O'Connell explained the importance of the case, and in doing so he paid a tribute to the justice, courtesy, and honour of Baron Pennefather, and, by implication, he passed a decided censure on his brother-judge. But the main object of the motion clearly was to indict the Solicitor General, for that he, with such remarkable discrepancies in his hands as existed between the depositions of Daly and his after-testimony, did press home against

the prisoners for conviction, and suppressed these facts
in his charges to the three juries. The debate opened
up the wide question — Whether counsel, with direct
testimony or circumstantial evidence before him as to
the innocence of a prisoner on trial, could in honour or
conscience either suppress such evidence or influence
the jury for conviction? The debate was singularly
interesting on account of the principle involved.
O'Connell's speech was remarkable for its wonderful
moderation, a fact on which he had to bear a good
deal of hostile chaff from the ministerial side of the
house. The Solicitor General's reply was singularly
feeble, wandering away to politics, and quoting O'Connell's speeches at dinner-tables and on platforms
against his studied moderation in the House. The
Member for Mallow, C. O. Denham Norreys, backed
up O'Connell in a lucid and argumentative speech, in
which he insisted that the point of debate was — Had
the Solicitor General in his possession at each of the
three trials the very depositions, etc., on which Judge
Pennefather directed the acquittal of the prisoners?
A Mr. North, defending the Solicitor General, attacked
O'Connell in a furious piece of declamation; and so
the debate raged during a sitting of Parliament, until
at last the heavy weight of votes on the ministerial
side bore down all opposition, and O'Connell's motion
was negatived by a majority of fifty-eight.[1] And so
the Doneraile Conspiracy passed into history, and is

[1] It was this victory that emboldened Doherty to bring on again at the Spring
Assizes the prisoners let out on bail.

now but a name signifying but little to the minds of
the peasantry.

The name of the Solicitor General[1] has passed into
oblivion so complete that I should never have heard it,
but that it echoed out of the recesses of history which
I have opened. If, however, there be any immortality
on earth, surely it will be that of the great advocate,
who, from the first years of his striking career, took up
the people's cause and defended it, often at the risk of
personal losses in the profession he had chosen to
follow, and sometimes at the risk of his life. Yet,
amidst all the triumphs of his career, political and
forensic, I understand that he deemed this rescue of
the Doneraile peasants and labourers not the least;
and, as he said in the House of Commons, it was a
case into which he threw his whole heart and soul.
And amongst the many incidents that he loved to
recall from a life full of every kind of dramatic episode,
I understand that he dwelt with particular pleasure on
that memorable night-ride through the mountains and
by the lakes of his native county; and with particular
emphasis on the tremendous contrasts between the
beauties and sublimities of Nature, as he saw it that
morning by hill and valley and river, and "the rascali-
ties of an Irish Court of Justice."

The peasants returned to the homes they thought
they should never behold again. They sat once more
by firesides which they thought were extinguished for

[1] He lived a short time in history as "Long Jack Doherty," a nickname given
him by O'Connell; he had realized £80,000 by his profession and speculations, but
died penniless.

them forever. And slowly a better feeling crept in between the people and the local gentry. The very gallant way in which many of the latter, at the risk of social ostracism, protested against what they rightly deemed a miscarriage of justice, touched the hearts of the people, and dissipated the unhappy hostility that had arisen from political causes. Providence has balanced very lightly this airy Irish nature. It swings to a touch. Where heavier natures creep slowly up and down according to the weight or pressure of circumstances, the Celtic temperament leaps to the weight of a feather; and you have sullen depression, or irresistible gaiety, murderous disloyalty or more than feudal fealty, in swift and sudden alternations.

During these momentous trials, for instance, O'Connell thought it his duty to challenge a Protestant juror. It was reported that this man had said, after the convictions on the first trial, that there should be a gibbet at every cross-roads in the county. A wave of indignation swept over the minds of the people at this truculent, unscrupulous expression. But lo! a witness testifies that the words were used in quite a different sense, and were condemnatory of Crown methods of prosecution, and sympathetic with the prisoners. "If this kind of thing is to go on," he said, "they might as well erect a gibbet at every cross-roads in the county." Quite a different thing! And so Irish anger swept around and evaporated in a cloud of incense about the popular magistrate. And so these sad winter days a great deal of public indignation ebbed away in a more

gentle and kindly feeling, or was diverted against that
class which has always been an object of particular
horror in Ireland, — the approver or informer.   There,
there is no relenting, no pardon!   The awful stain
goes down from generation to generation; and their
children and children's children are the pariahs whom
no man will willingly converse with, and with whom
any alliance, particularly of marriage, is regarded as
treasonable and dishonourable to the last degree.   Hence
every one of these hated wretches had to quit the
country, and even in foreign lands to change his name.
And even to this day, the old people will not speak
about them, except in a whisper; and then only when
they have looked carefully around them to see that no
one is listening, but friends.   But the magistrates,
against whom the conspiracy was supposed to have
been formed, remained in their country-seats and lived
honoured and revered by the people, and died peaceably
in their beds.   And then every remnant of the memory
of this drama was swept aside when the terrible spectre
of the famine appeared.   And as we read how, in
sudden torrential deluges in American sand-prairies,
beasts, the most hostile to each other, will gather and
congregate on some vantage point of safety to escape
destruction, and forget their natural antagonism in
the common instinct for safety; so, in view of that
dreadful scourge of 'forty-eight and 'forty-nine, all
lower feelings of caste and race were blotted out, and
in the common peril men forgot everything but the
common safety.   It was the new genealogy (alas! so

often interrupted since in favour of the spurious and
historical lineage which we have mentioned above), —
justice begat confidence; and confidence begat toleration; and toleration begat mutual understanding; and
mutual understanding begat love; and love begat that
Union which we all desire.

Here we shut up the cabinet of history, and pass
out into the gardens of tradition and romance.

CHAPTER VIII

GLENANAAR, the glen of slaughter, is a deep ravine, running directly north and south through a lower spur of the mountains that divide Cork and Limerick. The boundary line that separates these counties, and also the dioceses of Cloyne and Limerick, and the parishes of Ardpatrick and Doneraile, runs right along the top of the glen, and close to that boundary line on the southern side was the farm of Edmond Connors, one of the men who had been put back on the second trial in the Doneraile Conspiracy, of which we have just written. His farm lay along the slope of the valley, facing directly east. It extended right over the slope, and was terminated there by the wild heather of the mountain; and it stretched downwards to the river, always full even in summer, but a fierce, angry torrent in winter; and which took its name, Avon, or, as it is pronounced, Own-anaar, from the same terrific battle after which the glen is named. The house, a long, low building, thatched with reed, fronted the south; and, although very remote from village or town, the whole place — farm, field, and river, were as cosey and picturesque as could be found in Ireland. Edmond Connors, the proprietor, was, as we have said, a man of Herculean strength, broad-shouldered, deep-chested, strong-limbed; but you needed only to look at that calm, clear face, and those mild, blue eyes, that looked at you with a half-pitying, half-sorrowful glance, to see, as every one said, that Edmond Connors "would not hurt a child." He was, in fact, a superb type of a very noble class of peasants, now, alas! under modern influences, dying away slowly in the land. They were all giants, largely formed, strongly thewed. They rarely touched meat. At Christmas and Easter it was a luxury. Their dietary was simple and ascetic — meal, milk, and potatoes. But their constant exposure to rough weather, their incessant labour, and the iron constitutions they inherited from their forefathers and conserved by the purity and temperance of their lives, were better adapted than the feeble helps civilization gives to create a hardy and iron race. It was of such men and their forefathers that Edmund Spenser, a rabid exterminator, wrote in despair to Queen Elizabeth, that they were quite hopeless — these attempts that were made to destroy or root out such a people; for they were so hardy, so fearless of death, so contemptuous of fatigue and wounds, that even the savage efforts of Elizabethan and Cromwellian freebooters failed to destroy what Providence evidently intended to maintain and preserve. With these strong peasants, too, modern worries and vexations had no place. They had their trials; but they relied so implicitly on the maxims of their religion, which was also their philosophy, that they bore every reverse of fortune, and sickness and death, with the most profound and tranquil equanimity. A few times during their long and laborious lives, they might flash out in some sudden flame of anger, and then it was bad for those who crossed their path. But that died away in remorse immediately, and the old, calm, patient way of life was resumed again. It was really pathetic the way these gentle giants used to look out from their clear blue eyes, in which there was always a depth of sorrow hidden under their strong bushy eyebrows; and how patiently they took the events of life, and calmly the wildest vagaries of destiny. You could not disturb their equanimity. Tell them of the most wonderful or dreadful thing, and they accepted it without surprise or alarm. They would be the despair of a dramatist. He could not astonish them, or excite their enthusiasm. To sleep, to wake, to work, to pray, to die — that was the programme of existence. To wonder, to admire, to be angry, to be enthusiastic — they knew not the secret of these things. All things are ordered by a Supreme Will, of whom we are the puppets — that is all! Who does not remember them in their strong frieze cutaway coats, their drab or snuff-colored vests and knee-breeches, the rough home-woven stockings, and the strong shoes — all made, like themselves, for hard work and wild tempestuous weather? No Wordsworth has yet sung the praises of these Irish dalesmen; but this, too, will come in the intellectual upheaval that we are witnessing just now.

Since the time of the trial, and his merciful escape

from a horrible death, old Edmond Connors was
accustomed to remain even more alone than was his
usual wont. Always of a solitary turn of mind, he
began now to haunt the mountains continually. Sometimes he was seen sitting on the low parapet of a bridge
that crossed the mountain stream, sometimes on a
great boulder deep down in some primeval valley,
visited only by sun and moon and stars; and sometimes his great form was seen outlined against the
wintry sky, as he knelt and prayed on one of those
immense stones that form cairns on the crest of the
hills looking down into the glens and dales of Limerick.
What were his thoughts no one knew, for like all his
class he was a silent man, and rarely spoke but in
monosyllables.

There was a heavy fall of snow a few days before
Christmas of this year; and, as the weather was intensely
cold, there were none of the usual thaws, but the frost
knit the snow-flakes together and crusted them all over
with its own hard but brilliant enamelling. The whole
landscape was covered with this white, pure surface,
except where the river, now blackened by the contrast,
cut its cold, dark way between the clefts it had made
for itself out of the soft sand of the hills. The bleak,
dreary appearance of the landscape, however, did not
deter Edmond Connors from his daily ramble in the
mountains. His strong gaiters and boots defied the
wet of the snow-clad heather; and he trudged along
through slushy bog and across wet fields, only stopping
from time to time to look down across the white,

level plain that stretched its monotone of silver till it
touched the sky-line, and was merged in it. One
evening, just as dusk fell, about four o'clock, and the
atmosphere became sensibly colder, he turned his
footsteps homeward. His way led across the little
bridge down beyond the plantation of fir-trees on the
main road. As he came in sight of it he saw in the
twilight a woman sitting on the low parapet, with a
child in her arms. His footsteps were so completely
muffled by the soft snow that she was unaware of his
approach, until he came quite close to her, and she
woke up from her reveries and stared at him. She
was quite young, but the child in her arms told that
she was married. Her face would have been very
beautiful, except that it was now drawn tight as parch-
ment; and two great black eyes stared out of the pallor,
as if in fright at some undefined but yet unrealized
sorrow that was haunting her with its shadow. On
seeing the great, tall figure near her, she drew up her
black shawl hastily and covered her head, and turned
away. The old man seeing this, and thinking that
she had been suckling her child, and had turned away
in modesty, approached and said, kindly:

"God save you, honest 'uman! Sure 'tis a cowld
evening to be out; and a cowld rest you have got for
yerself."

The woman did not answer.

"Wisha, thin, me poor 'uman," said the old man,
kindly; "you ought to seek shelter to-night, if not for
yerself, at laste fer yer little child."

The woman remained silent, with averted face. He fumbled in his pocket and drew out a silver piece.

"Here, me poor 'uman," he said, extending the coin toward her. "I haven't much; but the Lord has been good to me, and we must be good to every poor crachure that wants it."

She put the hand aside with an angry gesture; and rising up to her full stature, she looked at the old man with blazing eyes.

"Edmond Connors," she said, "I know you, and you don't know me. But you go your ways, and lave me go mine. It will be better for you in the ind."

"Wisha, thin, agragal," he said, humbly, "sure I meant no harrum; but I thought it 'ud be murdher intirely to see you and your little *gorlach* on the road a night like this."

"Why do you talk to me of murdher?" she said. "Haven't you murdher on your own sowl? And isn't the rope swinging for you a-yet?"

"I have not murdher, nor any other crime on my sowl," he said, meekly, "though, God knows, I am a sinful man enough. But you're out of your mind, me poor 'uman, and you don't undershtan' the words you're spakin'."

"I wish 'twas thrue for you, Edmond Connors," she said. "I wish to God to-night that I was mad out intirely; and thin I could do what I was goin' to do, whin God or the divil sint you acrass my path."

"I don't know what you mane," said the old man,

now very anxious, "but if you wor thinkin' of doin' any harrum to yerself or yer child, may God and His Blessed and Holy Mother prevint you. Sure that's the last of all."

"Wouldn't it be betther for me to be dead and buried," she said, somewhat more calmly, "than be harried from house to house, and from parish to parish, as I am, wid every dure slammed in me face, and a curse follyin' me on me road?"

"That's quare," said the old man, "sure, haven't you the ring on your marriage-finger as well as the best of thim?"

"I have so," she said. "More bad luck and misfortune 'tis to me. 'Tis I'd be the happy 'uman if I could brake that ring, and put the pieces where they couldn't be found."

"At laste," said the old man, compassionately watching the blue eyes that stared up at him from the pinched, starved face of the child, "you should consider the child that God sint you; and if you cannot do anything to help yourself, or if you wor thinkin' of somethin' bad agin it —— "

"What could I be thinkin' of?" she said, defiantly. "If you have murdher in your own heart, Edmond Connors, that's no rayson ye'd suspect me of the same."

"I see, me good 'uman," said the old man, moving slowly away, "you're not from this neighburhood, tho' ye seem to know me name. No body in this parish 'ud spake as you have done. And," he said, with some little temper, "it 'udn't be safe for thim if they did."

It seemed to touch some latent sensibility in the wretched woman, for after some hesitation she called after him.

"I ax your pardon," she said, "for the hard words I said agin you just now. You didn't desarve them; and no wan knows that betther than me. If I could say all I'd like to say, Edmond Connors, there 'ud be short work wid your next thrial. But me mout' is shut. But only for this little crachure, me Annie, me only tie on airth, I'd very soon put the says betune me and thim you know. An' I suppose 'twas God sint you this cowld, dark night, to save me sowl from hell; for, Edmond Connors, the murdher I said wos on your sowl, and 'twas a lie, was very near bein' on me own."

The old man looked at her sorrowfully in the growing twilight. There was something in her aspect, something in her words with their mysterious allusions, that attracted and interested him. And the blue eyes of the child seemed to haunt him, and ask for protection.

"Now, me poor 'uman," he said, "you're back in yer sinses agen. Sure I know well how the hardship and distress dhrive people out of their mind sometimes. But it may come on ye agen; and remimber this is a Christian counthry, where any wan would be glad to take from ye that purty, weeshy little crachure in yer arms, and save it from the cowld river. Here, now,

take these few shillings, and buy somethin' warm for
yourself, for ye need it; and keep God and His Blessed
Mother ever afore yer sight."

She stretched out her hand, and it lingered long in
his great rough palm, whilst she fixed her glowing
eyes, shaded with anxiety, upon him. Then, in a
sudden impulse, she raised the big, strong hand to her
lips; and, dragging her wretched shawl more closely
around her, strode away. The old man stood and
watched her tall, girlish figure, as it swayed along the
road, darkly outlined against the white background of
the snow. Then he moved slowly homeward. As he
reached the crest of the hill through a short cut across
the heather, he turned round, and looked back. The
woman's figure stood forth clearly outlined against
the darkening sky. She, too, had stood still, and was
looking toward him. Seeing him still watching, she
raised her hand, and waved a farewell, and passed out
of his sight as he thought for ever.

He was more than usually silent, as he sat by the
fire that night, and watched the red turf and blazing
wood, as they poured from the open hearth great
volumes of smoke up through the wide chimney that
yawned darkly above. The eyes of that little child
haunted him. He was troubled in conscience about
it. He thought he should have asked the poor, lone
woman to allow him and his *vanithee* to be her protector. One mouth more was not much to feed; and
He who giveth food to the sparrows on the house-top
would help to feed a little child. He was quite angry

with himself, and once or twice he was about to rise
and go out, and follow the waifs. But he argued,
they are gone too far on their way now. Yet when he
came to the Fifth Joyful Mystery, as they recited the
Rosary that evening, the remorse came back, and
choked his voice with the emotion.

CHAPTER IX

NODLAG

CHRISTMAS morning came round; and the snow was still heavy in cleft and hollow; whilst on the open roads it had been beaten by many feet of men and horses into a sheet of yellow ice that made walking very troublesome and dangerous. The great white sheet was yet drawn across the landscape to the horizon; and on distant mountains it shone clear as amber in the light of the wintry sun. The eyes of men were yearning for the more soothing green colour of field and copse; for in this country, where we are so unaccustomed to snow, the eyes soon begin to ache at the dazzling whiteness, and seek relief in little spots or nooks of verdure under the shade of trees, or in hidden places, where the great crystal flakes could not penetrate.

The family had gone to early Mass, some to Ardpatrick or Ballyorgan, some down to their own parish church; for, despite the inclement weather, there was some pleasure in meeting friends on such a day, and exchanging Christmas greetings. The boys who had been home early from Mass went out with their sticks to hunt the wren; and *Hy, Droleen! Hy, Droleen!* echoed from copse and thicket, as the young lads shouted the hunting cry far away across the mountains. The rest of the family got back early from Mass also, and the deep hush of a Christmas Sabbath fell swiftly down over the entire land, for it was a matter of honour in Ireland that each family should be swiftly gathered together, and have their fireside consecrated against all intrusion on that day. So far is this rigid tradition maintained that it is most rare to find any one sitting down to the Christmas dinner who is not an immediate member of the family circle; and the happy-go-easy intimacy of other days, when a neighbour might freely cross the threshold with a "God bless the work!" is sternly interdicted on that day. The strict privacy of each household is rigidly maintained.

When night fell, all gathered together around the table, where smoked the Christmas dinner. This, too, was invariable in every Irish household. The roast goose, stuffed with potatoes and onions, the pig's head, garlanded with curly cabbage, a piece of salt beef, and an abundance of potatoes was, and is, the never-changing *menu* in these humble, Christian households. In places where there is a little more pretension, a rice pudding, plentifully sprinkled with currants, or a plum pudding, is in much request. And then the decks are cleared for action; and the great Christmas cake, black with raisins, is surrounded and steamed by smoking tumblers of punch; and all relax for a cosey, comfortable evening of innocent mirth and enjoyment around the glowing fire of turf and logs, on the sacred hearths of Ireland. And there are songs and dances *galore*, and absolute fraternity and equality, for servant boys and girls mix freely with the family on this great holiday of Christian communism; and many a quaint story is told and many a quaint legend unearthed, as the memory of the old travels back into the past, and the hopes of the young leap forward to the future. And all then was limited between the four seas of Ireland. America had not yet been discovered; and the imagination never travelled beyond the circle of the seas. And so there was nothing but Ireland to talk about, nothing but Ireland interesting; the Ireland of the past so dark, so tragical; the Ireland of the future so uncertain and problematical.

Late in the evening, or rather night, in this little home of Glenanaar, the thoughts of the family took a melancholy turn. The song had been sung, the story told; the girls and boys were tired after jig and reel, and the whole family circle were gathered around the fire now smouldering down in hot cinders and white ashes. The dim, crimson light predisposed them to meditation and even gloom, as the huge giant shadows were cast on the walls and upwards where the blackened rafters glistened under the dark, smoke-begrimed thatch. After a long silence, the *vanithee*, Mrs. Connors, with her hands folded upon her lap, said, looking intently at the fire:

"I hope we'll all be well and happy, this time twelvemonth! Sure, 'tis little we know what's before us! Who'd ever think last Christmas that we'd see what we saw this harvest?"

"There's no use in dhrawin' it up to-night, Bess," said the old man. "The comin' year, and every year of our lives, is in the hands of God!"

"Thrue for you," said the *vanithee*. "But, sure how can we help talkin' about what our hearts are full of?"

"'Tis all over now," said her husband, spreading his hands before the embers. "At laste, we may hope so. As long as the Counsellor is to the fore, the people are safe."

"You never know," said his wife, whose feminine instincts inclined to despondency. "It's clear as noon-day, that there's thim in the counthry still that 'ud swear black wos white, and night wos day."

"Ontil they're made sich an example of," said a deep voice from the settle, "that no wan of their seed, breed, or gineration shall be left to swear away honest lives agin."

"They say," added another of the boys, "that Cloumper Daly[1] is sperrited away already; but the other ruffian is under thrainin' agin be the police in Dublin to swear harder the nixt time."

"They're to be pitied, the poor, misfortunate cra-chures," said Edmond Connors. "It must be hard times that dhruv them to sich a trade."

"Wisha, thin, father," said one of the girls, who could make bolder on her parents than her brothers, "I wish you'd keep your pity for them that desarve

---

[1] "Cloumper Dawley" is the name by which the famous informer is still spoken of in the parish.

it better. Hard times, indeed! As if anything could excuse wholesale perjury and murdher!"

"You have your feelings, Kate," said the old man, "and sure I don't blame you. 'Twould be a lonesome Shrove for you, if Willy Burke hadn't done what he done."

This allusion to Kate's approaching marriage with John Burke only exasperated her the more.

"Yes, father," she said, "but as Donal here sez, what purtection have anny of ye, so long as anny of that dirty spawn of informers is left in the counthry?"

"'Twas a brave ride, surely," said the old man, not heeding. "I hard Dr. O'Brien say from the altar, that in a hunder' or two hunder' years' time, there'll be ballads and songs about it."

"You hard him say, too," said Kate, flushed and excited with the dance, and the thought of her lover's peril thus brought back to her mind, "that he hoped every approver and informer would clear out of his parish, and lave no trace behind them in wife or child."

"Go out, Donal," said the old man, not relishing this turn the conversation was taking, "an' bring in a creel of dhry turf and fagots for the fire. Sure we have some hours yet before bed-time, and the sight of the fire is good. And," he continued, turning around, as Donal promptly obeyed, "take a look at the cows in the stalls, and see they're all right agin the night. It is as cowld for thim crachures as it is for ourselves."

Donal, a "boy" of thirty-five or forty, went out into the keen frosty air; and first approached the outhouse

where the wood was kept. Having collected a goodly
bundle, he went over to the great long rick of black
turf, now blanketed under a heap of frozen snow. He
could not find the usual creel; so, lighting a stable
lantern, he went over to the byre where the cattle were
stalled for the night. Three of the beasts were comfortably asleep in their stalls; the remaining three
bent down their wet nozzles, and breathed on something that lay on the floor. Surprised beyond measure,
Donal went over, and stooping down saw his turf-creel,
and lying therein, warmed and saved by the breath of
the dumb oxen, was the sweetest and prettiest child
he ever saw. The little creature opened its blue eyes
at the lantern light, and stared and smiled at its dis-
coverer. The cows drew back. Their services were
no longer wanted. But one came back from the stalls;
and, as if loath to leave its little charge, put down its
wet nose again, and breathed the warm vapour of
breath on the infant.

The big Donal was so surprised that, as he said,
you could knock him down with a feather. But,
leaving the lantern on the floor, he came over leisurely
to the house, smiling at the surprise he was going to
give the family. Then he stopped a moment, debating
with himself what would be the most dramatic form
in which he could make the revelation. Like a good
artist he finally decided that the simplest way would
be the most effective; so he pushed open the kitchen
door, and said:

"Come here, Kate, I want you a minit."

"Wisha, thin," said Kate, reluctant enough to leave the warm house and go out into the frosty air, "'tis you're always wantin' somethin'. What is it now?"

When they were in the yard, Donal said to her:

"Keep yer sinses about you, Kate; for you'll see the quarest thing you ever saw now!"

"Yerra, what is it," said Kate, now quite excited, "is it a ghost or wan of the 'good people'?"

"'Tis a fairy whatever," said Donal, going over and letting the light fall down on the smiling face of the child. "Did ye ever see the likes before? what'll they say inside?"

Kate uttered a little scream of surprise, and clasped her hands.

"Glory be to God! Did any wan ever see the likes before? I wandher is it something good, or ——"

The dumb beast rebuked her superstition, for again she bent down her wet mouth over the child and breathed softly over her. And the infant, as if appealing against the incredulity of the girl, twisted and puckered its little face, as if about to cry.

"Here," said Donal, "ketch a grip of the creel, and let us take the crachure into the fire. And I suppose she's starving."

The brother and sister lifted the basket gently, and, leaving the lantern behind them, took the infant across the snow-covered yard, and pushed open the kitchen door.

"Here's a Christmas-box for ye that we found in the stable," said Donal, with great delight. "Begobs, whoiver sint it made no mistake about it. She's a rale little jewel."

The whole family rose, except Edmond Connors, who kept his place by the fire. He was always proof against sudden emotions of all kinds. They gathered around the basket which Donal and Kate brought over to the fire; and there was a mingled chorus of wonder, surprise, anger, pity, as the little creature lay there before them, so pretty, so helpless, so abandoned.

"Glory be to God this blessed and holy night, did any wan ever hear the like before?"

"T'will be the talk of the three parishes before Sunday!"

"Wisha, who could it be at all, at all? Sure that child is six months old."

"Sweet bad luck to the mother that abandoned ye, ye poor little angel from heaven! Sure she must have a heart of stone to put ye fram her breast this cowld, bitther night!"

"Wisha, I wandher who is she? Did ye hear of anny child about the neighbourhood belonging to anny poor, misforthunate crachure?"

The only member of the family who did not evince the least surprise was Edmond Connors himself. He continued staring at the little waif that lay at his feet, blinking up at him with her clear, blue eyes, as the ruddy flames from the wood and turf now leaped up merrily again. He at once recognized the child whom he had seen in the arms of the half-demented creature who had accosted him on the bridge; and he remem-

bered, and smiled at the remembrance, how earnestly
he had implored her to commit that child to the care
of some Christian household, who, for the love of God,
would preserve the little life and cherish it.

The *vanithee*, at last, impatient at his silence, said:

"Wisha, thin, Edmond Connors, wan would think
ye warn't in yer own house, ye're so silent, sittin' there
and twirlin' yer thumbs, and with yere 'Well! well!'
Can't you say somethin' to relieve our feelin's?"

"I think," said the old man, deliberately, and with
a little chuckle of amusement, "that it 'ud be no
harrum if ye warmed a little sup of milk and gave it
to the crachure ——."

"Thrue for you, faith," said his wife. "You always
sez the right thing, Edmond Connors, if you don't say
much!"

The milk was warmed; and the little creature drank
it eagerly, and brightened up after its simple supper.
And then began an eager search in its clothes for some
sign or token of its birth or parentage. This was
unavailing. The little garments were clean, and
sound, and warm; but no scrap of paper nor sign of
needle afforded the least indication of who the child
was, or whence it had come. And the uncertainty
gave rise to a warmer debate — about the religion of
the child, and whether she had been christened, and
what might be her name.

"Av coorse, she's christened," said one of the girls.
"Av she was the blackest Prodestan' in Ireland, she'd
have her child baptized."

"Begor, that's true," said another. "An' faith, it might be some fine lady that's tired of her little baby ——"

"Nonsense!" broke in Mrs. Connors. "There's not a dacent woman in the land would abandon her child like that."

"Take my word for it," said one of the servant girls, "the mother that carried that child is no great things. Perhaps 'twas that mad 'uman who was around here a couple of weeks ago."

"The mad 'uman!" said Edmond Connors, for the first time turning around. "What mad 'uman?"

"Some poor angashore of a crachure, that kem round here a couple of weeks ago; and asked wos this where Edmond Connors lived," said his wife. "We tried to be civil to her; but she cursed and melted us all, yourself in the bargain."

"And had she a child wid her?" asked the old man innocently.

"We don't know. She had some bundle in her arms whatever. But we thought she wos getherin' up for the Christmas time. But whoever she wos, she wos no great things. We wor glad when she took her face off av us."

"But what are we to do with the child, at all, at all?" asked one of the girls. "And why did her misfortunate mother pick us out to lave her with us?"

"I suppose she thought we'd keep her," said her mother.

"And won't you?" said the old man, looking at the child and the fire.

"Won't we? Did any wan hear sich a question?" said Mrs. Connors. "Faith, I'm sure we won't. Nice business we'd have rearing a child that might be ill-got. We've enough to do, faith, these times to keep ourselves, with everythin' threatenin' around us. We'll take her down, next Sunday, plaze God, to the priest, and let him see afther her."

"And why should the priest do what Christians refuse to do?" said the old man. "Why should. he have the burden of rearin' her?"

"He can put her in somewhere," said his wife. "An' perhaps, there may be some lone crachure who'd take her off his hands for a thrifle."

"Thin you won't throw her out amongst the cows to-night?" said the old man, sarcastically.

"That's a quare question," said his wife. "Yerra, what's comin' over you at all? Sure you used to be as fond of childre' as their mother. But we'll keep her a few days; and thin ——"

"What night is this, Bess?" asked the old man, rising up, and speaking solemnly, his back to the fire and his hands clasped tightly behind him.

There was something in the tone assumed by the old man that hushed the whole place instantly into silence. He so seldom manifested any sign of temper, or even assumed a tone of authority that, when he spoke as he now did, his words came weighted with all the earnestness of a power that was seldom asserted. His

wife, who, in ordinary every-day life, was supreme
mistress and ruler of the establishment, bore her momentary dethronement badly. She shuffled about
uneasily, and affected to be very busy about household
affairs.

"I suppose 'tis a Christmas," she replied without
turning round, and in a very sulky tone.

"And do you remember what happened on this
blessed night?" he said, now removing his hat and
placing it on the *sugan* chair where he had been sitting.

"I suppose I do," she answered. "The Infant
Jaysus wos borned in the stable of Bethlehem. Have
ye anny more of the Catechism in yer head?"

"And I suppose," said the old man, "that if that
poor woman and her husband (God forgive me for
speaking of the Blessed Vargin and holy St. Joseph in
that way) kem to the dure with their little Child a few
nights after, and asked Bess Connors to take the baby
from them for a while, Bess Connors would say: 'Next
dure, hones' 'uman!'"

"You know very well, Edmond Connors," said his
wife, now thoroughly angry, "that Bess Connors would
do nothing of the kind."

"I know you long enough, Bess," said the old man,
"to know that. But whin God sint this little crachure," here he stooped down and took the smiling
child up in his great arms, "do you think He sint it
as a sign and token of nothin'? And whin the same
all-merciful God saved me from the gallows and a
grave in Cork gaol, where I might be rotting to-night,

instid of bein' here amongst ye, wouldn't it be a nice
return to throw out this little orphan into the cowld,
hard wurruld outside? No!" he said with emphasis.
"If God has been good to us let us be tindher wid wan
another."

There was no reply to this. The young men would
have liked to side with their father, but they were
afraid of their mother's keen tongue. The girls were
bolder; and the elder, Joan, or Joanna, a very gentle,
spiritual being, said meekly:

"I think father is right, mother. We mustn't fly in
the face of God."

"Here," said the mother, completely conquered,
"let ye nurse her betune ye. I wash me hands out of
the business intirely."

"Take the child, Joan," said the father, handing
the infant over to his eldest daughter. "So long as
there's bit, bite and sup in the house, she shall not
want, until thim that owns her, claims her."

"Do so, and nurse her betune ye, and may she
bring a blessing on yer house, Edmond Connors," said
his wife. "But av it be the other way, remimber that
ye got yere warning."

"What will we call her?" said Joan, taking the
infant from her father's arms. "We must christen
her agin be some name or anuther."

"We'll call her Bessie for the present," said the old
man. "The laste honour we can pay yer mother——"

"Be this and be that ye won't," said his wife in a
furious temper. "I had always a dacent name, an'

me family before me wor dacent, an' I never brought
shame or blame on thim —"

"Here, here," said Donal, to end the discussion—
"annything will do. Call her *Nodlag*,[1] afther this
blessed night."

And *Nodlag* remained the child's name.

---

[1] Pronounced *Nŭlŭg* — Irish for *Christmas*.

CHAPTER X

THE defeat of the Crown in these half-political, half-social trials had been so utter and complete, that it was generally regarded as the merest formality that the prisoners, let out on bail, should be again summoned before the Judges. Besides, the belief in O'Connell's great forensic abilities, so well manifested before the Special Commission, created the hope that amounted to certainty in the public mind, that no matter what pressure was brought to bear by the Crown, no jury could convict on what had already been proved to be the perjured and suborned evidence of approvers. In fact, it was fully believed by the general public, that the Crown would not renew the prosecution. Hence, during the months of January and February, great contentment reigned in the humble cottage at Glenanaar. The early spring work went on as usual, and no apprehensions darkened the brightness that always shone around that peaceful Christian hearth. Nodlag, too, was a ray of sunshine across the earthen floor. Gradually she grew into all hearts, and even the *vanithee*, struggling a long time against her pride of power so rudely shattered on Christmas night, yielded to the spell of enchantment cast by the

97

foundling over all else. The men of the household
never went out to work, or returned from it, without
a word or caress for Nodlag; the girls went clean mad
about the child; and often, when no one was looking,
the *vanithee* would remain a long time by the child's
cradle, talking motherly nonsense to it, and always
winding up with the comment:

"'Twas a quare mother that put you among the
bastes a Christmas night, alanna!"

Edmond Connors, too, was completely fascinated by
her childish charms. He would often go in and out
of the room where her cradle lay to caress her, and
when she was brought near the fire, and he could look
at her, long and leisurely, he would plunge into a
deep meditation on things in general, and wind up
with a "Well, well, it is a quare wurruld sure enough!"
But the secret of her abandonment and her parentage
was jealously guarded by him. He knew well that
if he so much as hinted that that winsome child was
the daughter of the perjured ruffian, Daly, who had
tried to swear away his life and who had sent decent
men to transportation, not even his supreme authority
would avail to save the child from instant and peremptory dismissal from that house. When he found the
secret safe, for all the inquiries made in the neighbouring parishes had failed to elicit any information about
the child or its parents, although it was still the common talk of the people, he often chuckled to himself at
the grim joke he was playing, and he could hardly
help saying in his own mind, as he saw his daughters

fondling the child and his sons kissing her — "If ye only knew!" Then, sometimes, there would come a sinking of heart as he thought of the possibilities that might eventuate from his approaching trial, and the significant hint from the wretched woman: —

"An' isn't the rope swinging for ye a-yet?"

At last, the Spring Assizes came around; and the three men, Connors, Wallis, and Lynch, were ordered to Cork for trial. It was a surprise; but still regarded as a mere matter of form. The Solicitor General, Doherty, was again to prosecute; and he came, flushed from his triumph over O'Connell in the House of Commons, and determined to prove by the conviction of his prisoners that the famous Conspiracy was as deadly, and as deeply spread as he had represented. Public interest was not so keen as on the first trials at the Special Commission; and therefore that secret and undefined pressure of public opinion did not lean so heavily on judges and jury. The prisoners were not aware of this; but came into court with hope high in their hearts that this was but a mere formality to be gone through to comply with the law. They would be acquitted by the Solicitor General himself in his opening speech.

As they passed into the dock to surrender to their bails, Edmond Connors was aware of the dark figure of a woman, clad in black, and with a black shawl tightly drawn about her head, as she stood so close to the door that her dress touched him lightly. The yeoman on guard apparently did not notice her, or

made no attempt to remove her from a place usually
occupied by officials. As her dress touched the old
man, he looked down; and she, opening her black
shawl, revealed the pallid face and the great wild eyes
of the woman he had accosted at the bridge. At first
he shuddered at the contact. Then, some strange
influence told him that it was with no evil intention
she was there. Yet, his thoughts began to wander
wildly, as his nerves sank under the fierce words of
the indictment, charging him with intent and conspiracy to murder; and the words of the woman would
come back: —

"An' isn't the rope swinging for ye a-yet?"

To their utter dismay and consternation, too, O'Connell, their champion, their deliverer, did not appear;
but there was the arch-enemy, Doherty, "six feet
three in height, and with a manner decidedly aristocratic." On went the dreadful litany of their imputed
crimes; on went the appeals to prejudice, sectarian
and political; on went the smooth, studied language,
all the more terrible for the passionless tones in which
it was uttered; and alas! there was no stern friend here
to cry, "Stop! That is not law!" Counsel exchanged
notes, looked up, hesitated; but it needed the fearless
and masculine tribune to block that stream of deadly
eloquence. Overawed by the position and personality
of the Crown Prosecutor, and afraid to get into close
contact with him, they were silent. And then the
approvers came on the table.

It would seem to ordinary minds incredible that the

evidence of these ruffians, completely disproved on the score of self-contradiction, and rejected by the mixed jury at the Special Commission, should ever be demanded again. But it was. The scene in the tent at Rathclare, the document of assassination duly signed, the supplementary evidence that was furnished to support and buttress a tottering cause, were all again paraded, until Daly, turning around to identify the prisoners, surprised the court by affirming that he could not swear to Edmond Connors ; that to the best of his belief he was not there. Nowlan succeeded Daly, corroborated every word sworn to by that worthy, and wound up his evidence by the solemn declaration : —

"But there's wan pris'ner there, that shouldn't be there; and that's as innocent as the babe unborned; and that is Edmond Connors. He had nayther hand, act, or part in the Doneraile Conspiracy!"

There clearly then was but one course. Jury consults; and hands down a paper to the Judge. And Edmond Connors is dismissed from the dock — a free man. As he passed out with a courteous, but dignified · —

"I thank ye, gintlemin!"

he felt a cold hand touch his own. He pressed it tightly, as much as to say:

"Yes, I understand. I owe my life to you, for having protected your little child."

Such is the strange magnetism that flashes from soul to soul in this world, when the mighty current is directed by kind thoughts, helpful deeds, and divinely-human sympathies.

He whiled away the day in handshakings from friends, and weeping congratulations from those who were dear to him. For the friends of all the other prisoners were there; and where there was a common cause, there was a common triumph. He lingered around the city, though anxious to get home to his little paradise beneath the black hills. He felt himself bound in honour to wait and share the certain trium-phant acquittal of the men whose shoulders touched his in the dock. But, as the evening shades closed in, and no news came from the courthouse, he decided to get out the common cart, with its bed of straw and the quilt, in which the peasantry then, and now, used to travel from place to place, and he made all his preparations for his night-journey homewards. Donal, his eldest son, was just turning his horse's head from the city, when a wild shout arrested them.

"We might as well wait and be home with thim," said the old man.

A few of the crowd came up. There was, alas! no triumph on their faces, but the pallor of great fear.

"What is it? how did it turn?" asked the old man.

"Wallis acquitted; Lynch, convicted and sentenced to be hanged," was the reply.

"God presarve us!" said the old man. "'Tis only the turn of a hand between life and the grave."

The crowd melted away; and the two men, father and son, passed out beneath the stars.

After a good many exclamations of fear, anger, pride, joy, they both sank into silence, as the horse jogged on swiftly enough, for his head was turned to home. A thousand wild thoughts chased one another through the old man's brain — the thought of his narrow escape from death, of the loyalty of that poor woman, of the strange instinct that had made him adopt her child — a deed of charity now requited -a hundredfold. Then he looked forward and began to calculate the chances against the child. If the least whisper of the truth were known — and why should it not transpire at any moment? — he felt he could not retain the child, and this would be a breach of faith not only with the woman, but with all his own most cherished principles. He felt he needed an ally, and that ally should be his son, who had first discovered Nodlag, and who, when his father died, should succeed to the duty of her protector and father. But how could he break the terrible revelation? and how would Donal take it? Would he have manliness enough to rise above the traditions of his class and do what would be most noble and generous? Or would the inborn instincts of the Ceit revolt at the thought that the child of such blood should be harboured as one of their family? It was really a cast of the die, how Donal would take it; but it was absolutely necessary to make the revelation, and, with a silent prayer to Him who sits above the stars, the old man coughed, and said: —

"Are you awake, Donal?"

"Yerra, why wouldn't I be awake?" said Donal, rubbing his eyes; for he had been dozing. "Where are we?"

"I knew you were dozing," said his father; "and sure small blame to you. We're between the half-way house and Mallow."

"The night is so dark," said Donal, illogically, "I didn't know where we were. Did we pass the half-way house?"

"An hour ago," said his father. "Don't you see the owld castle of Ballinamona over there on the height?"

"Sure enough," said Donal. "We'll be in Mallow in an hour. I wandher what time is it?"

"Betune three and four in the mornin', I think," said his father. "We'll have the light soon."

"'Tis mortial cowld," said his son, whipping up the horse. "Why didn't you stop at the half-way house? Sure any wan would want a dhrink to-night."

The old man was silent. The occasion was not auspicious. Then he resolved it must be done.

"Donal?"

"Yes, sir!"

"I have somethin' to say to you that's on me mind. Did you notice annythin' in the Coort to-day?"

"Nothin' but the usual blagardin' and ruffianism," said Donal. "I'm glad we're done with judges, juries, and informers forever."

This staggered the old man; but he knit his brows and went on.

"Thin you didn't remark the evidence of Daly and Nowlan?"

"I did," said Donal, drily. "Maybe the grace of God is tetching the ruffians; or, begobs, maybe they got a bribe."

"That's it," said the old man, gleefully. "They did. Daly was bribed."

"I didn't think you used do much in that way, sir," said Donal, half joking, half resenting. "An' it must take a big bribe to get thim ruffians to spake the truth."

"No, thin," said his father. "It was a little, weeshy bribe enough; and 'twas God sint it."

"I'm glad you're left to us, sir," said his son; "but, be all that's holy, I'd rather swing than tetch the palm of these thraitors to creed and counthry."

The omens were growing more inauspicious; but the old man was determined.

"Donal," said he, "can you keep a saycret?"

"Did you ever know me to blab anything you ever tould me?" said his son.

"No!" was the reply. "An' that's the raison why I'm goin' to tell you somethin' that I wouldn't tell to any wan livin', excep' the priest and yourself."

"It must be a grate saycret out an' out," said his son. "Perhaps you would want to sware me?"

"Yes, I do," said his father, "although the word of sich a son as you have been, Donal, is as good to me as if you kissed the Book! Pull up the horse for a minit!"

Donal drew the reins; and they came to a standstill on the hump of a little bridge that crossed a brawling river.

"Where are you?" said the old man, feeling for his son's hand, like the blind patriarch of old.

"Here, sir!" said Donal, placing his strong, rough hand in the palm of his father's hand, which instantly closed over it.

"I want you to swear by the Gospels which we haven't wid us, and by Him who wrote thim Gospels, that you'll never breathe to morchial bein' what I am tellin' ye now; do you swear?"

"I do," said the young man, rather frightened at the solemnity of the place and scene.

"Will you also swear that whin I am dead and gone, you will be a father to that child you found in the cowhouse a Christmas night?"

"Nodlag?" said Donal, utterly amazed.

"Yes, Nodlag," replied his father grasping the son's hand more tightly.

"Av coorse, if you wish it," said the son, reluctantly. "Whatever is there is yours; and will be mine only because you giv' it to me."

"An' I do give it to you, Donal, my son," said the old man, affectionately. "For never did man rear a better boy than you. An' now go on, an' I'll tell you all. 'Twas little Nodlag whom you brought in from the cows that cowld, bitter night, that saved me from the gallows to-day."

Wondering, fearful, not knowing what to think,

Donal whipped on the horse, and his father, sitting by him, commenced his dramatic tale.

"Do you remimber the women talkin' that night about the mad crachure who wos carryin' about a bundle wid her at the Christmas time?"

"I do well. I saw her meself; and the divil's own bad tongue she had, especially for yerself," said Donal.

"Did you see her in Coort to-day?" said his father.

"No!" said Donal. "I can't say that I did."

"She was there thin," said the old man. "She bribed Daly and Nowlan in my favour; and Nodlag was the bribe."

"Thin she **is** Nodlag's mother?" cried Donal in amazement.

"She is," said his father, trying to suppress his excitement. "And now remember your oath, Donal. *She — is — Daly's wife!*"

The young man was so stunned by the information that he remained speechless for some minutes, trying to piece things together. He was dazed by the information. Then, suddenly, the horror of the thing seemed to smite him, and he said, in a suppressed but terrible way:

"Thin, be all that's holy this blessed night, out she'll go on the road the minit I crass the thrishol."

"Is that the way you keep your oath?" said the father, pleadingly.

"I'll say nothin' to no wan," replied his son. "But out she'll go; and may the divil fly away wid her an' all belongin' to her."

"There's more ways of breakin' an oath than by shpakin,'" said his father. "You can't do what you say you'll do, but which," he added, determinedly, "you *won't* do without tellin' what you know."

"Thin, who's to prevint me?" said his son, sullenly.

"I'll prevint you, and God will prevint you," said the old man, solemnly. "Glenanaar is mine till I dhrop; and no wan will tetch that child so long as my name is Edmond Connors."

Donal knew well the iron determination of his father when he had made up his mind to a particular course of action; so he dropped his threatening manner, and pleaded with his father on another side.

"The Connors of Glenanaar were never disgraced till now," said he. "I never thought I'd see the day whin me father would bring shame and sorrow upon us."

"Dhrop that, I say," said the old man, "or maybe only wan of us 'ud see your mother to-night."

"To think," said the young man, sullenly, "that the house that sheltered a dacent family for four ginerations should cover the child of an informer — oh, my God! how can we ever shtand it?"

"By houlding your tongue, and keeping your oath," said his father.

"And do you mane to say, or think, that this won't be known?" said Donal. "I tell you 'twill be known before a week's out; for there never yet was dug a grave that could keep a saycret deep enough from *thim we know*. And thin — thin they'll burn down the house before our eyes."

"The saycret is in God's keepin' and yours," said his father. "And *He* won't tell it."

There was a long silence between father and son, for now the day was breaking beyond the hills; and very soon the sun would be peeping above the dark shoulder of Knockroura. They soon entered the suburb beyond Mallow Bridge. Not a soul was stirring. Dogs barked at them from behind stable gates, as the deep wheels of the cart rumbled over rough stones; but these sounds of life were soon quiet, as they rolled over the wooden bridge that spanned the river, and heard the deep murmur of the waters beneath. Here, a sudden thought seemed to strike Donal; for he suddenly reined in the horse, and confronted his father.

"Father," said he, in a trembling voice, "forgive me for what I said agen you just now. Sure I never thought that you were to blame. What could you know more than me that night you sint me to the cowhouse? Sure, I ought to know that if you knew that night who it was we were bringin' in to our house, you'd have towld me to thrun her out in the pit. Father," said he, dubiously, noticing the silence of the old man, "say you never knew that it was an informer's child you were bringin' in upon a dacent flure that night; an' I'll forget all."

"I knew it well," said the old man, solemnly. "'Twas I asked the mother to lave her child wid us."

Donal said not a word, but whipped up his horse. In the afternoon of that day he made up his mind that his father had gone mad. The terrors of death and disgrace had unhinged his mind. It was all a pure fabrication of a demented mind. And he felt he could now keep the secret well. Time would reveal everything, if there was anything to reveal. Meanwhile he would watch and note all things carefully. And — Donal felt a real glow of pleasure as the thought occurred to him — they could keep *Nodlag*, who, unknown to himself, had really grown into his great, big heart.

Edmond Connors felt a sensible relief when, as they jogged along the road homewards, Donal manifested the greatest concern about him; and, once or twice, whistled softly to himself the *Cailin deas Crúidhte nam-bó*

CHAPTER XI

FORESHADOWINGS

DID Donal believe his father was really insane?
No! but he tried to believe it, or rather persuade his
judgment that it was so. That is, he wanted to fling
away into the background the strange, and indeed
terrible revelation his father had made; and cloak its
awfulness by the belief that his father was the victim
of a delusion. Hence, he tried to make no change in
his manner toward Nodlag; nay, if anything, he was
more affectionate than before, and his sisters jested
and said:

"Begor, Donal, it is clear you are goin' to wait for
Nodlag; but you'll be the bald old bachelor thin!"

And his father said to himself:

"Did Donal understan' me rightly? He's the
wandherful play-actor intirely, knowin' what he
knows!"

By degrees, however, the ever-haunting idea of her
parentage created a strong revulsion in the mind of the
young man. He became moody and discontented;
and, as is usual in such cases, he placed the blame
everywhere but on himself. Most of all, he threw the
whole responsibility on the child. From time to time,
in his lonely communings, the horror of the thing

would burst on his imagination; and he would pull in
the horses when he was ploughing, and take off his
hat, and wipe his brow, and say, half aloud:

"Good God! think of it. Yonder, in my mother's
house, taken to her bosom, kissed by my sisters, is the
child of the informer, who has sent one dacent man
to the gallows, and a half-dozen good neighbours to
Botany Bay. An' I can't say a word. Gee-up! It
bates the divil hollow!"

Then, one day, the dread of what would happen if
the secret were discovered suddenly struck him, and
intensified his aversion. His own words to his father
came back:

"They'll burn the house about us; and shoot every
mother's son of us."

Would they? Faith, they would, and never think
the smoke of a pipe about it. If it were whispered
abroad that Daly's child was harboured, clothed, fed,
at Edmond Connor's house, their lives would not be
worth a moment's purchase. There were a hundred
ruffians in a circuit of five miles, who would make a
holocaust of the whole house and family. Yes! but
where's the remedy? To reveal the matter to even
one, would be disastrous. He might put it on the plea
of his father's insanity; but then who'd believe him?
And there was his oath, taken under the stars that
momentous night! No, clearly there was nothing to
be done but await the development of events.

And so the years went by, the child growing steadily
into the affections of mother, sisters, and brother at

Glenanaar, but most of all, into the deep, soft heart
of Edmond Connors himself. Donal alone regarded
the child with indifference, if not aversion. The
shadow of a forthcoming revelation seemed always to
hover around her to his mind. She became a very
sweet, winsome child, every year seeming to add some
new charm to her beauty. She was quite unlike her
mother, who was dark and sallow of complexion;
whereas Nodlag was exceedingly fair, with large, innocent, blue eyes and a great wealth of yellow hair,
which she tossed into her eyes and face, as she ran
around the yard or across the fields, or leaped lightly
over the river that ran zigzag beneath the farm in the
valley. Often, however, when she was alone, and free
from observation, she had a peculiar habit of suddenly
standing still, and waiting and listening, as if she
heard a voice afar off, and awaited its repetition,
thinking herself deceived. On such occasions she
leaned her head gently downwards, and sometimes
put up a warning finger, as if to arrest her own attention; then, after a pause, as if she had been mistaken,
she ran around gaily again. This mood would seize
her at all times; and as she grew in years, it became
more persistent, so much so that, even at meals, she
would forget herself, and pause to listen for the strange
voice. So, too, if she leaped a brook, or mounted a
ditch, she would stand transfixed for a moment, and
lean and listen, and then leap on lightly as before.
By degrees, this peculiarity began to be noticed; and
she was questioned about it.

"What's the matter, Nodlag?　What do you hear?"
the old woman would ask.

And Nodlag would give a start of surprise, and
laugh, and say:

"Oh, nothin', ma'am.　I don't hear nothin'."

But it gave rise to a great many surmises, the more
common interpretation being that it was her cruel
mother, who, in some far place, was repenting, and
calling, calling for her abandoned child.

She was not more explicit, however, with the old
man, — her protector and friend, as she knew instinct-
ively.　She became, as she advanced toward the years
of reason, the companion of his walks across the mountain and down the valleys; and he used to feel an unusual thrill of pleasure, as he lifted her over a brook,
or across a stile, or took her up in his strong arms and
carried her across a tract of wet bog or moorland, or
over one of those deep ravines cut by the winter torrents
out of the soft, pebbly sandstone.　He once ventured
to ask her more particularly what she waited and
listened for, when those strange moods seized her.

"Oh, nothin', daddy.　Only I thought some one
was callin'."

"Was it like the way the boys are called to dinner,
acushla?"

"It was, daddy!"

"Or was it like the way they call after the cows?"

"It was, daddy!"

"Or was it like the chapel-bell for Mass on a Sunday
morning?"

"It was, daddy! Ding-dong, ding-dong, an'
mo-o-o-o-o!" as she tried to imitate the echo of the
bell.

And as all this was very vague, and left things just
as they were, they ceased to ask her questions, but
all agreed that she was a "quare" child, out-and-out,
and altogether.

One day in the early spring of the year in which
Nodlag attained her majority of eight years, and was
classed amongst those who can distinguish good from
evil, the gentleman who possessed rights of shooting
over the mountains came in to Edmond Connors'
cottage. He had had a good day, for several brace of
wild fowl hung from his shoulder, and he appeared
tired. Things had now settled down somewhat; and
better relations had sprung up between the gentry
and the peasantry of the neighbourhood. So he was
welcomed with a *Céad míle fáilte;* and took his glass
of milk with a little potheen mixed, as humbly and
gratefully as possible. He put his gun into a corner, sat on the *sugan* chair, and sipped his tumbler
of milk slowly. When about to leave, he glanced
anxiously around the room, and toward the doors
of the double bedroom across the kitchen; and said
at last:

"By the way, I heard you had a remarkably handsome child here, — a little foundling?"

"Yes," said the old man, somewhat anxiously, for
he had an intuitive fear of the "gintry"; and always
suspected, even under the most friendly exterior, dan-

gerous and hostile motives. "Is Nodlag there, Joan?" addressing his eldest daughter.

"She is not," said Joan. "She's gone down to the forge with Jerry."

"It was good and kind of you," said the stranger, "to take in a homeless waif like that; and to have all the expense of rearing her, in addition to your own family."

"As to that," said the old man, watching the gentleman anxiously out of his mild, blue eyes, "the crachure is no expinse. One mouth, more or less, does not make sich a difference."

"No, but she'll be growing, and will be soon a young woman," rejoined the stranger. "And that will mean responsibilities which few men but yourself would face."

"Well, sure if she grows, God bless her! she'll be the help, too; and sure the girls will be laving us, wan by wan; and we'll want some woman around the house," said the old man.

"True! I heard, indeed, that one of your daughters was about to marry young Burke ——"

"Begobs, your Honor, you have all the gossip of the parish picked up. We thought you knew nothin' but the best covers for the woodcock or the plover," said Edmond Connors, with mild sarcasm.

"When you're out all day alone with your woodranger, you must hear things," said the gentleman. "And we have a deeper interest in our tenants and neighbours than we get credit for."

"That's thrue, too," said the old man, still on the alert for all that was to follow. "We never suspect how many friends we have, till we need them."

"I wish to show my friendship for you, Connors," continued the gentleman, "by telling you that I'll take that child off your hands, educate her, rear her, and put her in a position in life where you'll be proud to see her."

"I am much beholden to yer Honor," said his host. "But for all you're worth in this world, and they say 'tis a good dale, I wouldn't part with that child. But, here she is herself," he said, as Nodlag ran into the kitchen, flushed by her ride on the bay mare, which had been just shod, down at the forge. Donal entered by the front door just at the same moment.

"Good-day, Donal," said the gentleman. "I hope you're well. And this is the little one. What's that you call her? Come here, little one, come to me!"

But Nodlag shrank terrified from him, and put her two arms around the old man's leg for support and protection.

"Well, 'tis a quare name, sure enough," said Edmond Connors. "We call her Nodlag, because 'twas on a Christmas night we found — God sent her," he said, checking himself before the wistful eyes of the child.

"Well, Connors," said the gentleman, preparing to depart, "please yourself about my offer. I'll take the child, and relieve you of all further responsibility about her. I promise you she'll be cared for well, — nearly as well as you can care for her yourself."

"I'm very much obligated to you," said the old man, this time searching the face of Donal, who was listening attentively. "But she's one of ourselves now; and we can't part with her."

There was a deep silence for a few moments, during which the child's grasp tightened around the legs of her protector; and then Donal, looking up, said, as if that discussion was well over and ended: —

"You had a good day on the mountain, Sir. That's a heavy bag."

"Yes, indeed," replied the gentleman. "I have never seen so many birds on the hills before. The place is thick with woodcock and gray plover. I think we are near cold weather. The birds are migrating in large coveys to the South and West."

"And the sky is as black as midnight," said Donal. "I think the snow is comin'; and I wish it was, to take away the bitther cowld."

"So Linehan says. He thinks we're near a big fall. In that case the sooner I'm near home the better. Good evening!"

"Good-bye and good luck!" said Donal.

"Donal," said the father when the stranger had departed, "wouldn't it be well to gether in the sheep from the hills? It may be a big fall; and there's twenty young lambs, or so, I think."

"There are twenty-four," said Donal. "Yes, I'll get Owen and wan of the min; and we'll gether them in."

"An' my lamb, daddy!" said Nodlag, her eyes wide open in fear and sorrow, "I must go and save Nanny."

"She's not far," said the old man, "but you can go out, and wait for the boys; and they'll search for you."

Nodlag went out; and Donal turned fiercely on his father.

"Why, in the name of God," said he, "didn't you take his offer? It would rid us of all our troubles."

"It might add some others," said his father, meekly. "In any case, I have made a promise, and I'll keep it."

"Sure 'twas God sint Mr. Dunscombe with that grand offer," cried Donal. "It was the best chance we ever got; and it mightn't come agin."

"What was the best chance that might never come agin?" asked Mrs. Connors, coming in from the yard. "I'm thinkin' we're in for somethin' hot an' heavy to-night; and we haven't a hundred of flour in the house. But what wos the offer, Donal, ye were spakin' to your father about?"

"Nothin'!" said the young man, sulkily.

"It can't have been any great things, thin," said his mother, nettled at the reply.

"'Twas only Mr. Dunscombe wanted to get Nodlag!" said the old man, in the interests of peace.

"An' what did you say?" she asked, fiercely, for she had acquired a great love for the child.

"What 'ud I say; but that God sint her to us, and we'll keep her?" replied her husband.

"It would be the quare thing, out an' out, if you said anythin' else," she answered. "And was that what you called a great chance, me *bouchal?*" she demanded, angrily turning to Donal.

"I think," he replied, sullenly, "that, as the child didn't belong to us, it was a good chance to get rid of her, especially whin she 'ud be well done for."

"You never showed that child a fair face since she kum into the house," said the mother. "Begor, you begrudge her the bite and sup we giv' her, as if it would lessen you — and thim you want to bring in here to us."

This was an allusion to Donal's projected marriage, — a subject of painful interest always to mothers, who are obliged to abdicate the moment the bride crosses the threshold of the door. It nettled Donal, because this very matter had been a subject of debate between himself and his future bride, who had tried to make it one condition of the marriage contract that Nodlag should be sent away. Nay, this very question, and some delay about her sister's arrangements with young Burke, were the main causes of the delay in his own settlement. He had, then, a double reason for wishing that Mr. Dunscombe's offer had been accepted by his father.

"How do we know who or what she is?" he answered in a high temper.

"You know as much now as the night you brought her in the creel, and put here there be the fire. But you have the cowld hard heart, Donal," said his mother. "But take care! 'Tis dangerous to thrample on the widow or the orfin."

Donal was about to make another angry reply, which would have imperilled the sacredness of his oath; but his father, going to the door, looked up and said:—

"I'm thinkin' if you spind much more time in codrawlin', ye'll be lookin' for a needle in a bundle of straw, whin you search for the lambs this awful night."

CHAPTER XII

THE GREAT SNOW

So, indeed, it was. A double darkness had come
down from sky to earth; and the great eclipse of the
heavens began to break into tiny flakes of light, which,
hung in the atmosphere, made the darkness deeper,
and then shone in a great sea of pearly whiteness,
when the soft clear crystals heaped themselves into
fleecy masses upon the earth. It was the first fall of
the "Great Snow," which commenced that night of
the 15th of February, 1837, lasted for three days, and
remained two months on the ground, blotting out
every trace of verdure, and imprisoning hundreds of
people, who, far away from the towns, had to endure
the horrors of a half-famine during those miserable
weeks. At nine o'clock that night there were three
feet of snow in the yard and fields around Glenanaar;
and deeper drifts in the hollows beneath hedges, or
piled against stable walls, where the light wind had
drifted them, and no stronger wind could dislodge
them. From time to time, Donal and Owen and the
servant-men came into the yard, sweating and panting,
as they flung down a sheep or a lamb, which they had
saved. And every time they went forth, their quest
became more dangerous and trying, as their strength

grew less beneath the strain, and the snow mounted higher and higher in soft hillocks, which concealed dangerous places, and made by their very sinking and yielding beneath the feet the task of walking painful and laborious.

It was ten o'clock, and the snow was yet falling in larger and thicker flakes, when the boys announced that all the sheep had been brought into safe shelter, but that a few lambs had been lost in the snow.

"Thank God," we won't miss 'em, said the *vanithee*. "Was Nodlag's lamb brought in?"

"Nodlag's?" said Donal, half dazed and blinded from the snow and the fierce exertion he had made.

"Yes," said his mother. "Her pet lamb, with the blue ribbon around her neck."

"I don't know," said Donal, wearily, and half asleep on the hard settle.

"Where is Nodlag herself?" said Edmond Connors, turning around from the fire.

"Where 'ud she be, but in bed these hours?" said his wife. "Look, Joan, and see how's the child!"

Joan took up the candle, and entered the bedroom, where Nodlag's tiny cot lay close up against one of the larger bedsteads. She returned in a moment with a face full of terror.

"Nodlag is not here!" she said.

"I thought so," said the old man, rising up. "Whilst we were thinkin' of nothing but our sheep and lambs we've allowed God's child to be taken from us."

"She was with the boys," said Joan, looking at Owen and Donal.

"No, she wasn't," said Donal, sullenly. "At laste, she wasn't wid me."

"Nor wid me," said Owen. "I never laid eyes on the child since Mr. Dunscombe left the house."

"She wint out into the yard," said the old man, "and I tould her wait for ye outside, and go wid ye."

"She must have gone off by herself thin," said Owen, "for sorra an eye I put on her, since the snow begin."

Edmond Connors said not a word; but went over and took down his yellow leather leggings from the rack near the fire, and drew them on, and buttoned them.

"Where are you goin', father?" said his daughter, Joan, in dismay.

"Where am I goin'?" he cried. "I'm goin' to seek after that child. Do you mane to think that I'm goin' to lave her out there in the bitther cowld to perish?"

"Ye're takin' lave of yer senses," said his wife. "Run out, Donal; run out, Owen; she can't be much farther than the ploughed field."

"I'm afeared 'tis a poor search we're goin' to make," said Owen, rising wearily. "Come, get the lantern, Jerry, and let us see what we can do."

And Donal rose sulkily and followed his brother. Their clothes were wet through with the snow, and a great steam ascended from them as they stood up to go.

"Give 'em a dhrop of whiskey," commanded the old man. "They may have to go farther than they think."

They needed it; for weakened by long exertion as they were, they had to summon all their strength for the search now before them. It was quite possible that they would have refused to undertake it but that they expected it would be a short one. The child, they reasoned, could not have gone far from home. They would find her in the outhouse, or somewhere sheltered under one of the hawthorn trees that crowned all the ditches and fences on the farm. When, however, their search in the vicinity of the house was fruitless, and no answer came to their muffled cries: "Nodlag! Nodlag!" across the snow, they became anxious, and agreed to separate, — Owen and Jerry taking the hills behind the house, and Donal going down toward the river. In a few seconds they were out of sight and hearing of each other, as they moved in different directions, each a ghostly heap of snow, and quite indistinguishable from rifts and white hillocks, or burdened shrubs or trees across the dreary landscape.

It was weary work; and Donal was alone in that terrible night-quest. Every limb and muscle ached with pain, as they were strained by the violent and quite unusual exercise, for the young man had to leap and throw himself forward from rift to rift; now falling into wet slush, now stumbling forward, and trying to catch a foothold for a further leap, and always flashing his lantern to and fro in the darkness, and shouting "Nodlag! Nodlag!" across the valley. But no reply came. Only the soft, silent snow sifting down from the blackened heavens, glinting one moment a golden colour in the light of the lantern-candle, and then sinking into the soft drift, where it was lost.

Donal began to lose temper. It was only the peremptory challenge of his father that drove him out from the warm kitchen on such an errand. Somehow he had come to persuade himself that this child of misfortune, this inheritress of evil, would be as swiftly and mysteriously taken from them as she was sent. He could not imagine her growing up like other girls, and passing on to honourable wifehood and motherhood. There was something uncanny about the whole affair, and it would end dramatically and mysteriously as it had begun. Is this the end, here and now? What could be more opportune, more appropriate, than that the child of shame and sorrow should be buried deep in the snowdrifts? It is an easy death, they say. The cold numbs the senses, and then there is sleep and unconsciousness, and death comes gently in the sleep. He sat down beneath a willow, which was so loaded with snow that there was just a tiny space of wet grass beneath. There he began to think. Then the very fate that he dreamed and half-hoped for Nodlag came to himself. He got numbed, and a strange, drowsy feeling came over him. He tried to shake it off, but couldn't. His aching limbs yielded to the momentary rest, the lantern fell from his hands, and he sank into an uneasy slumber. He had a horrible dream. The last things he saw were the great broad flakes reddened in the lantern-flame; and he thought these were turned into flakes of fire that fell on him, one by one, and burned through the clothing into his flesh, and made him one hot, piercing blister. He flung them aside and rubbed his hands of them; but down they came, mercilessly tormenting him, until at last he woke with a shudder, and saw to his infinite relief that it was the cold snow that was enveloping him and paralyzing his hands with cold. He leaped up, rubbed his palsied hands, beat them under his arms, until a little warmth came back, and, after a little thought, took up the lantern again and strode homewards. But the dream came back. His conscience upbraided him. It said plainly: "The wish is the deed! To abandon is to destroy! Go back!" And he feebly argued: "Am I to roam about all night, looking in vain for what may never be found? Is not my own life in peril? Was I not near death a few minutes ago?" And then again the thought would arise: "How will my father look if I go back without the child? How will his keen eyes pierce me? He'll say nothing; but he'll never forgive! He will tell me forevermore by his silence that I am a murderer."

This thought determined him. He made a savage resolution to find that child, living or dead, or to be found dead himself. He would not return home without her; and, with his strength fast ebbing away from fatigue and cold, he knew what that meant. He turned his face from the direction of home and went down toward the river. It rolled by in the darkness, a dark, turbid Styx, its blackness made deeper by the white

banks of snow that leaned above it and over it. There
was the chill of death in the look of it, and a sound of
despair in the swish of its waters, as they swept in
mad tumult from side to side.

"God help her if she has fallen in there!" he murmured.

He raised the lantern and tried to throw its light
across the roaring torrent. A circle of crimson fell on
the banks of snow at the other side as he walked slowly
along by the river; and — his heart stood still! There
was something dark in the midst of the circle. It was
the foot of a child! With sudden, renewed energy he
leaped down the drifts along the bank until he came
to a wooden bridge, frail and uncertain, for it consisted
of but one plank and a fragile hand-rail. The snow
was sifted lightly upon it, because it got no foothold
on the narrow board, and there in the white powdered
crystals were unmistakably the print of Nodlag's feet.
He flashed the lantern on them for a moment, then
leaped across the bridge, and sped up along the bank
at the other side, throwing the light before him. In a
few seconds he was on his hands and knees shovelling
away the soft snow which enveloped the child, and at
length revealed her little figure, with the dead lamb
clasped to her bosom. He flung this aside into the
stream, and sitting down and opening up his great
coat, he gathered the child into his arms. She was
apparently dead. No sign of life appeared in the blue,
pinched face, or closed eyes, and she hung limp and
listless in his arms. In a moment a sudden and com-

plete revolution took place in his feelings toward her.
All the aversion of the last few years grew into a
sudden, overwhelming love for the seemingly dead
child. He felt that he would gladly give his life there
in that awful wintry night to bring back life to those
dead features and limbs. The powerlessness, the piti-
fulness of the little waif, the remembrance of her sad
destiny, appealed to him so strongly that he wept like
a child. And then he prayed to God as he had never
prayed before, to give him back that soul that seemed
to have sped on its eternal errand. Half-frantically
he beat the little hands in his strong palms, rubbed
and fomented the stiff limbs, breathed on the stony
face, which his tears also washed. For a long time
(it seemed to him years in his agony) no sign of life
appeared; and he had made up his mind to lie down
there beside her and let them be found dead together,
so that no man should say he had failed in his duty,
when he suddenly noticed that the little hand shrank
from the hot glass of the lantern. He redoubled his
efforts, drew the lantern closer, and shed its soft heat
over the little limbs; and in a few moments the purple
colour on the cheeks gave way to a soft rose-tint, and
opening her eyes she said, wearily: —

"Who's that? Is that Owen?"

The words cut him like a knife. He knew how the
heart of the child, which he had steeled against himself, softened out to the kindlier brother; and here in
the first moment of consciousness, the instinct of trust
revealed itself.

"No! 'Tis I, — Donal! Don't you know me, Nodlag?"

"Why are you batin' me, Donal? What did I do?" For he was still chafing gently and slapping the little hands. But the little appeal almost broke his heart.

"I'm only thryin' to dhrive away the cowld, Nodlag. Do you know me now?"

"I do. But where is Owen? I'll go home with Owen."

He said nothing. But leaving the lantern behind him, he took up the child, and folding her close to him that the warmth might vivify her, he said:

"Tighten your arms round my neck, Nodlag, an' don't let 'em go. And may God and His Blessed Mother give me strinth to reach home. But I am afeared you and I will have a cowld bed before mornin'."

For now he felt that his strength, momentarily excited by the emotions he had just experienced, was again rapidly ebbing away; and he began to fear that he could never face that hill and the long fields before him, filled deep with the drifts that every moment grew higher and higher. And the terrible flakes, falling so silently, so noiselessly, so mercilessly, blinded his eyes, and weighed heavily on his shoulders, and clogged his feet. And here in his arms was a burden, which, as Nodlag fell into a sleep again, had become more passive and helpless than before. But Love, pure, unselfish Love, especially the Love that grows out of the black root of Hate, is a powerful thing; and Donal felt himself driven forward, as if a power impelled him, and took from him the office of rescue; and on, on he went, lifting his feet, as if in a treadmill, yet cautiously feeling his way, for he knew the value of the burden which he bore, and the principle of honour had yielded to the stronger propulsion of love. But nature is nature; and, as he threw out the disengaged arm, blindly feeling his way before him, and took great, long strides, feeling for crevices and hollows, he became aware that his mind was beginning to wander. He struggled against it; but in vain. He shouted aloud with the full strength of his lungs; and he thought he heard answering voices. But the delirium from cold, hardship, and hunger, was seizing upon him. He was in the dock; and the Judge was placing the black cap upon his head, as a preliminary to the death-sentence for the murder of Nodlag, when a woman's form, clothed in black, shot up from the ground, and flinging out her arms wildly, commanded the Judge to desist. Then the lights of the courthouse began to flash and flicker before his eyes. The woman turned to him, and cried: "Donal! Donal! Nodlag! Nodlag!" Then everything began to reel around. He felt a burden falling from him; there was a general upheaval and cataclysm; and he himself, in the general horror and disruption, fell forward, dead.

CHAPTER XIII

A WEDDING AND A WARNING

THE lights that he saw in his delirium were the lanterns of the rescuing party, who had been sent forward to search for him, after their unavailing quest for Nodlag in the mountains; and the voices were the voices of his brother Owen and the men-servants. When he awoke from the stupor and delirium he found himself lying on the hard settle in the kitchen, propped with pillows; and as the cells of memory began to awaken, and he wandered over the events of the night, he turned suddenly, and said:

"Nodlag?"

"Thanks be to the great God," said his mother, coming over, "you're yourself agin."

"Nodlag?" he said, impatiently. "Where is Nodlag?"

"She's all right. She's in bed; and nothin' the worse for her sousin'."

He relapsed into silence. They gave him some drinks of milk and whiskey. But for a long time he could not catch on to what had occurred; and the dream of his delirium was yet haunting him. Then he asked:

"Who saved us? Where were we?"

"You were near enough," said his sister, "in the ditch at the end of the church-field. But a miss is as good as a mile. You must change, and be a good boy now, for you were never so near your ind before."

"Was it so bad?" he asked.

"'Twas, and worse. You were talking all the *raimeis* in the world."

"I felt my mind wandering before I fell," he said. "It was the quare thing, out and out, altogether."

"Betther get on to bed, now," said his mother. "'Tis time for us all to be there."

"What time is it?" said Donal.

"Just four o'clock!" said his mother. "And the boys must be up at five."

The next day he was all right, except for the intense muscular pains in back and shoulders. His father said nothing; but looked at him with his keen, kind glance, and gripped his hand with a fervour that was more than eloquence. Little Nodlag lay unwell in the inner room. The chill had brought on a slight attack of pneumonia; and when Donal entered she looked very ill and feverish. But she fixed her great shining eyes upon him, and said not a word. The strong man shook with emotion. The very sense that he had saved her intensified the great love newly-born in that night and on that drift where he had found her.

"We lost the lamb, Nodlag," he said. "He wint down the river. I found him dead in your arms, when I pulled you from the snow."

"Was he dead?" she gasped.

"He was, and cowld and hard as a stone. But I'll give you another, whin you're up and around."

"This is the second time Donal saved you, Nodlag," said his mother, coming in. "Begor, you'll have to marry him now, whether you like him or no."

"She doesn't want me," said Donal, in a bantering tone; "'tis Owen she wants. She wouldn't believe it was I saved her from the snow and the river."

The large shining eyes of the child were fixed on him. Then she did a pretty thing. She put aside the hot drink which Mrs. Connors was offering her, and asked Donal to give it to her. He held the vessel to the child's lips, and she drank eagerly. But his hand trembled. His mother wiped her lips with a handkerchief; and the child made a sign.

"Stoop down," said his mother, "she wants you." The big man stooped; and Nodlag put one hot arm around his neck, and drew him closer. He pressed her hot lips with his own, and went out to have a good cry.

When they were gathered around the fire that night, old Edmond Connors in the centre, looking, as was his wont, dreamily at the blazing wood-blocks, there was a good deal of banter and fun, which Donal had to bear.

"Begor, Owen, you're cut out altogether. Nodlag and Donal now are bound to one another; and 'twould take the Pope himself to brake it."

"No matther," said Owen, "we must get somebody

else, I suppose. 'Twill be a quare story if we can't pick up some likely colleen at Joan's wedding."

"There'll be the power an' all of people here, I suppose," said Donal. "Where'll we put 'em?"

"Aren't the barns big enough for the whole parish?" said the old man. "But, if this weather lasts, the neighbours won't come."

"Won't they, though?" said Owen. "'Tisn't snow, nor hail, nor wind will keep the boys and girls away from a good wedding."

"Wisha, thin, Donal," said Joan, who was anxious to turn away the conversation from herself, "wasn't it the quare things you wor sayin' last night, whin you wor brought in?"

"What things?" said Donal, anxiously looking at his father.

"Never mind!" said the old man. "Shure you were out of your min' with the cowld and the hardship; and you didn't know what you were sayin'."

"You wor talkin' and talkin' about jedges, and black caps, an' informers, an' Daly and his wife, and Nodlag." 'Tis quare how things mix themselves up in drames like that."

"I remimber," said Donal, cautiously, "jest before I fell, I thought I was in the dock, an' the jedge was puttin' on his black cap, whin a woman, a great tall woman stood up, and stopped him. An' thin I heard voices: 'Donal! Donal! Nodlag! Nodlag!' an' I fell."

"'Twas we wor callin'," said Owen. "An' 'twas the devil's own job to make you hear. An' sure 'twas well we didn't miss you both; for ye were like a big snowball for all the world."

"How is the night?" said the old man, anxious to change the conversation. "Do you think ye'll have everythin' in for the weddin', Bess?" he said to his wife. "How many gallons of sperrits did ye ordher?"

"We ordhered thirty," said the *vanithee*. "But sure we can get more."

"An' the rounds of beef?"

"They're all right!"

"An' the hams?"

"They're all right," said the wife, impatiently. "Can't you lave thim things to ourselves; and not be interfaring with our work? Did you settle wid the priest yourself?"

"I did, God bless him!" said her husband, "an' 'twas aisy settlin'. He'll have twinty weddings that day, and more cummin' in; but he'll be here at three o'clock to the minit, he says; so that we can have nine hours rale *Keol*, before Ash Winsday breaks upon us!"

And they had, — real, downright, tumultuous, Irish fun and frolic. From North, South, East, West, the friends came, as heedless of the snow that lay caked upon the ground, and the drifts that were piled in the ditches and furrows, as a Canadian with his horses and sleds. There was the house far off — the objective of all the country that night — with its small square windows blazing merrily under the fierce fires upon the hearth; and afar off, clearly outlined against

the white pall on the ground, were the dark figures of
the guests who had gathered to do honour to a family
on which no shadow of a shade of dishonour had ever
rested. And they feasted, and drank, and danced;
and, late at night, the old people gathered around the
fire in the kitchen, and told stories, whilst the youngsters, to the sound of bagpipes and fiddle, danced themselves into a fever in the decorated and festooned
barn. And Donal led out Nodlag, and insisted on
dancing an Irish reel with her, much to the disgust of
his intended bride, who watched the child with no
friendly eyes, and half determined that the moment
she became mistress of Glenanaar farm, out that waif
and foundling should go, and seek a home elsewhere.
But no shadow crossed the mind of the child, now
thoroughly recovered from her illness; but she danced,
and danced with Donal, and Owen, and Jerry; and
some old people shook their heads, and said 'twas the
fairies brought her and left her, and that somehow
there was something uncanny about it all.

At last, twelve o'clock rang out from the kitchen
timepiece — an old grandfather's clock, an heirloom
in the family for generations — and Lent broke solemnly on the festivities of the night. Some of the
youngsters, a little heated, insisted on keeping up the
fun till morning, and quoted as an excuse for additional
revels the old distich:

> Long life and success to the Council of Trint,
> That put fast upon mate, but not upon drink!

But the elders were inexorable. This was the day of

ashes and humiliation, the first day of penance, and all should yield to the Church's behests in this grave and solemn matter. So, in the moonlight of that March night, the great crowd dispersed with many a good wish for the happiness of the young people who commenced to carry the burden of life together that solemn night.

As they said goodbye! after many a *dhoc-a-dhurrus*, young Burke, the bridegroom, whispered to Donal: —

"Light your pipe, and walk down a bit of the road with us!"

Donal did so. Burke and he had been always close friends, even before they assumed this new relationship. They allowed the cars to go on before them with their female relatives, and trudged along the hardened snow, smoking leisurely.

"'Twas a pleasant night enough!" said Donal, not wishing to make too much of their profuse hospitality.

"Nothin' could be grander," said Burke. "It bate every weddin' in the parish."

He went on, smoking silently.

"I hope you'll be good to Joan," said Donal; "there isn't, and 'tisn't because I say it, a better girl nor a claner housekeeper in this counthry."

"Do you doubt me?" said his companion, half-offended.

"Divil a doubt," said Donal, "but we were fond of Joan, an' we'll miss her."

Burke was again silent.

"You've somethin' on your mind to tell me," said

Donal. "Wasn't everythin' right, marriage-money an' all?"

His companion gave him a rude shove.

"Thin you have somethin' to say," cried Donal. "Out wid it, man! What have you to be afeared of?"

"I'm afeared of nothin' for meself," said Burke. "But I'm afeared for ye."

Then suddenly turning, he asked fiercely:—

"Who's that girl ye have up at the house?"

"Girl? What girl? We've no girl there but Norry and Peggy!"

"I don't mane thim. We all know who thim are. But who's that young *thucka* ye danced with to-night?"

"I danced with many a one," said Donal, on his guard. "With your sisters, and your cousin, Kate Heaphy, and Lucy Kelly, and ——"

"I don't mane thim naither," said Burke. "I mane that youngster whom ye tuk into yere house, and who's been wid ye since."

"Oh! Nodlag!" said Donal, waking up.

"That's her! Who is she? Where did she come from? Who're her belongings?"

"Ask me somethin' aisy," said Donal, fencing and parrying the question.

"Do ye mane to say, Donal Connors, that nayther you, nor your father, nor your mother, know who the divil's breed it is ye are keepin' on a flure that was wanst dacent enough?"

"You've taken a little dhrap too much to-night,"

said Donal, "altho' ye seldom do it, and 'tis a good man's case. All that I can tell you is, that no sign or token has come to us to tell us who the girl is, since the night I found her meself amongst the cows."

Burke walked on in silence, till they came to the forge just at the cross-roads above the bridge where old Edmond Connors had interviewed Nodlag and her mother. Here he stood still, and hailed the cars that were beneath them in the hollow where the bridge was sunk. He held out his hand.

"I see ye don't know it, nor suspect it," he said in a hollow voice, "tho' it is the talk of the country-side, and is spoke of where you wouldn't like to hear. *Thiggin-thu!* Well, I'm your brother-in-law now; and wan of the family. So I put you on your guard. If the boys," he whispered, hoarsely, looking around cautiously at the time, "find out that what they suspect is true, there'll be a bonfire at Glenanaar before St. John's Eve."

"Yerra, what is it all about?" asked Donal, affecting great ignorance and alarm. "What do they suspect? Or, what harrum can a poor little *girsha*, like Nodlag, be to any wan? If they want to do mischief, haven't they Bond Lowe and his likes ——"

"There are worse than Bond Lowe," said Burke, meaningly. "The thraitor within dures is worse than the inimy without."

And swinging his hands loosely, he passed on, and overtook the cars that held his young bride and the members of his own family.

Donal stood still for a moment, shocked at the unexpected revelation of his father's secret. Then, when he thought of all he had suffered for Nodlag that night, three weeks gone, when he rescued her from the snow, and the winning ways of the child, and her utter helplessness, he muttered between his teeth: —

"Why the d——l can't they keep their selves quiet? There's always some blackguardin' and ruffianism brewing betune them. What's it to thim who Nodlag is, or where she kum from? But, be the powers ——"

"Fine night, Donal Connors," said the cheery voice of the blacksmith, Redmond Casey, or, as he was popularly known, "Red" Casey, partly as an abbreviation of his name, and partly explanatory of a red shock of hair which was always victoriously engaged in a deadly struggle against the black dyes of the smithy. He was a young man, and had taken over the business on his father's death a few years previously. His aged mother was his housekeeper; and his smithy was, as is usual in Ireland, club and news-shop and House of Parliament for half the country-side. Here, in the fierce light of the mighty fire, fanned by the huge bellows, and to the music of the clanging sledge and anvil, were all subjects of parochial, national, political, and ecclesiastical affairs discussed, — the only silent man being the smith himself, who pared and cut, and measured and nailed, drinking in every kind of information, but saying nothing. He stood this night of the wedding, calmly smoking at the door of his forge. He had been kept busy up to the last moment, "frosting" and "kniving" the horses that had borne the merry crowds to and from the wedding.

"'Tis a fine night, Red," said Donal, coming over. "I'm sorry you couldn't be with us."

"So was I; but there was no help for it. Ye broke up airly."

"We did. The ould people would have no more dancin' nor sportin' after twelve o'clock. An' now we have to face the black tay in the mornin'."

"Well, but ye'll be havin' your own wedding soon," said Red. "An' I hope we'll have a rale night of it."

"I hope so," said Donal, moving homeward.

"I say, Donal," said Red, as if suddenly recollecting himself.

"Well, Red, what is it?" said Donal.

"'Tis a family business, an' I suppose I shouldn't interfare," said Red, blushing in the darkness. "But they say your intinded, Donal, don't want Nodlag on the same flure wid her, an' the ould woman here does be lonesome sometimes ——"

"You mane you'll like to have her here?" said Donal.

"That is, av there's no room for her at Glenanaar," said Red.

"So long as there's bit, bite and sup yonder," said Donal, solemnly, "Nodlag will have her place at our table, no matter who comes in ——"

"Oh, I meant no offince," said Red.

"An' I take none," said Donal.   "An' at laste, it is somethin' to know that she has a friend in you, Red, if all fails her."

"That she has, and some day I may have the chance to prove it," said Red.   "Good-night!"

CHAPTER XIV

A MIDNIGHT SYNOD

IT was in an old gray keep, one of the square fron-
tier-fortresses, built in Queen Elizabeth's time, that
the midnight synod was held. The castle rose from
a little swell, or knoll, which probably was in ancient
days the moraine of some mighty glacier that had slid
down from the mountain valleys and pushed the
detritus of sand and earth before it. It was built of
gray limestone, and "stood full square to all the winds
that blow."

Here, in past ages, were entrenched the mail-clad
warriors, who held the whole country-side against the
rapparees; and here this moonlit, frosty night, with
the snow still glittering all around, were gathered the
descendants of these same rapparees, as fierce, as
generous, and as vindictive as their sires of three hundred years gone by. Some sate on the stone steps that
led to the upper stories of the old castle; some leaned
against the heavy walls; and two or three were on the
summit, hidden behind the parapets, sentinels against
the approach of strangers or enemies. They were all
young men, of the farming and labouring class. A few
were still members of the Whiteboy *vendetta*. All had
worn the white shirt in their time. Two were the sons
of the Dan Lynch who was executed at the same assizes

at which Edmond Connors had been acquitted. Years had wrought no change in their hearts, although time and trouble had laid heavy hands upon them. The smouldering fires of hatred were newly lighted by the startling report that had gone far and wide over the country. These boys, too, were first cousins to Nano Hegarty, Donal's future bride.

There were few preliminaries. At least, there were no synodical prayers.

"Boys," said young Lynch, "ye know what ye're here for. It has gone round the counthry that the seed and breed of that infernal ruffian, Cloumper Daly, is in our midst, left here by her father and mother. And, the question is, what's to be done?"

"Is that what we're summoned for?" said a young farmer, no great friend of the Lynch's.

"'Tis, and isn't it enough?" hotly replied Lynch. "Do ye mane to say that we're goin' to stand by, and see that Hellspawn amongst dacent people, who never had shame, altho' they had their fill of sorrow at their dure?"

"'Tis a quare thing, though," said the former speaker, "that we should be called upon to make war upon a slip of a child that never did nobody harm. How can she help those from whom she was got?"

"'Tis aisy for you to talk, Connor Brien," said Lynch, "but if you knew what it was to rise in the mornin', and think of your father swung by the throat by thim Sassanachs in Cork; and he, before the High God, innicent ——"

Here the poor fellow's emotion smothered him; and he could not proceed. But it had the effect of the most deadly eloquence upon his audience.

"Thrue for you, Dan," said a great, burly fellow, rising. "'Tis only whin it comes home to our own dures, that we feel for other's troubles."

"If I thought," said another, "that the spawn of that sarpint was amongst us, be the Holy Moses, 'twould soon go down the river, or up the sky in smoke."

"We're all of wan mind in that matther," said a peacemaker. "But, before ye go farther, wouldn't it be well to know what 'tis all about?"

"What the divil, man," said young Lynch. "Don't we all know what 'tis about? Are our heads growin' onder our oxters that we haven't hard what everyone is sayin'?"

"Aisy now, aisy now, Murty," said the peacemaker. "Does anny man mane to tell me, that Edmond Connors would give food and shelter to any wan of that seed, breed, and gineration?"

"They say he don't know it," replied the other. "All he knows is, that he picked up the child on a Christmas night, and kep' her out of charity. That's all."

"An' how can anny wan prove she's Cloumper Daly's child?" asked another who was for peace, and who was tired enough of violence.

"There's no proof if you come to that," said Murty Lynch. "But Cloumper Daly's wife wint to America without her child; and the child at Connors's was found about the same time."

"Yerra, what proof is that?" asked the pleader. "And was there anny more onlikely place on the face of the airth for Cloumper Daly, or his wife, to put their child than at the dure of the man whose life they wor swearing away?"

"Begor, that clinches the matter, Dan," said a young fellow, who had been hitherto silent. "Sure, in the whole wurruld they couldn't find a worse spot than Glenanaar. Ould Ned Connors would have pitched her straight to the divil."

"But sure, man, I tell you he didn't know it; nor does he know it till this day. Thin, ye heard what Dunscombe said to his wood-ranger, just before the great snow fell?"

"No! no! what's that?" said many voices, whilst all faces were turned up expectant.

"Is it Linehan you mane?" said one, to make quite sure of the personality.

"Yes, Thade Linehan ——"

"The divil a much I'd give for what that ruffian and rint-warner would say," cried a boy, who had been prosecuted by Linehan for poaching. "He's not much better than an informer himself."

"No matter for that!" said Murty Lynch, angrily, as he felt the tide of opinion setting against him, "the divil himself will tell the truth whin it suits his purpose."

"Well! well! what did Dunscombe say? Let us hear it!" cried a dozen voices.

"What did he say?" repeated Murty, to emphasize the answer. "He said he made an offer to ould Ned Connors about that child, which he'd be sorry for not takin'."

"What was the offer?" cried the incredulous ones. "It must have been a chape bargain that Dunscombe offered for. He'd split with the divil himself."

"He offered to take the child, and do for her, and rare her up a lady ——"

"An' make a souper of her?"

"He didn't say that."

"He meant it."

"Well, I see ye're all agin me," said Dan Lynch. "But, be this and be that, I'll take the thing into me own hands, as ye haven't the heart of a h_re ——"

"Yerra, now, aisy, Dan," cried the great big giant. "You know us as well as any wan ——"

"I know you, Dinny; an' I know you're a man, an' a man's son."

"You know well, Dan," said the giant, soothed by the flattery, "that I'd face all the landlords, an' agents, an' bailiffs in Munster; an' if it come to that, I'd think no more of spitting one of thim thin I'd think of spearin' a salmon in the close saison. But 'tis different alte-gither, whin it comes to talkin' of doin' away wid a little slip of a colleen, that never did no harrum to no wan."

"An' who the divil talked of doin' away wid her?" said Lynch, angrily. "I never mintioned it, av ye did."

"Hallo! me bouchal, is't that ye're afther?" said the

giant. "Ye want to save yere own skin; and let uz pay the piper. Is that it?"

"Ye're a parcel of white-livered *kinats*," said Lynch, now losing all control of himself. "'Tis aisy to see that none of ye, nor of thim belongin' to ye, ever swung for yere creed or counthry."

"Begor, you're right, Dan," said one of the "boys," passing his finger inside his collar. "That's a cravat that must be cut to be loosened. None of us ever wore it."

"'Tisn't too late a-yet," said Lynch, moving away. "High hangin' and the divil playin' is what some of ye will see before ye die. Come, Murty! Come, Darby! All the sperrit is died out of the counthry!"

And he and his brother and the one follower left the meeting.

"Wisha, in the name of God," said one of the boys, rising up to return home, "is that what we're brought here for this cowld night, whin we ought to be in our warrum beds? Begobs, some people will soon call a meeting if they want to snare a hare, or spear a salmon."

"Lynch thinks we're obligated to him and his, on account of his father," replied the giant. "An' if it wor a clear case, and somebody besides a woman or child consarned, I'd not be for backin' out of anything in fairity. But, be the hole in my coat, I'm not goin' to pick a quarrel with Edmond Connors, nor his family, bekase he chuse to take in a little *gorlach* of a child on a Christmas night."

"I was spakin' to his son-in-law, John Burke,"

replied the former. "He tould me he gave a hint to
Donal, which he wouldn't have done, only he had a
sup in him the night of the weddin', — an' sure if he
hadn't it thin, whin would he have a right to it? An'
he tould me, from the way Donal took it, he had no
more idee of it than the babe unborned."

"Av coorse," said the giant, "ould women's talk
will go far an' wide across the counthry. Give 'em
the tay an' the snuff, an' begob, they'll invint stories
and romances for ye, as long as from here to Bantry
Bay!"

"But why are the Lynches so hot about it?" was
asked. "Sure, it can't be they want to revinge the
murdher of their father on such a child as that?"

"No! but there's another weddin' comin' on, I'm
tould," was the reply. "Donal Connors is bringin' in
Nano Hegarty from out there beyant Ardpatrick, and
sure she don't want any wan to share the flure wid
her."

"Thin Owen and the sisther go out, I suppose?"

"Av coorse, they do. An' av she could turn out
the ould couple wid them, she think no more of it
than of saying, 'Hurrish!' to the pig."

"An' that's Dan Lynch's game, is it?" cried the
others, in a chorus of indignation. "Wisha, thin, bad
luck to him, the naygur, to think we were goin' to bind
ourselv' to help Nano. 'Twill be manny a long day
afore we'll come to a meetin' of the Lynches again."

And the boys dispersed, one by one, each taking a
different pathway across the snow-enveloped fields.

The great giant, Thade Ryall, and one young lad, who always accompanied him, lingered behind.

"Have you a steel and flint about you?" asked Thade.

"I have," said the boy, searching his breeches pocket.

"An' a piece of spunk?"

"Here you are! 'Tis dyin' for a dhraw I am myself this cowld night."

Thade Ryall lit his pipe by striking fire from the flint and steel, and catching the spark on the spunk; and smoked for a long time leisurely. Then, he handed the pipe to his companion, and, wiping his mouth with the back of his hand, he remarked:

"I'm thinkin' to-night's meetin' won't ind here!"

"I'm thinkin' the same," said the other, reluctantly joining in the dialogue.

"What are you thinkin', Jim?" said the giant.

"I'm thinkin' I'd like to hear you talkin', Thade," said Jim, innocently.

"'Tis the pity the weed is not grown in Ireland," said Thade. "What a manifacturer and conshumer and gineral daler you would be!"

"Go on, Thade! Go on!" said Jim, economizing every valuable moment.

"The top of a rick of turf, a sunny day, and the wind from the south to timper it, and a well-blackened dhudeen, and the tin box full ——"

"Shtop, av ye don't want me to shtrike you! What the divil do ye want grigging a poor fellow like that fur?" said Jim, as the delectable vision rose up before him, and the stern contrast was all around.

"Well, as I was about saying, whin ye interrupted me wid yere minanderings," replied Thade, "I don't think the Lynches will shtop their hand afther to-night."

"What can they do?" said Jim.

"What can anny wan do whin the divil inthers into him? Whin I kim out that moonlight night tin years ago, d'ye think I had any notion of drivin' thim slugs through the Ameral's carriage? An' av I knew his daughter was wid him, don't ye think I'd sooner turn the muzzle upon meself?"

"Whisht!" said Jim, cautiously. "Do ye hear nothin'?"

"Nothing at all," said Thade, unconcernedly. "And whin you, Jim Cassidy, as good and riligious a boy as ever broke his mother's heart, lie in wait that night for George ——"

"Whisht, for God's sake, whisht!" said Jim, rising up. "The walls have ears. Here's yer pipe, and bad luck to ye wid it."

"I thought I'd get it out av ye," said Thade, coolly smoking. "Nothin' but wan thing could take the pipe from your mouth, Jim!"

"But what were ye saying about the Lynches?" asked Jim, crossly, for he felt he had been cheated.

"Nothin' pertickler, 'cept they won't shtop there."

"Ned Connors is a dangerous man," said Jim.

"I know a more dangerous man," said Thade.

"Who?"

"Donal Connors. He's the wan man I'd be afeared to meet, av his timper was up."

"I think I'll put him on his guard," said Jim. "He did many a good turn for me."

"You can't," said Thade, sententiously.

"Why can't I?" said Jim.

"Haven't you yer oath, you ruffian?" said Thade. "Didn't ye sware on the crossed shticks not to revale iss, aye or no, that 'ud happen here?"

"Thrue for you, begobs," said Jim. "Shure I forgot meself. But it will be no harrum av I have it convayed to Donal, that he may expec' a visit, but that they won't shtay long."

"Well, that's another question," said Thade, balancing the morality of the thing in his mind. "It's wan thing to tell, another thing to convay. Well," he said at length, "I suppose you may, but don't let the Lynches ever hear it, av ye vally yer life, an' don't care to be tied to the settle."

"Are ye done, Thade?" said Jim. "It's mortial cowld here."

"Take another *shaugh*," said Thade.

"N-no!" said Jim. "But I'll take the lind of a loan of your 'baccy-box till to-morrow. Ah!" he said, lovingly, as Thade handed him the little flat tin box, "Sure, 'tis atin' and drinkin', and sleepin' — all thegither!"

A few nights later there was a little scene at the forge. A few of the boys met as usual to talk over events; and the conversation turned upon Nodlag.

"Whatever they say, the Lynches are right," said one, lighting his pipe at the forge furnace.

"They might be, if they could prove themselves," said another.

"That's just it!" said a third.

"No wan manes anny harrum to the girl," said the first speaker, "but it is clear this is no place for the likes of her aiquals, afther all that occurred. Begobs, people have their feelings; and 'tisn't Ned Connors should go agin them, whatever tie he has in the girl."

"The right thing would be to frighten him, without hurtin' him; and let him sind her on the road, where he picked her up," said the first.

Red Casey was swinging his sledge with great strokes on a horseshoe that was held redhot by a boy with a long, forked tongs. He caught the conversation, however; and lifting high the sledge in the air, he said:

"The man that puts a wet finger on that girl, by G——, I'll smash his skull as aisy as I shtrike that shoe."

He brought the heavy sledge down with a fearful thud, and the red sparks flew fast and thick all around. The boy, who held the horseshoe, let it fall in terror; the rest slunk silently from the forge.

And Nodlag, the cause of all this commotion, slept calmly the sleep of innocence, and dreamed out her little span of happy oblivion till the dawn.

CHAPTER XV

THE OLD ORDER CHANGETH

DURING that eventful year, Owen Connors and his sister left the old home at Glenanaar, — the former, to take up a situation in Limerick, and the latter to become companion to a maiden aunt, who was also her godmother, and from whom great things were expected, as it was supposed she had "lashings of money." The great snow had disappeared, reluctantly enough, as even far into the month of May white patches still could be seen, nestling in ditches and deep down in ravines, where the sun could not pierce. But the roads and byways were open; and the spring work progressed gaily, the ground being softened and warmed for the plough and harrow by the genial influence of the snow. Except for the departure of Owen and his sister there was very little to trouble the peace that always slept over that cottage at Glenanaar; and even this sundering of ties, as close as life itself, was accepted with that mute resignation, so closely resembling the aspects of fatalism, which has always been a characteristic of the Irish peasant.

Donal's marriage took place a few weeks before Advent. It had been deferred for many reasons; for a little difference about business details in Ireland is often the occasion of the "breaking-off" of a match,

or at least of considerable delay. And the Hegartys
were always notorious for driving a hard bargain.
The families had met at fairs in Kildorrery, Kilfinane,
and elsewhere; had spent hours in public-houses,
arranging, debating, changing, and settling the details
of the marriage contract. At length it was decided,
according to the singular but universal custom, that
the old people should surrender the farm, and all
farm assets to their son, Donal; that they should receive
in lieu thereof from the Hegartys the sum of £200;
that they should have the right to a room in the house,
and their maintenance; and in lieu thereof, should
there be any difficulty about deciding what is meant
by "proper maintenance," they should have each £15
a year; and, finally, the grass of three sheep. This
kind of arrangement is the universal custom. Sometimes it works well. More frequently it is the occasion of much heart-burning. But there seems no
other way of settling so complex a question. At last,
after coming to an understanding on these knotty
points, the great question about Nodlag's future was
discussed. It was at a famous fair, held in Kilmallock
on the eve of All Saints' Day, and known as Snap-
Apple Fair, from the ancient customs and amusements
connected with All Hallows' Eve from time immemorial
in Ireland. There were present old Edmond Connors,
now grown feeble enough; Donal; and the father and
mother of Nano Hegarty. They met in an upstairs
parlor of a public-house, kept by a "friend," who
magnanimously kept away all the other customers

who were unable to find room downstairs. The usual rather squalid fencing and sparring that goes on, on these occasions, gave way before the calm, dignified, attitude of old Edmond Connors, who simply made one quiet, determined statement, and no more.

"Av she was wan of yere own flesh and blood, we wouldn't mind," said Mrs. Hegarty, referring to Nodlag, "altho' it is ushal to give up the place clear on these occasions. But a *thucka*, who came from no wan knows where, and who was got by no wan knows who — begor, 'tis the quare business intirely."

"There's isn't much use in argyin' the matther," said Edmond Connors. "As I said at the fair at Kildorrery, Nodlag must remain, and be thrated like wan of oursels."

"Can't you lave her as a servant-girl?" said old Hegarty. "We'll put her on good wages, an' you'll have nothin' to complain about. Come now, Ned, 'tis only a thrifle of a misondhertsanding," he said, in a wheedling tone. "'Twould be the quare thing, out and out, an' althegither, that such a *thescaun* should stand atween us. Spake, Donal!"

"Av she was to remain as a servant-girl, there 'ud be nothin' to prevint those who are comin' in " (this was the delicate way Donal referred to his future wife), "to give a month's notice at anny time, and turn her on the wurruld."

"Oyeh! shure now, you're jokin', Donal," said Mrs. Hegarty. "The idee of Nano doin' annything that you wouldn't like; and she so fond of you!"

"Didn't she say, Kate," said her husband, "when the Begleys wor comin' around matchmakin', that she'd have Donal Connors, and no wan else in the wide wurruld; and that she'd rather beg the whole wurruld wid him than wear silks and satins wid others?"

"Indeed 'n' she did," said Mrs. Hegarty. "An' more'n that. She often said to meself, sez she, that she'd marry Donal, or no wan; and shure now here he is turning his back upon her, as if she wor the blackest shtranger."

"I'm not turnin' me back upon Nano," said Donal, uneasy under the accusation, "but nayther me father, nor I, will do a wrong thing to an orfin for anny wan."

"An' is the poor little crachure an orfin?" said Mrs. Hegarty, seizing on the word. "Sure, they say her father and mother, bad scran to them, are safe and sound in America."

And she screwed her eyes into the face of old Edmond Connors as she spoke.

"How can they say that," he replied, "whin nobody but the grate God knows who her father and mother might be?"

"Av coorse, av coorse," said old Hegarty. "But people will say the quarest things: but shure, av 'twas thrue, you'd be the last man in Ireland to keep sich a wan under an honest roof."

Donal fidgeted a little; and his father grew white beneath the eyes. But in all other outer appearances he remained perfectly composed.

"I never mind what people do be sayin'," he said.

"They'll let no wan pass. But what do they say, Mrs. Hegarty; for 'tis better to have the thruth out, than keep it in?"

"Tell him, Kate!" urged Hegarty. "'Twill kum better from a 'uman!"

Kate couldn't see this at all. She could not perceive where the feminine element came into the matter.

"Wisha, betther let it alone," she said, pulling up the hood of her black cloak. "Let there be an ind to the matther, as we cannot agree."

Then her husband assumed an attitude of great determination, as of one about to make a tremendous sacrifice.

"Come, Ned," he said, "I'll tell you what I'll do. I'll give you an' the ould 'uman the grass of anither sheep, an' a new feather-bed that was never slep' on, av you sind away that—" here he was about to use an opprobrious expression, but a glance from the keen blue eye of the old man stopped him, and he added — "*gorlach.*"

Edmond Connors rose up, a signal that negotiations were at an end, when Hegarty seized him, and put him back in the chair.

"Wisha, thin, Ned Connors, you're the divil intirely at dhrivin' a bargain. We'll give in to you here. But," he said solemnly, raising his finger and emphasizing his words, "av anny harrum comes av it, the blame be yours, not mine!"

"No harrum can kum," said Donal, "excep' to those who wish harrum. An' let thim beware!"

So then it is decided by the Fates that Nodlag shall
not be cast upon the world to beg her daily bread, or
otherwise degenerate; but shall get shelter, and clothes,
and food, not as a menial, but as a legitimate member
of a family. For herself, poor child, now bursting
from childhood into girlhood, with all its dreams,
aspirations, and ambitions, she knew nothing of all
that men were conjecturing about her mysterious past,
or plotting about her uncertain future. But she wept
somewhat when Owen and his sister, amid many
kisses and tears, and other signs of love, crossed the
threshold of the old home, which they should never
re-pass but as strangers; and then went about her
daily avocations as usual, — took up the sod of turf,
and her well-worn books every morning, and hied her
to where the old hedge school was hidden near the
bridge that crossed the Own-an-aar, and conned over
her Voster, and her Carpenter's spelling-book, and
won the admiration of the old schoolmaster for her
obedience and intelligence; and got back in the evening
to her humble dinner of potatoes and milk, and the
warmth of the beloved fireside, where every day she
became dearer and dearer. And sometimes the old
listening habit would come upon her, and she would
stop at the bridge to hear the far-off voice. Or, in the
middle of her lesson about the bad boy that used to
say, "I don't care," she would suddenly pause, and
put her hand to her ear, and listen; and the old man,
who had heard something of her history, would look at
her compassionately, and her companions would nudge

one another. "There's the Fairy-Child agin listening for the good people. I wondher whin will they come, and fetch her away?"

At home, she was queen and mistress by virtue of her right and faculty of loving. One thing troubled her these latter days. She often found Donal watching her intently; and she vaguely conjectured, by that curious instinct or presentiment such sensitive minds possess, that the advent of the new mistress would mean in some way or other a disruption of the blessed peace that always hung around this Christian household. The feeling was shared, in great measure, by old Mrs. Connors, who felt that, the moment the deed assigning the farm to Donal and his future wife was attested, her supremacy was over — her long reign of nearly fifty years was at an end.

"There'll be changes, alanna," she used to say, drawing out and combing carefully Nodlag's yellow tresses, "an' they won't be good for you nor me. But all the same, we'll be together, an' sure that's a great matther."

"Will she bate me, granny?" the child would ask.

"No, alanna. She won't, because I won't lave her. But there's many a way of killing, besides chokin' with butther, agragal!"

"Wisha, don't be makin' the child lonesome wid that kind o' talk," the old man would put in. "We'll be all together, Nodlag, till death us do part, as the Catechiz says. What did you larn to-day, alannav?"

And Nodlag should go over her whole lesson, line

by line, the old man nodding his head, and putting in a word here and there.

Then, in the early winter, the fatal day came. A stranger crossed the threshold of Glenanaar as its mistress; and the old people sank down into the condition of dependents. Clearly, Donal's heart was not altogether in the matter. He went about his work, but with none of that light-heartedness and enthusiasm one would expect from a newly-married man, who had found the desire of a lifetime. His wife, cautiously, but firmly, took up the management of the little household; and quietly, but unaggressively, assumed absolute control. The old people cowered by the fireside; took their meals in silence; and submitted patiently to their lot. But one could see how the sense of her dethronement and subjection was telling on the old woman. Once or twice, through sheer force of habit, she gave little orders through the house, which were at once silently, but firmly, countermanded by the young mistress. Then she appealed to the filial affection of Donal to support her. But he, through a sense of justice, and possibly to avoid a chronic condition of hostility between the old order and the new, said:—

"Better let Nano manage, Mother! She understands the matther betther."

And the old woman bowed her head in a resignation that broke her heart. It was pitiful to see her going around the old familiar places, as if she were not only a stranger, but an intruder; to watch her face when another voice than hers gave orders to Peggy or Larry;

to hear her pitiful appeal even to the beggars that
thronged the door:

"I have nothin' for you now, honest man. I am as
poor as yourself."

It is true the bonds between her husband and Nodlag
and herself grew closer after her abdication and consequent humiliation; but every one that knows the im-
perious and arbitrary manner with which these grand
old "Irish mothers" reigned and ruled over their
households will easily understand how the new order
cut into the very heart of this good old Christian
mother. The old fires gradually died out; the spirit
waned; a general listlessness supervened over the former restless activity; and before the autumn came
again, or rather in its earliest days, she fulfilled her
own prophecy:

"Ye'll be berryin' me at the fall of the lafe."

There were fewer friends left therefore to Nodlag;
but these were fast and true. She was everything now
to old Edmond Connors; and Donal, forever watching
her with those keen, sorrowful eyes, was cautiously
kind. His wife, bitterly hostile as she was, refrained
from any open demonstrations of dislike. But gradually, as a clever, vindictive woman might, she reduced
Nodlag even below the level of a menial. The girl
was taken from school and put to hard work. The
servants, imitating their mistress, and cognizant of the
secret that was no longer a secret, for the whole parish
knew it, treated her with contumely. By degrees, and
under one excuse or another, she was quietly kept

away from the family meals, and even the servants would not eat with her. And all was arranged, quietly and without offence. Donal was not blind to this. He saw through his wife's manœuvres clearly; but he had no opportunity of interfering. He swallowed his wrath in silence, and went about his work, moody and distracted. But he took every opportunity of consoling the lonely girl for her hard fate. Whenever he went to fair or market, he brought home a *fairin'* to Nodlag, sometimes a cheap brooch, or a hair-comb to keep back her rich hair; sometimes it was a *Book of Fate*, found by Napoleon in the Pyramids of Egypt, sometimes the *Key of Heaven*, or the *Garden of the Soul;* but in some mysterious way they rapidly disappeared, leaving Nodlag disconsolate. Once, in a fit of fury, the new mistress smote the girl across the face, and her cheek and eye were swollen. Donal asked what had happened. Nodlag would not tell. Then he called his wife into his bedroom. He was one of those quiet men, who give way sometimes to paroxysms of rage.

"Nano," he said with a white, terrible face, "you shtruck Nodlag. If ever you shtrike her agin, you'll remimber it to the day of your death!"

CHAPTER XVI

WHAT OF THE FATES?

THIS did not smooth matters much for the poor girl. Her life very soon became a misery and a martyrdom. As her intelligence developed with her physical strength she began to perceive, at first dimly and reluctantly, then swiftly and certainly, that her lot in life was a peculiar one. She had become faintly conscious of this at school, where she was isolated from the farmers' daughters around, who would have made her school-life a burden, were it not for the friendship the master evidently entertained for her. But, sometimes, an awkward question would be put by some stupid fellow: —

"Why do they call you Nodlag? That's a quare name. An' what's yere other name?"

The significance of the fact that she had no name beyond a kind of nickname gave her the first inkling of her isolation from her kind. She made one or two inquiries which were answered evasively; and then, with the ease of youth and perfect health she forgot all about it. Now, it all came back with tenfold force; and as she gradually understood that she had no family name, no family connections, no relations, no friends, in the usual sense of the word, her peculiar position gave her many hard, bitter hours of sombre and melancholy reflection. For now she sprang into womanhood with that swiftness characteristic of highly nervous and sensitive organizations. She grew swiftly tall; and without a trace of weakness or delicacy she became a jealous contrast to the coarse, heavy, lumbering figures of the farm-yard. She was, in fact, in her sixteenth year, a tall, handsome, mountain girl, who could leap the Ownanaar at full flood, and jump lightly from the ground on to the back of the tallest horse in the yard. And as her thick hair deepened in hue and became an auburn colour, her long, straight features, slightly browned and freckled, took on a delicacy and refined tone that was specially exasperating to those with whom she was brought into daily contact. But all this superiority, unnoticed by the modest girl, did not tend to relieve her from the ever-painful feelings of her loneliness and isolation; and, once or twice at school, and more frequently, in the farm-yard and fields, she heard herself called by a name, the opprobrium of which she took long years to realize. Once or twice, she approached Donal with a question; but then shrank from the dread of the revelation. She felt that she could not bear to be told of some secret shame, or misfortune, that would blight all her after-life. In her ignorance, she had at least the consolation of knowing that she did love and was beloved. Why she could not say; but at least it was a salve for the ever-present sore, that whatever secret was kept in the archives which she feared to open, at least it could not estrange

from her the affection she prized above all things else
on earth. The suspicion that a revelation, even to
herself, of that secret might force her into a conscien-
tious disruption of those sweet ties that made all the
happiness of life prevented her from seeking a knowledge that might be fraught with evil. So she determined to remain silent, and accept the uncertainty
with all its present rewards. For she could not be
insensible to her own personal attractions. Instinct
told her that she had great advantages, not only over
these poor girls who slaved in the farm-yard, but even
over their mistress herself; and modest and humble
though she might be, she could not be insensible to
facts that left an ever-growing impression on her
imagination. Then, sometimes, she felt that, with all
the coldness and aversion with which she had been
treated, and was still treated, even by neighbouring
families, there was somehow blent a note of admiration; and it was not altogether a maiden's fancies, or
mere vanity, that made her feel that the eyes of people
rested on her face and figure, going to or coming from
Mass; and there was sometimes a little feeling of
exultation, which died away again into despondency,
when she had to pass through an avenue of cars and
carts, and was ungreeted, save by that cold stare of
silent admiration.

She became dimly conscious, however, that besides
her friends at Glenanaar, now reduced to Edmond and
Donal, there was one other spot where her presence
was greeted like a sunbeam. This was at the forge,

down near the bridge. There was always a welcome
and a warm corner for her near old Mrs. Casey, as she
sat by the kitchen fire; and there was no mistaking the
cheery salutation:

"*Milé failte, alannav! milé failte!* What a stranger
you're becoming! We didn't see you sin' Sunday.
Did we, Reddy?"

"No, Mother! Nodlag is getting so big now, she
has too much to do, besides comin' to see us!"

Here was a note of impatience that meant much.
But it was very sweet, nevertheless, to the lonely girl,
who made the humble cabin almost her home, not so
much in the way of residence, as by a kind of pro-
prietary right she assumed in arranging and managing
Mrs. Casey's humble belongings. For ever since she
was a child it was Nodlag's invariable custom, whenever she came to the forge, to fling aside the parti-col-
oured shawl which served as a snood; and letting her
long hair fall down, she would move around the little
kitchen and bedroom, setting all things to rights, clean-
ing there and tidying there, until everything came to look
spick and span under her dainty touch. And the old
mother would bless her from her *sugan* chair, and say:

"If God 'ud only sind us a daughter like you!"

And the young smith, with his grimy shirt open,
revealing his strong chest, would lean on his sledge
with blackened arms, knotted and gnarled with huge
muscles, and sigh and think:

"If that purty picture could remain, what a blessed
life would be mine!"

But now Nodlag had grown to womanhood; and the jest and the laugh had died away from the young smith's lips. A deeper feeling than his cheerful child-affection had taken hold of him; and he became silent and shy and reserved. A new life had entered his veins. The great transformation had taken place. To the unconscious Nodlag the change was alarming. She could not interpret it. Old Mrs. Casey was as kind, as loving, as solicitous as ever. Her welcome to the forge was unstinted in its warmth. But the attitude of the young smith was a puzzle. Instead of the broad, deep gaze into her blue eyes, he looked at her in a shy, furtive manner; answered rather shortly, and never now performed the chivalric courtesy, to which she had been accustomed from childhood, of lifting her, or helping her, into the saddle. She concluded, after a good deal of reflection, that Redmond's mind was also poisoned against her; that the deep secret of her life had averted his face from her forever. She little knew how deep a hold she had of that strong, manly heart. She little deemed that a hundred times a day a very smutty, but not unhandsome face, crowned by a mass of rusty hair, fairly well dyed with soot, stared through the little square window of the forge up along the winding road that led to Glenanaar; and that his honest heart leaped with pride when he saw her well-known, shapely figure come swaying down the white road, or bending with every movement of the white or bay horse she was bringing to his forge. Why didn't someone tell her the boy's mighty secret?

Or why didn't Redmond himself speak, and solve the riddle of his future happiness forever?

Well, he did; but not to Nodlag. He took Donal into his confidence in his shy, reluctant way.

"I think," he said to Donal one day, as they smoked together leisurely after the horses had been shod, "Nodlag is not lookin' as well as we'd wish her."

"I didn't notice," said Donal, somewhat alarmed. "Do ye think she's looking badly?"

"Maybe 'tis the way she's growin'," said Redmond, "she's runnin' up very fast for her age!"

"I'm afeard she's not as continted as she ought to be," said Donal, sadly. "Thim that ought to be a mother to the lonely girl are more inclined to be a stepmother."

"'Twould be aisy enough to betther that, begor," said Redmond.

"What do ye mane? How?" asked Donal, sharply.

"I mane that me and me mother would be the happy pair, if Nodlag could make her home here, and lave where she isn't welcome!"

"That's dacent of you, Red," said Donal. "An' I suppose you know all — I mane all that the people does be sayin'?" he corrected himself hastily.

"I do, and perhaps more," said Redmond. "An' I don't care a *thraneen* for all that the gossips can say agin her. There's not a girl like her in the County Cork or Limerick."

Donal looked at him inquiringly; and a great light began to dawn.

"Me father," he said at length, "could never do widout her. She reads for him, and sews for him, an' works for him; that is," he said, after a pause of shame, "whin she's allowed by her supariors."

"There's somethin' in that, surely," said Redmond. "But your father, Donal, is binding a good deal, and wakening, since your mother's death; and if anythin' should happen to him, what would become of Nodlag?"

"Thin I should take care of her," said Donal.

"Av coorse, av coorse," said Redmond, coughing violently, for the smoke had gone the wrong way, he said. "But you know Nodlag now is no child; an' we know what wimmen are, whin they git jealous-like."

"Thrue for ye, Red," said Donal, with a smile of meaning playing around his mouth; "but if Nodlag is no longer a child at Glenanaar, she wouldn't be a child ayther down here."

Redmond coughed again violently, until his face was as red as his hair.

"I know what you mane, Donal," he said. "But —" here he stopped suddenly, as if to gather his faculties together. Then he continued, "But I wouldn't ask her to come here, onless I had a right."

"That manes only wan thing," said Donal, reflectively.

"Only wan thing," said the smith. "If you and your father consint, I'm satisfied to make Nodlag my wife!"

"But tare an' 'ouns, man," said Donal, highly delighted, "what about Nodlag herself? Have you spoken to her, or is it all arranged betune ye?"

"Never a word on the matther passed my lips," said Redmond. "'Tis you, Donal, must do the good turn for me!"

"Begor, I will with a heart and a half," said Donal, "tho' 'twould come much betther from yerself. But have you thought, Red, of what it all manes?"

"Have I?" said Redmond. "Was there anny other thought in my mind for the past twelve months but what I'm spakin' now? God forgive me! Manny's the time it came uppermost in me prayers, and even at Mass!"

"And do you think 'twill serve your bisness?" said Donal.

"'Twill, and it 'twon't," said Redmond. "If they could do widout me, they might. But you know there's not another blacksmith within six miles!"

Donal thought long and deeply.

"You know," he said at length, "that Nodlag has nothin' but what's on her!"

"An' did I ask for anythin'?" Redmond said, half angrily. "Did I mintion money, or annything else, Donal Connors?" he continued. "Come now, as man to man, did I?"

"No," said Donal. "Red, you are a brave, good man, and if Nodlag likes you, me father and me will be the happy couple."

"Thin, you'll spake to Nodlag?" said Redmond,

anxiously, "and lave me know her answer as soon as you can."

"I will," said Donal, drawing his horse's reins over his shoulder; "an' 'twon't be my fault if she doesn't say yes to you!"

"God bless you, Donal," said Redmond, fervently; "and may it come to my turn yet to do as good a turn to you!"

Here, then, was the solution of a good many difficulties, if Time and Fate would allow. A fair vista of an honoured life stretched smilingly before the feet of the lonely girl. It was only the little Yes, to be enlarged and emphasized into the more solemn I will, and all would be right forevermore. But here come the Fates, and Chance, and Evil; and, lo! down rush the clouds and rain, and blot out the sunshine and the glory, apparently forever.

But Donal's heart was singing with delight, as he trudged lazily up the hill; and he often smiled as he imagined the surprise and the delight of Nodlag when he broke the matter to her. He turned over in his mind the hundred ways in which he would make the solemn communication with most effect. Would he broach the matter in the comic and bantering style so usual in Ireland; or would he speak to her seriously, as a father to a child? Or would he put it enigmatically, or by way of parable, pretending that it was a piece of match-making going on in another parish, and with no reference to herself, until she gave her opinion? He decided, at last, that this was the "shuparior plan"; and he arranged his story as neatly as possible towards a successful issue.

And the young smith swung to his work with redoubled efforts, for now that he had cast the die he was anxious for the result. A thousand times he told himself that he would be contumeliously rejected; and he often regretted his smutty face and sooty hair. No girl could see beneath such a grimy appearance the pulsations of a strong, brave, loyal heart. And then, again, hope revived. Donal's eloquence, and her own loneliness and dependence, would do all. And, as he rang his small hammer on the anvil in short, quick strokes, he knew that the musical steel echoed the word that was in his heart: Nodlag! Nodlag! and Nodlag!

CHAPTER XVII

AN OLD MAN'S DREAM

ON the evening of that day in which Redmond Casey had given his solemn commission to Donal, old Edmond Connors, returning slowly from his walk through the fields, sat weary and tired on the parapet of the little bridge that curved itself above the Own-anaar. The years, and perhaps much musing and sorrow, were telling on the great, muscular frame of the old man. And everyone said that since Donal's marriage, and the death of the *vanithee*, Edmond Connors had aged more than twenty years. He often, too, fell into fits of drowsiness. He slept before the hot fire in the kitchen; he slept outside against the south wall of the barn, where the sun shone fiercely; he slept sitting on a boulder above a mountain torrent; and people said he was breaking up, and that this somnolency was a forerunner of death. And this evening, as he sat tired, there on the mossy wall of the bridge, Edmond Connors fell asleep, and dreamed, in the fitful way of the old or the troubled, that Nodlag had gone from him forever. He did not know why or wherefore. He vaguely conjectured that Nano, Donal's wife, had made her life unbearable; and that himself and Donal could not prevent it. He only remembered that the girl had come into the kitchen, flung her arms around his neck, kissed him on forehead and cheek and lips, and passed out the back door of the kitchen without a word. He was moaning sadly in his dreams, when a light finger touched him, and he woke. He saw standing over him a tall woman, with great black eyes, shining out of a pinched and sallow face, and above it a crown of the whitest hair he thought he ever saw. He rubbed his eyes, and stared, not knowing whether this, too, was not part of his dream. The woman spoke.

"Edmond Connors, you don't know me?"

"N-no," said the old man; "are you alive, or am I dhramin' yet?"

"You are wide awake, now," the woman said, looking down upon him. "Listen! I want somethin' from ye!"

"I have nothin' to giv' ye, me poor 'uman," said the old man, feelingly. "Whin God giv' it to me, I shared it with His poor. I've nothin' now, but what does not belong to me."

"You have somethin'," she replied, "that belongs to me. I have come to claim it."

"You're makin' a mistake, me poor 'uman," said the old man. "Edmond Connors never kep' as much as the black of yer nail from annywan. You mane somebody else!"

"No!" she cried. "I mane you! I want me child!"

The dream and the reality rushed together through

the brain of the old man. He did not know "which was which." He looked up at the woman, and said faintly:

"Nodlag?"

"Yes!" said the woman, apparently remorseless. "I have come to claim back the child you have called Nodlag. Her right name is Annie Daly, and she is my child!"

"And are you the 'uman that met me on this bridge fourteen or fifteen years ago, whin the snow was on the ground, and — she was a little child in yer arrums?"

"I am," said the woman.

The old man paused.

"And was it you that lef' that little infan' to the mercy of God on that cowld Christmas night in the byre among the cattle?"

"It was," said the woman, unmoved.

"Thin, as you giv' up yer mother's rights thin, what right have you now to claim her back?"

"The same mother's rights," she answered, "and the sthrong hand of the law."

"To the divil wid you and yer law," cried the old man, starting up in a fury. The word "law," so utterly hated by the Irish peasant, as synonymous with every kind of injustice and brutality, set his cold blood aflame.

"To the divil wid you an' yer law," he repeated. "You an' yer law darn't put a wet finger on *my* child. I've saved her from worse than ye, an' as long as God laves me the bret' of life, nayther you nor yer law will take her from me."

The woman now sat down on the mossy wall, and pulled the old man down beside her.

"Listen to rayson, an' common sinse, Edmond Connors," she said. "'Tis thrue I put me child into your hands that Christmas night. Your byre was warmer than the cowld river. If I remimber right, 'twas you yourself that axed me."

"'Twas," said the old man; "you thought to murdher that weeshy, innicent crachure that God giv' you, and I said many a Christian family would be glad to take her frum ye."

"Did ye know at the time to whom ye were shpakin'?' asked the woman.

"No! But I knew well 'twas Annie Daly, daughter of the man that was swearin' away me life, that was brought in from the bastes that night."

"You did?" said the woman.

"I did," he replied. "An' I clung to her since, and she has growed into me heart, as none of my own childre' ever growed; and, be the high Heavens, nayther you, nor your law, nor any livin' morchial man will take her from me, ontil she puts me in me coffin and sees the last sod above me grave."

The woman was silent for a few minutes.

"You did a good an' charitable act, Edmond Connors," she said at length, "but didn't ye ever get back annything in return?"

He did not catch her meaning for a few minutes.

Then, as the recollection of the trial dawned upon him, he cried, as he felt for the woman's hand, and grasped it firmly: —

"Yes, *mo shtig, mo chree*, an' I have never forgot it. But for you, me bones would be blaching this manny a year, beside poor Lynch's, in Cork gaol."

"'Tis to save you from somethin' worse," said the woman, disengaging her hand, "that I've come acrass three thousan' miles of stormy ocean, and am here now in the teeth of those who'd murdher me, if they knew me."

"I'm at a loss to know what you mane, ma'am," replied the old man. "I have only a few years, it may be a few months, to live, an' I'm not sorry to be goin' to the good God ——"

"People like to die in their beds, and to have the priesht wid them," she replied, "no matther how tired of life they are."

"An' wid God's blessin', that's how I'll die," he said. "I've been prayin' all my life agin a 'sudden and unprovided death,' and God is sure to hear me in the ind."

"He'll hear you, but he won't heed you," said the woman, rising up, and pulling the black shawl over her head, as the preliminary of departing. "As you don't take me advice, Edmond Connors, this blessed evening, a worse death than the Cork gallows is before you."

"What wrong have I ever done to morchial man or 'uman," he cried, anxiously, "that anywan should murdher me?"

"'Tisn't to the guilty, but to the innicent, the hard death comes," she replied.

"But I have never made an inimy in me life, 'uman," he cried, passionately. "I've always lived in pace with God an' me nabors."

"I don't say 'tis on your own account," she replied. "But I hard since I kem back to this misforthunate country that your sacret is out, an' the bloodhoun's are on yer thrack."

"Why don't you shpake to Nodlag hersel', and let her decide?" he said, after a long fit of musing.

The wretched woman gave a short, hoarse laugh.

"An' do ye suppose for a moment she'd listen to me story?" she said. "Do ye suppose she'd lave you for the likes av me?"

"Nodlag is a good girl," said he, seeing how much he was gaining. "If you can shew her that you are her mother, she'll go wid you to the inds of the airth."

"I don't want her to kum wid me," said the wretched mother. "I want her to go where she'll be cared for well, without puttin' any wan's life in danger!"

"An' where might that be?" he asked.

"She can go among the gintry," the woman answered. "They'll sind her where she'll be safe, and where no wan can find her; and she'll be rared up a lady, instid of bein' slushin' and moilin' for Nano Haygerty!"

"And be brought up a Prodestan', I suppose?" said the old man, looking at her keenly.

"That's nayther here nor there," said the woman. "Her belongin's have got more from Prodestans than Catholics anny day."

"Av they have, 'tis the dirty wages they got," the old man said. "And Nodlag never yet did anything mane, to say she'd do it now."

"There's no use in talkin' to you," the woman cried, lifting the shawl high on shoulders and head. "Keep her, Edmond Connors, keep her. You've a better right to her than me, and may it be a long time till the Death comes between ye to part ye! But there's blood before me eyes these nights I have been spindin' out there on the heather and the furze; and I misdoubt me if there's not blood to be shed like wather. But I have warned ye, Edmond Connors, I have warned ye! An' yet, may the Blessed Vargin be 'atween ye an' her inimies, for all ye have done for me child!"

She took his hand, raised it to her lips, and kissed it passionately, as she had done so many years before; and then strode away with her swift, swinging step across the road, and down through the moorland.

"Am I dhramin' still?" said Edmond Connors. "I'm so ould and wake now, I don't know whin I'm asleep or awake. But 'tis quare, out and out, that Nodlag should be comin' up so aften."

Hence, when the old man returned home, he could scarcely keep his eyes off the girl. He stared at her, and watched her, wherever she was, and whatever she was doing; stood up, and followed her figure from the kitchen when she went out; sat down resignedly and

kept his eyes fixed upon her as she sat beneath the
lamp, darning his stockings, or polishing his brown
gaiters. She was getting somewhat alarmed at the
persistency of his gaze, when, late at night, looking
around cautiously first, to see if Nano was in the
kitchen, he beckoned the girl to his side.

"Whispher, alanna," he said, "and don't spake loud,
for fear thim would hear who oughtn't to hear. Did
ye see anny wan strange to-day?"

"No, sir!" said Nodlag, surprised. "There was no
sthranger round the house to-day."

"No 'uman," he asked, "with a yellow face, and
big eyes, and gray hair?"

"No, sir!" answered the girl. "There was no wan
of that kind about, at laste as far as I know."

"Don't mintion to anny wan that I asked the question," he said.

He fell into a fit of musing that seemed to last very
long to the young girl. Then he woke up suddenly to
see her face near his.

"What was I sayin'?" he cried. "Oh, yes! Don't
mintion to anny wan what I was sayin', Nodlag. But,
whispher! Come closer, Nodlag!"

"Yes, sir! What can I do?"

"Nodlag, sure you won't lave me?"

"Leave you, sir?' Certainly, I won't."

"Promise me that you won't lave me till you see the
hood of the habit pulled down on me face, and the last
sod flattened above my grave."

"Sure, you know, sir, I'll never lave you," said

Nodlag, crying. "Where 'ud I go from you, who have been father and mother to me?"

"Thrue for you, child," the old man whispered. "More than father and mother, if ye knew all. But ye didn't see the white-haired 'uman I was spakin' about?"

"No, sir," she said, now believing that he was grown delirious. "There was no wan of that kind here, at all, at all!"

"Thin, you'll say nuthin' to nobody about what I was sayin'," he whispered. "'Twas all a dhrame! 'Twas all a dhrame!"

She went back to the table and resumed her work, but from time to time he called her over, when there was no one in the kitchen but themselves.

"Say nothin' about it, Nodlag! Say nothin' about it! 'Twas all a dhrame! 'Twas all a dhrame!"

CHAPTER XVIII

A LIFE FOR A LIFE

DONAL was quite wrong when he said that Nodlag had nothing but the clothes she wore. She was, unknown to herself and the world beside, the heiress of Edmond Connors, her more than father. The old man, feeling that time was narrowing for him, and that he should soon sleep with his fathers down there beneath the elms at Templeroan, had gone into Kilmallock, and apportioning equal shares to Donal, Owen, and their unmarried sister, had left by will, duly drawn and signed, the rest of his money, and such property as he might die possessed of, to Nodlag. And lest this might not be strictly legal, he had called her for the first time in his life by her baptismal name, Annie Daly.

How the double circumstance, the legacy and the revelation of the name, became known to Donal's wife, it is difficult to ascertain. But the knowledge was conveyed to her in some way, and by her own minute and vigilant inquiries she placed the matter beyond doubt. Needless to say, it doubly intensified her dislike for Nodlag, until that hatred became an obsession. The thought that *her* fortune, the money accumulated with such infinite pains by her father and mother, and even by the labour of her own hands, should go to this girl was maddening. On one excuse or another she left Glenanaar, and went home to her parents for a few days. When she returned she was unusually silent, and her manner towards Nodlag had changed almost into an attitude of kindness. Donal's spirits rose, and, after waiting many days for a favourable opportunity, he opened the subject of the young blacksmith's suit to Nodlag. He was so cheerful that he spoke with a light heart, and with that bantering manner that best bespeaks friendship amongst the Irish peasantry. He met Nodlag on the bridge that crossed the Ownanaar, the bridge where he had discerned Nodlag's tiny footprints the night of the great snow.

"Did you dhrive the yearlings up the glen?" he said.

"I did," answered Nodlag. "They're up in the high field."

"'Tis a grand year, glory be to God, for near everything," said Donal, not looking at the girl.

"'Tis, indeed," said Nodlag. "Everythin' is thrivin', thanks be to God!"

"I suppose you'll be a bit lonesome now, lavin' the ould place?" said Donal, breaking in at once on the subject in a whimsical manner.

She started, and turned quite pale. Had the voice for which she had been listening all these years spoken at last?

"What do ye mane, Donal?" she said, almost crying; "am I goin' to be turned away at last?"

"Faith, an' you aren't," he said, buoyantly, "But, begor, I'm afther thinkin' you are goin' to be *took* away from us; and sure 'tis we'll miss you."

"I thought there was somethin' goin' on," she said, "from the way the Missis was talkin'. I knew she begredged me the flure, but I never thought, Donal, you'd turn agin me."

And here she broke down utterly, and, putting her apron to her eyes, wept bitterly.

"Why did you take me out of the snow-drift, Donal Connors," she said, amidst her sobbing, "up there under the ash-tree; an' why didn't you lave me die, and go to God, instid of turnin' me now adrift on the world? You know I have nayther father nor mother; I don't know who I am, or what I am, or where I came from. All that I ever knew was that I thought I had a father an' a frind in your father, Donal; an' if you and him now are goin' to turn agin me — well, sure, I've no right to complain," she said, in a sudden burst of gratitude, "ye both have been more than father an' mother to me, and, whatever happens, I'm not likely to forget it."

"Like all women," said Donal, smiling at her sudden emotion, "you're running away wid the question. What I was thryin' to say was, that a likely young colleen like you won't be long widout a husband, an' a good one."

Nodlag blushed scarlet, and dried her tears.

"You're jokin', Donal," she said. "You know as well as I do, that there's not a dacent boy in the whole neighbourhood would look at me, whatever it is, is agin me."

"I know wan dacent boy enough," said Donal, "that has worn his two eyes a'most blind lookin' at you, or for you. At laste, I know the sun never shines for him unless you're to the front afore him."

"Whoever he is," said Nodlag, her woman's heart leaping up at the thought that she was thus singled out for admiration, "he has never spoke to me; an' whatever be his manin', he never intinds to make me his wife."

"I'm not so sure of that," said Donal; "in fact, I kem to offer you his hand, as they say; and the divil's own black wan it is."

"What's the great saycret, Donal?" said Nodlag, anxious to turn away for a moment from the revelation of a happiness that seemed too great. "Who am I, an' where did I come from?"

"That I can't tell you. But I can tell you this, that, unless you throw away your chance, you will be, in a very short time, Mrs. Redmond Casey."

The declaration threw both into a reverie. Donal, having spoken, and seeing the success of his intervention on his friend's behalf, was plunged in conflicting emotions of delight and regret. It was a happy thing for Nodlag and for them all. It would mean a new life for her, surrounded with all kinds of affection, and a happy emancipation from the sordid trials to which she had for so many years been subjected. For himself it would mean peace at least. And yet he thought

there would be a big blank in his own and his father's
life. There would be a gap at the fireside, where they
would miss her bright presence, and her gentle voice,
and her silent but affectionate ministrations. He felt
it was a change and a sad one.

Nodlag's memory was running rapidly over the past,
trying to recall every little incident indicative of the
newly-revealed affection of Redmond; and her imagination fled forward to the future, and she saw herself,
no longer the unnamed dependent on the charity of
others, but the honoured wife of a decent tradesman;
and she was thinking how she would make up for all
this blessedness by her loving solicitude to his mother
and himself, when the morning reverie was suddenly
broken by the shrill, sharp voice of Donal's wife: —

"Wisha, thin, Donal Connors, aren't I well in my
way, huntin' and seekin' for you all over the farm,
and you nowhere to be found? Wouldn't it be betther
for you to be above driving out Hickey's pigs from the
grass-corn than colloguing an' codrauling with that
idle *thucka*?"

"Are the pigs in the grass-corn?" said Donal, lazily
raising himself from the wooden parapet of the bridge.

"They are! An' 'tis mindin' thim an' your bisness
you ought to be; an' let *her* do somethin' to airn the
bread she's atin'."

"Thin, why didn't you drive out the pigs yersel'?"
said Donal. "'Twouldn't be the power and heap an'
all of throuble to dhrive out a few little bonniveens,
sure?"

"I have enough to do, slushin' an' slavin' for you an' your ould father, mornin', noon, an' night," she retorted. "It was the cowld, bitther day for me I came upon yer flure."

"Think over what I've been tellin' ye, Nodlag," said Donal, following his wife. "You see it can't be a day too soon."

All that day, Nodlag's heart was singing its own jubilant song of triumph and affection, as she went around, doing little things here and there. The poor girl walked upon air, and saw a new colour and shape in all things. This sudden transformation in her life was so much more than she ever expected, or hoped for, that she found it difficult to still the beatings of her heart. It was like a beautiful dream come true. For often down there at the forge, as she went around and tidied things for old Mrs. Casey, she couldn't help thinking how much better she would do her work of benevolence if she had a right to the place, and it was a housewife's duty. How often she dreamed of the new curtains she would loop up over the diamond panes; and the flowers she would place in the windows, and the new chairs she would get in place of the old *sugan* chairs now tattered and frayed and worn. And what broods of chickens she would rear, and what fresh eggs she would have for Redmond's breakfast, and all the other airy fantasies of young and hopeful girlhood. And now 'twas all come true. Yes! Donal would not deceive her. Redmond had asked her to be his wife; and she had — No! Her heart stood still.

She had never answered Donal. But he understood, and would make all right. She leaped so suddenly into happiness that it was almost too much for her. The servant-girls, who, following their mistress, disliked her, noticed it. They said to one another:—

"Begobs, you'd think she had come into a fortune, or found a crock of goold. What's the matther, I wondher!"

Alas! And the cup of hope and love was dashed from the lips of the poor girl in one instant; and it was only after many years and many bitter trials that it was proffered to her lips again!

It was the early spring-time, and night fell sharply at six o'clock. There was no moon and the thick banks of gray clouds shut out the feeble light of the stars. Supper was over in the house; the dishes and cups had been washed and laid aside on the dresser, and the mistress had done an unusual thing. She had allowed, nay ordered, the girls to go up to the dance at the cross-roads that branched to Ballyorgan on the right, and to Ardpatrick on the left. The old man, half asleep, was nodding over the fire. Nodlag was reading by the light of a paraffin-lamp in a corner; reading, to her surprise, undisturbed, for her mistress rarely allowed her that luxury without breaking in with sundry commands to do this or that work about the house. Donal was in the bawn-field looking after the lambs and ewes. Donal's wife was busying herself in the bedroom.

Just as the clock struck nine the front door, opening

on the by-road, was opened noiselessly, and, one by
one, six masked men came into the kitchen. Nodlag,
with her back to the fire, was the first to see them.
She gave a little shriek, and her heart stood still.
Instinct told her that it was on her account they had
come — that this was her life's great crisis. She stood
up, with white face and eyes dilated with terror, as
she noticed that the two last of the intruders carried
firearms.

"What's the matter, alanna?" said the old man,
turning around.

She couldn't reply. She merely pointed with her
finger.

The old man arose from his chair slowly and with
difficulty, and confronted the intruders. His faculties
had become so weakened by age that here again he
found it difficult to distinguish a dream from a reality.
But the trembling figure and white face of Nodlag
assured him that this was no delusion. Here were
six masked men, and their presence boded no good.

"Run out for Donal, Nodlag!" he said, turning to
her.

"Stop where ye are," said the leader of the gang in
a voice that he sought to disguise, "av ye don't want
yere brains blown out!"

"Who are ye, and what in God's name do ye want
in a dacent house, an' at this hour of night?" asked
the old man.

"'Twas wanst a dacent house enough," said the
man, "but it is no longer so. It is cursed, and blighted,

and banned, in the eye of every dacent man, 'uman, an'
child in the three parishes."

"That's quare enough intirely," said the old man.
"I never hard that priest nor minister had ever anythin'
to say agin' us."

"'Tisn't priesht, nor ministher," replied the other,
"but informer and approver, who sint manny a dacent
man to the gallows; and whose spawn," he cried passionately, pointing to Nodlag, "you have been rarin'
to turn on you an' yours in the ind."

"Oh, wirra, wirra! Oh, ochone, ochone!" cried
Donal's wife, coming out from her bedroom, and in a
paroxysm of fright. "Oh, who are ye, at all, at all,
and what do ye want? Oh, sure take annythin' ye
like, and go away like dacent boys! Oh, where is
Donal, at all, at all; and the girls? Oh, spake aisy to
them, sir, or they'll murdher us all."

"We don't want you here, hones' 'uman," said the
ringleader. "Go back to where you kem frum, an'
hould yer tongue."

"I will, indeed. But sure you won't kill him, nor
do him anny harm. Sure, av 'tis atin' or dhrinkin' ye
want, ye can have the besht ——"

"Hould yer tongue, 'uman," he cried, rudely pushing
her aside till she fell on the settle, "an' let us do the
bisness we're sint to do. That is," he said, turning to
the old man, "to warn you to-night, Edmond Connors,
to sind out from you that girl, an' let her beg her bread
as she ought to do, from house and house ——"

"That I'll never do," said the old man, firmly.

"Who tould you, you ruffian, that this is Cloumper
Daly's child? Not that 'twould make much difference ——"

"Who tould me?" said the fellow, fumbling in the
breast pocket of his coat. "Doesn't every man in the
parish know it? Do you deny it? Nobody knows
better than you!"

"Lave me go, sir," said Nodlag, coming forward
bravely, now that the truth flashed certainly on her
mind. "Lave me go! I have been here long enough!"

"No," said the old man, pulling her softly towards
him, "you and I go or stop together."

He did not know how prophetic were his words.

"But wance more, you ruffian," he cried, fiercely,
for all the old lion-spirit was now aroused, "what do
you know of this girl? An' how do you say she's
Cloumper Daly's daughter?"

"You d—d ould hypocrite, here are yer own words
fur it," said the fellow, showing a sealed paper. "Who
wrote, or got wrote, 'Annie Daly' there?"

The old man looked, and his face fell. It was his
own will, that had been stolen.

"I see it all now," he said, looking over to where
his daughter-in-law was crouching on the settle, "I
see it all now. I'm in the way, and she's in the way
of those who are well behoulden to both of us. I think
I know who ye are now; but whoever ye are, let me
tell ye, that nayther Nodlag nor I will lave me house,
where me fathers and their fathers lived before me,
ontil we are put out by the shtrong hand of the law."

"Ind the argyin'," cried the rough voice of one of the ruffians behind; "we can't be stayin' here all night."

"Wance more, I put it to you for pace sake, and to prevint bloodshed," said the leader, "let her go, and do you remane in pace."

"Oh! For the luv of God, Mr. Connors," cried his daughter-in-law, who now saw the unexpected determination of the old man, and feared that matters would end in a way she had not anticipated, "give in to them. Sure the girl is big and shtrong enough to airn her own bread now."

The old man looked at her with such anger and contempt that she shrank from him and rushed into the fields to summon her husband.

"I gev you my decision," said the old man, turning once more to the intruders. "I say whatever is mine and Donal's is hers, so long as we live."

"Thin, be all that's holy," said the ruffian, levelling his musket at Nodlag, "we won't shtand it. I'll give you while I do be countin' twinty ——"

He held the musket still levelled towards Nodlag, his eye running along the barrel, whilst he commenced: "Wan! Two! Three! ——"

He had scarcely said these words, when a dark figure leaped from the door, and flew through the kitchen; and a strong hand caught the would-be murderer by the neck, and swinging him round and round, at last pushed him towards the wall to wrest the deadly weapon from his hand. The other ruffians, thinking there was help at hand, fled through the door, and up along the road. The old man had pushed Nodlag into the recess of the fireplace and had stood before her to protect her. The two strong men struggled wildly, but Donal, having his two hands free, had driven the fellow up against the whitewashed wall and pinned him there.

"Don't shoke me, Donal Connors," said the ruffian, gasping for breath, as Donal squeezed and twisted his neckerchief. "Unhand me, or be this and be that ——"

To relieve the suffocation, he had to part with the weapon, which he flung on the floor. The moment it struck the ground, the flint touched the steel, there was a frightful explosion, and the whole kitchen was filled with smoke, as some heavy body fell with a thud upon the hearthstone.

But, unheeding this, the two men, now equally matched, struggled desperately for the mastery. Donal Connors had the reputation of being the fiercest fighter and most powerful wrestler in the country, and was reputed a dangerous antagonist when his passions were excited. His opponent now, an equally powerful man, felt he was fighting for his life, and he threw into the combat all the energy of desperation. And, when he had got his right hand free, he caught Donal by the collar and the blue necktie; and the two men swung around the kitchen, now flung against the settle, now against the door, now dragging each other along the mud floor, which their rough boots had powdered into dust, and again, erect, with white faces and panting breasts, and breathing hotly into each other's mouth the silent hatred and determination that this was to be a death-struggle and nothing less. They were strangely silent, and struck but few blows. At last, swinging round in their death-embrace, they stumbled up towards the fireplace; and here the would-be murderer tripped over some heavy body, and fell towards the fire, dragging Donal with him. In an instant, the latter was up, and planting his knee so firmly on the ruffian's chest that the ribs seemed to crack beneath the pressure, he tore the black mask from the fellow's eyes, and revealed the face of — *his wife's brother*.

"I thought so, you ruffian," he cried; "you'll pay dear for this. Nodlag, come here!"

No Nodlag answered; but turning around he saw his father, lying senseless across the hearthstone, his legs shattered and splintered by the heavy slugs discharged from the blunderbuss, and the hot blood pumping from the severed arteries, and making a ghastly dark pool in the lamplight.

He rose up at the awful sight, and lifting his hands to Heaven, he shrieked:

"Great God in heaven to-night! Nodlag! Nodlag!"

But Nodlag, like one insane, had fled shrieking into the darkness.

CHAPTER XIX

A FLIGHT AND A RETURN

THREE years had rolled by, and, although the tragedy in the homestead at Glenanaar was still fresh in the memories of the people, and was often a topic of discussion around the winter's hearths, it was cast into a background of utter insignificance when the great national tragedy commenced; and after many a hope and fear, it was seen that, without doubt, Famine and all its ghastly train of evils was far and wide upon the land. Looking back on that appalling period in our history, the great wonder is, not that so many perished in the famine, but that so many lived, and lived in comfort, in the years previous to that dread visitation. When old men point out to-day places where whole villages then existed, each with its little army of tradesmen, — fullers, spinners, masons, stone-cutters, carpenters, etc., we, whose economic conditions are not yet up to the normal standard of living, ask ourselves in amazement how did the people then live. The land is as rich to-day as ever; the population has dwindled down to one-half of what it was then. If to-day the struggle for existence is still keen, what must it not have been then? And yet, the remnants of the ancient peasantry assure us, and they themselves are the best proof of the assertion, that the men

of those bygone days, nurtured exclusively on potat..s
and milk, were a far more powerful race than their
descendants; could endure greater hardship, and ac-
complish greater work. But when the potato was the
sole sustenance of the people, we can imagine what a
horror, slowly creeping on their minds, finally seized
them with utter panic, when, in the autumn of '47, and
again in the autumn of '48, that strange odour filled
the atmosphere, and told of the deadly blight. Even
to-day that word has an ominous significance. Men
seem to grow pale at the thought of it. The farmer or
labourer sniffs the air on one of those sweet autumnal
evenings, and goes into his cottage a depressed man.
A newspaper report from the far west of the country,
that the "blight" has appeared, makes men still
shudder. What must it have been in these far days,
when no other food was to be had; when the granaries
of the great prairies were yet unlocked, and a whole
people might perish before the hands of the charitable
could reach them.

And they did perish; perished by hundreds, by
thousands, by tens of thousands, by hundreds of thousands; perished in the houses, in the fields, by the
roadside, in the ditches; perished from hunger, from
cold, but most of all from the famine-fever. It is an
appalling picture, that which springs up to memory.
Gaunt spectres move here and there, looking at one
another out of hollow eyes of despair and gloom.
Ghosts walk the land. Great giant figures, reduced to
skeletons by hunger, shake in their clothes, which hang

loose around their attenuated frames. Mothers try
to still their children's cries of hunger by bringing
their cold, blue lips to milkless breasts. Here and
there by the wayside a corpse stares at the passers-by,
as it lies against the hedge where it had sought shelter.
The pallor of its face is darkened by lines of green
around the mouth, the dry juice of grass and nettles.
All day long the carts are moving to the graveyards
with their ghastly, staring, uncoffined loads. In the
towns it is even worse. The shops are shuttered.
Great fires blaze at the corners of streets to purify the
air. From time to time the doctors send up into the
polluted air paper kites with a piece of meat attached.
The meat comes down putrid. At the government
depots, here and there, starving creatures dip their
hands into the boiling maize, or Indian meal (hence
and forevermore in Ireland the synonym of starvation
and poverty), and swallow with avidity the burning
food. A priest is called from his bed at every watch
of the night. As he opens his hall-door, two or three
corpses fall into his arms. Poor creatures! here was
their last refuge! Here and there along the streets,
while the soft rain comes down to wash more corrup-
tion into the festering streets, a priest kneels in the
mud over a prostrate figure. He is administering the
last rites, whilst a courageous bystander holds an
umbrella above his head to guard the Sacred Species.
No graves, but pits, as after the carnage of a great
battle, are dug in the cemeteries; and the burial service
is read over twenty corpses at a time. Those who

have managed to escape the dread visitation are flying panic-stricken to the seaports. They heed not the coffin-ship, nor the sea-perils before them. Anywhere, anywhere, out of this pestiferous, famine-stricken Gehenna! The ships are full. Those who are compelled to remain behind on the quays send up a wail of lamentation. The dread spirits of Fever and Famine haunt them. There is no exorcism so powerful as to dispel them. There is nothing but flight, flight! The panic has lasted even to to-day.

One dark, iron-gray, bitter evening in the month of March, 1848, Redmond Casey was looking through the smoke-begrimed pane of glass which lighted the smithy. Work was dull; and he had time to dream. And his dream was the dream of the last three years, the figure that had so often darkened that mountain road before him in sunlight and moonlight, and the face that had made the sunshine and the moonlight brighter. He had been a very lonely man these three years. His fancy which had painted all kinds of lovely things, with Nodlag the central radiance, had been rudely dashed to pieces by the hand of Fate; and the tragedy at Glenanaar, which had almost ceased to interest the people around, was as vivid as ever to him on account of his great personal loss. Work, of course, that blessed panacea, more or less had dissipated the memory of his sorrow; but now and again this would come up with startling clearness to remind him of the swift and sudden calamity that had made barren so many years of his life.

As he looked out over the cold, bleak landscape, he saw the closely-shawled figure of a woman coming up the road with slow, painful steps; and then, after a moment's pause, turning into the little boreen that led from the smithy to the road. Here, evidently, her strength failed, for, putting out one hand, as if she were blind, she groped for the ditch, and then fell against it heavily. Redmond rushed into the cottage, and cried to his mother: —

"Run out, mother! There's another of thim poor crachures in the ditch!"

"The Lord betune us and all harrum," cried the mother. "Will it ever ind?"

She took up a porringer of milk (into which she poured a little hot water), and a piece of home-made loaf, and went out. Making her way with some dread and caution, she came within a few feet of where the fainting woman was lying; and afraid of the fever to approach nearer, she placed the food on a large stone, such as is always found near a smithy, and shouted: —

"Here, poor 'uman, here is milk and bread for you! Thry and rouse up, alanna, and God 'ill give you the strinth."

She turned and passed into the house, afraid to remain longer in such a dangerous vicinity; and the unfortunate woman, making one last effort for dear life, raised herself by a great effort, tried to walk forward a few steps, and fell. Then, after a few moments, she raised herself on hands and feet, and thus crept and crawled along the ground towards the now thrice-tempting food. She had to pause a few times, and Redmond, watching through the smithy pane, tried to catch a sight of her face. But she held her head so low that he could not see it. At last, after many painful efforts, she came within reach of the stone, and was just putting out her hand to seize the porringer of milk, when a huge, gaunt sheep-dog leaped over the neighbouring ditch, upset the milk, caught up the bread in his lank, gaunt jaws, and sped up the boreen towards the road. The woman raised herself from her stooping posture, and, flinging up her arms with a gesture of despair, fell senseless to the earth.

Just at the moment, however, that she lifted face and hands to heaven in the agony of a final supplication, the young smith caught a glimpse of eyes that were unchanged amidst the general and terrible transformation of famine, and of one stray lock of auburn hair that had freed itself from the hooded shawl; and with one wild leap he tore through the smithy door, along the boreen, and in a moment had the fainting girl in his arms. He raised her weakened and emaciated form as if it were a child's, and bringing it into the house, he laid it on his mother's bed, and shouted in a suppressed whisper: —

"Mother, quick, quick! A little milk at wanst. An' a dhrop of sperrits in it!"

The mother, amazed at his temerity, was too panic-stricken to remonstrate. She only moaned and lamented over the fire: —

"Oh, Lord, Lord! he has lost his five sinses, an' brought the faver and aguey into the house! Oh, Red, Red, what's come over you at all, at all?"

"Mother," he cried in a hoarse whisper, bending down his face to hers, "if Nodlag dies, I'll never forgive you, living or dead!"

"Nodlag! yerra, glory be to God! your sinses are wandering, boy. Nodlag! what Nodlag?"

But Redmond saw no time was to be lost in asking or answering questions. He put a small tin vessel of milk hastily on the fire, and went over to the cupboard to get the bottle of whiskey. As he did, he took a swift, secret look at the poor girl. To all appearance she was dead. Her shawl had been flung aside, and her features were now quite visible. But, oh! what a dread change! Beneath the cheek-bones, her face had sunk in in dreadful hollows, and her neck was thin and withered. There was a blue line across her lips. Her forehead (though her temples were sunken), and the thick masses of auburn hair that crowned it, alone retained their graciousness. The young smith poured some spirits into the black, hollow palm of his hand, and rubbed the blue lips lightly with his fingers. This he repeated several times, only interrupting the process to go over and dip his grimy finger into the vessel containing the milk, to test its warmth. After some time he had the satisfaction of seeing a slight colour come back to the marble face. He then took up the vessel of milk, and said to the weeping and distressed mother: —

"Mother, for the love of God, keep quiet! This is no time for keening. Here, lift Nodlag's head, and lemme see if I can get a drop of milk into her mouth!"

The mother, with some fear, yet with many an endearing Irish expression, raised the head of the poor girl, whilst Redmond tried to force a little milk between her lips. For some time the attempt was ineffectual, and life seemed to be flickering under the broad wings of death, as a candle-flame flickers blue and thin in a strong wind. But at last she swallowed a teaspoon of the milk, then another, and another, until at length her eyes opened, and fell first upon the face of the young smith. She continued to gaze at him earnestly for a few seconds, then she whispered, "Red!" and lay back wearily, yet refreshed, on the pillow. Though it was like the opening of the gates of Paradise to Red Casey, he went out and wept like a child.

All that night mother and son watched the poor famine-stricken girl, until, coming near the dawn, she fell into a deep sleep, so calm and with such regular breathing that Mrs. Casey, now completely over her fright, ordered Redmond to bed.

"Lave her to me now!" the good mother said. "Lave her to me! Sure, whin God sint me back her I wanted to be my daughter three years ago, sure she ought to find her mother still."

And Redmond kissed his mother, and said: —

"Mother, you were always good, and I have never been as good as I ought to you."

A few days rolled by, and the magnificent constitu-

tion of this mountain girl, reared in hardship that
strengthened and purified, asserted itself, and she was
able to go about again, and do little bits of household
work. As her strength came back, there came with it
a new and more spiritual beauty, as if sorrow and
hunger had worn away all grosser tissues, and left her
a kind of transparent and almost unearthly loveliness
that made Redmond afraid to look at her. There
grew up between them, too, a kind of shyness, that
made Redmond afraid to be alone with her for a
moment; and Nodlag, on her part, seemed to court the
society of the mother rather than the companionship
of the son. And one day, a few weeks after her prov-
idential rescue, Nodlag took down her black shawl,
whilst Redmond was from home on business, and after
kissing the old woman, who never noticed how expressive it was, she passed out of the humble cottage and
faced the world again.

Red Casey was thunderstruck when he returned
home. This was the second time his hopes were
blasted. In his anger, he attributed Nodlag's flight
to everything but the real cause. He blamed his
mother; he blamed Nodlag; he blamed himself for
having allowed so close and splendid an opportunity
to pass. Then he became suddenly practical. He
asked his mother which way Nodlag went. He was
determined to follow the girl, and bring her back, or
lose her forever. The old woman could not say
whither Nodlag went. She thought she only went
down to the well. Red, at once, tore off his leather

apron, burnt here and there by the smithy fire, and putting on a rough cap over his sooty, red hair, he sallied forth. He went up the hill quickly, and leaping a gully, he ascended an abrupt height, whence he could trace the roads for miles. He could see no trace of the girlish form of Nodlag. Sad at heart, he retraced his steps, and moved down along the western road, his head sunk on his breast, and no hope in his mind. He had passed halfways across the bridge where old Edmond Connors had challenged Nodlag's mother, on that snowy evening when Nodlag was but an infant, and the mother in her wretchedness was debating with herself whether her child would not be happier there in the death of the torrent than in the dreadful life that stretched sullenly before her. Something dark caught his eye, and in a moment he saw the girl sitting on the bridge-wall. She looked pale and frightened, as if she had been guilty of some crime, and this disarmed the anger of the young smith. He came over, and sat down on the parapet near her. She was trembling all over.

"I couldn't stay, Reddy," she said. "Indeed I couldn't. 'Twouldn't be right."

"Did me or me mother trate you badly?" he said, stiffly.

"N-no," she said, weeping, "God knows I am ever so thankful. I'd be in my cowld grave to-day but for you, Redmond Casey, and your good mother; and how could I forget that?"

"Thin somebody has been putting some quare things

into yer head," he said. "As if the bit you ate, and small enough it is, God knows, could make a differ to me mother or me."

"It isn't that ayther," she sobbed. "Sure I knew ye never begredged me. But I couldn't stop, an' I'd be far away now, only the wakeness kim on me again."

"Thin, in God's name, can't you come back to where you're a hundred times welkum?" said Red, utterly failing to comprehend the girl's delicacy of feeling. "An' av you think you're a burden, sure we'll make you work for the bit you ate."

"Oh, no, no, no!" she wept. "I can't go back at all, at all, Redmond Casey. I'll go along, and maybe some wan of the farmers round about will employ me. There are few handy for work now, God help us!"

"Well, whatever you plase," said Redmond, rising up, and looking down on the white face of the girl. "But, before we part, Nodlag, I'd like to clare up wan thing."

Nodlag looked up.

"Did Donal Connors give you me message the day his father was murdered?"

"He did," said Nodlag, the colour mounting to her face.

"An' what did you say?" said the young smith, watching the play of her features as if life and death hung upon her word. She was silent.

"Did you say yes?" he demanded.

"You know I did, Redmond Casey; but why do you torment me now?"

"'Tis you're tormenting me," he replied. "If the same question were put to you now, would it be the same answer?"

"How could it be, when things are so different now?" she replied.

"How are they different?" he demanded.

"I didn't know all thin," she replied, "till that dreadful night. I know all now. How can I be the wife of any honest man?"

"That depends on the man himself," said Redmond, gaily, as he felt he was gaining ground.

"It manes sorrow and shame to him to have me his wife; it manes every finger pointed agin him; it manes that 'twill be thrun in his face at fair, at Mass, and at market; it manes that nobody will come nixt or nigh him; it manes —" here she stopped suddenly short in her self-accusation.

"An' if wid all the manes and the manings," said Redmond, "be wants you still to be his wife, an' if he will put his smutty fist in the face of the wurrld" (here Redmond put a literally smutty fist in the face of an imaginary world), "an' if he takes you, as the priest says, 'for bether for worse,' will you still say no?"

She looked up into his sooty, honest face, and there was something in that look, for now he took upon him the right of command, and said simply, Come!

A few minutes later she entered the house as its mistress.

"I found Nodlag, mother," said Redmond, "and the divil is in it, if I lave her go agin."

Before the week Nodlag changed her old name forever (though we have taken the liberty to retain it), and became Mrs. Redmond Casey.

CHAPTER XX

HAGAR AND ISHMAEL

THIS, then, was the history of Nodlag, told me, from time to time, there in the twilight of his sickroom, by her son, who still retained, after all his travels, and the many and varied experiences that tend to harden the human heart, the tenderest and most chivalrous love for his mother. Her strange history — that of a pariah amongst her own tribe — seemed to separate her in his imagination from all other beings with whom he had been brought in contact; and the singular birth-taint which he had derived from her, and which, as he imagined, would cling around him to the end of life, identified him in so mysterious a manner with her, that he had come to regard himself and her as beings apart, with the destiny of a common misfortune, not of their own making, but inherited. But here, as his own personal experiences commence, I shall give the narrative in the first person, and as far as may be, in his own words. He had read a good deal, picked up a knowledge of some languages, and had cultivated the art of speaking, as most of his countrymen in America strive to do. But the narrative was a sad one. It was Ishmael telling the story of Hagar and himself in the wilderness.

"My earliest recollection of my mother was of a

tall, thin woman, very gentle and affectionate, but very
reserved in manner. I particularly remember her
very bright blue eyes, and her hair, which she always
wore in tiny waves of auburn low down on her temples,
and caught up by a fillet behind her ears. She never
went from home, but to Mass on Sunday. She seemed
to find all the pleasure of life in her domestic duties,
in the love of her husband, and the care of her children.
When reason began to dawn for me, I was the only
child remaining. My two sisters had gone out to
service, for owing to emigration and the famine, servants were not to be had except at enormous wages.
My only brother, too, was apprenticed to a carpenter
in the County Limerick. I was the only one left at
home, and I got a good deal of petting, which I repaid
a hundredfold by such love as son never had before
for mother."

Here he stopped, not for the last time, for his emotion subdued him. The shame and sorrow that had
hung around his mother's memory had made her dear,
very dear to him.

"I only remember," he resumed, "her face and
figure, and one small habit she had, of listening at
strange times, as if rapt in a dream, listening as if to
the sound of far-off bells, or to a voice calling, calling
out of the night. You know, Father, that we who
have travelled and seen the world get rid of a good
many of these old superstitions; but, somehow, since
I came back to Ireland, the glamour of the old times
seizes me, and I am really afraid I'd turn back if I

saw one magpie on the road. But my mother had that strange habit. She would lean down and listen with her hand to her ear; and sometimes my father would make great fun of it, and say: 'Nodlag! Nodlag! who's calling now?'

"But I had little time to notice things, for as soon as ever I got through Voster and Carpenter's Spelling-Book, I was taken from school, and put at the anvil. I had a taste for it, for I remember, when very small, how I made a valiant effort to pick up a hammer from the floor, and when, after many days' trial, I succeeded, I remember my father shouting 'Hurrah!' and my mother kissed me. Then, when I became able to lift and swing the sledge, my father said I had book-learning enough, and now I should do something for my bread.

"Ah! how well I remember that forge and its surroundings, — the great black walls, hung here and there with horseshoes and all kinds of rusty iron-work; the deep night of its recesses that was only lightened by the ruddy blaze from the great fire; the huge bellows which sent sparks dancing all over the coal-strewn floor; the horses coming in, some terrified, some submitting quietly to the operation of shoeing; my father, lifting up the hoof into his leathern apron; the smell of the burnt cartilage; the tap, tap of the hammer; the shrinking of the poor beasts; but, most of all, the metallic music that echoed all day long from the anvil, and which beat time in my mind to many an old rune or song about Ireland and her sorrows.

"For that was the first lesson I learned,—long before I knew my prayers or my Catechism,—that Ireland had suffered, and had been wronged in an appalling manner; and that it was the bounden, solemn duty of every young Irishman to fight for that sad motherland, until her wrongs were avenged and her rights achieved. Ah me! how it all comes back, in the light of experience and memory, and how now I understand a hundred little things which even then were a puzzle to me. For the very rebel songs that I hummed as I beat out the long iron rods on the anvil,—'The Risin' of the Moon,' 'The Wearing of the Green,' even the simpler love melodies, such as 'Come, piper, play the Shaskan Reel,' I noticed were never heard in my father's cottage. Neither did he ever take part in the furious debates that were held in the forge by the boys who used to drop in for a chat or on business. He was a silent man; nevertheless, I couldn't understand why he never railed against England, nor broke out into enthusiasm about Ireland. He listened, worked, and said nothing.

"I, on the contrary, was a furious rebel. I outdistanced the most fanatical Fenian there by my diatribes against England. I astonished every one by my quotations from Mitchel, Davis, Emmet. I chaunted the most furious sword-songs I could discover. I electrified every one (at least, so I thought) by my declamation of Meagher's Sword-Speech. I lay awake at night, plotting and dreaming how I could fling shells and balls into whole British regiments and annihilate them;

I saw myself the hero of a hundred fights. Somehow, my enthusiasm was taken coolly. It fell flat on the souls of these young fellows, whom I knew to be sworn Fenians. They would listen to my most furious oratory, look at one another, and smile. I didn't understand it then; I understand it well now. They did not believe in me. How could they with all they knew?

"I had grown a great, tall lad of sixteen years, when the famous rising of '67 took place. For weeks before, we young fellows had been out on the hills, not so much engaged in active service ourselves, but as scouts or pickets to give warning to the Fenian detachments, in valley or wood, of the approach of the police or the redcoats. Many a moonlit night did we watch, shivering in the icy winds that pierced us through and through, and no thought of danger in our minds, only a fierce jealousy of the sworn soldiers in the great Irish Republic, and a far-off ambition, which set our pulses bounding, that we might attract the notice of some one of the Irish-American officers, of whom at that time the country was full.

"I well remember the night poor Crowley was shot in Kilclooney wood. I remember his funeral, down through mountain, town, and village, amidst a mourning population, to his grave by the sea. It was an awful evening, and we were gone clean mad with hate and anger. It was then I committed one of the worst sins of my life."

"The Yank" turned round, as if to deprecate my wrath.

"I cursed, hot and heavy," he continued, "the priest who refused, for some reason, to have the chapel-bell tolled that evening as we passed, a deep, serried mass of men, through the streets of Fermoy."

It brought up at once to memory a picture that had been fading and slumbering away; and, as the whole scene flashed back, I could not help starting with surprise and, perhaps, a little enthusiasm.

"We were mad, mad," he said, regretfully, "and we did curse the Government and that priest."

"He wasn't altogether to blame, my dear fellow," I said, laying my hand on his arm.

"What? How?" said the Yank. "Do you think he was justified in refusing such a little mark of respect to the dead patriot?"

"Perhaps not. I was as mad as yourself about it ——"

"What, you? Surely, you weren't there!" he cried in amazement.

"I was," I replied. "I remember that black March evening well. We, a lot of raw, young students were massed on the College Terrace; and I remember how we watched with beating hearts that great, silent, moving multitude of men. But when the yellow coffin containing the mangled remains of poor Crowley came in sight, swaying to and fro on the bearers' shoulders, we lost ourselves out and out. We saw the body, or thought we saw it, rent and torn and bleeding from English bullets; and some of us were crying, and some of us were cursing, and more wanted to scale

the College walls in spite of priest and Bishop. But
I heard afterwards, when we had come to the use of
reason, that there were at least extenuating circumstances in the Administrator's Case."

"Perhaps so," he said, incredulously. Then, after
a pause: —

"But I was about to say as a set-off that I ever after
enshrined in my heart of hearts the memory of that
young curate, who, more or less at the risk of his own
life, knelt by the fallen Fenian, and had his anointing
hands stained, — no, by the living God!" he exclaimed,
sitting up suddenly rigid, and flinging out his right
arm, whilst sparks seemed to leap from his eyes, "*not
stained, but consecrated with the blood shed for Ireland.*"

The paroxysm was so sudden, I was struck dumb,
and could only watch him, — his livid face, and the
blindness of battle in his eyes. Presently, the tension
relaxed, and his soul came back to his body. But it
was an eloquent revelation of What-might-have-been.
In that mood, and under that spell, these men of '67
would have stormed the gates of Hell.

For a few minutes he remained silent. Then,
turning around, and clenching his right hand until it
was quite bloodless from the pressure, he said
sharply: —

"Father?"

"Yes?" I replied.

"Bind your people to you with chains of iron and
links of steel. The day the priests are torn from the
people is woe, woe to Ireland!"

He paused again, and his great hand relaxed its tension, and the pupils of his eyes contracted, and I saw he had come back to reality once more.

"Pardon me," he said, passing his hand across his forehead, "where was I? I was talking about something. Oh, yes! I was about to say that wherever we were on vedette duty, on hill, or mountain, or valley, I was never left alone. Other lads were sent out, one by one, and kept their solitary watch, a mile or so apart. I had always a comrade, who stuck to me like a leech. Fortunately, I had such a dislike for peelers and soldiers, that I never spoke to one in those days. If I had been seen alone in conference with them, my life would have been forfeit. And, here is the curious feature of my story. Not a breath of suspicion ever attached to my father. He was implicitly trusted by the chiefs of the organization. He knew all their secrets. I thought this was because he was so silent and cautious. Possibly. But I know now that suspicion attached only to my mother and me, so tremendous is the importance the Irish attach to 'blood.' His marriage made no difference to Red Casey, so far as the public opinion of his honour and integrity was concerned. My parentage made all the difference in the world to me. I had tainted blood, and nothing will ever get the Irish imagination over that."

"Oh, nonsense!" I said. "We've outgrown all that a long time ago. These things are now forgotten or exploded."

"I wish I could believe it, Father," he replied.
'Do you remember my nervous anxiety, that neither
my name or history should be known?"

"Perfectly; but I thought and still think it absurd.
Events now succeed each other so rapidly, and the
newspapers supply such daily relays of most interesting
intelligence, that we have ceased to linger on the past."

"I don't know," he said, dubiously. "The old
saying is there, ready to be quoted against me any
moment — 'What's bred in the blood will break out
in the bone.' Isn't that it?"

There was little use in trying to dissipate such foolish
fears. I let him proceed.

"The strangest thing of all was that my father
shared the superstition or suspicion. Although deeply
attached to my mother, she shared none of his secrets.
He left his housekeeping altogether in her hands; but
political or other secrets he rigidly withheld. And
though I think, — nay, I am sure, he loved me, for
being like him in appearance, and for my great strength
and agility, somehow he never trusted me. When I
broke out into my rhodomontades about Ireland's
misgovernment and England's perfidy, he was always
silent. He never encouraged me. And I knew even
then that he had arms concealed in the haggart, — a
coffin-load of rifle-barrels, well greased, with cartridges
to match, but I knew no more where they were than
you do."

"I think he was quite right not to trust the discretion
of a mere lad," I said.

"It wasn't that," he replied. "He trusted me in all kinds of business matters, but he was silent as the grave there. But the strangest thing of all was, that neither by word or sign was ever the slightest hint given me that my birth was tainted. You'd imagine that somehow it should transpire. Never. When I heard my father call my mother 'Nodlag!' I thought it a pet name. That was all. And you know we were brought up so rigidly, and in such strict seclusion from the company of our elders, that there was no chance of my ever discovering the secret. But I often wonder that not one of my schoolmates in a temper, or through mischief, ever hinted at it. Probably they were afraid of me, on account of my great strength and courage, or probably it was some delicacy, such as you often find amongst our people, that kept them from taunting me with such a terrible and ineradicable birth-taint.

"But it was almost a joke, though a gruesome one, that I should be always so fierce against the detested tribe of informers. Just then the State-Trials of the prisoners who had taken part in the rising of '67 were proceeding in Cork, and my cordial detestation of the Crown Prosecutors, especially of 'Scorpion Sullivan," was nothing to the hatred I had for the wretched approvers who had turned Queen's evidence against their comrades. How I stormed and raged I remember now with a smile. But my companions only listened and said nothing. I called them white-livered poltroons for not flaming up, like myself. They never resented it. They only smiled. I consoled myself by the reflection that I was the only genuine patriot in Ireland."

"A pretty common delusion," I interjected, "and not limited to ardent and impassioned youth, but the attribute of every age and condition. Well, if it is not exactly modest, at least it is not ignoble. Go on!"

"No," said he, with a meaning smile, "even Sam thinks he is the only one left of the race of Emmet and Wolfe Tone."

"Sam has at least one attribute of another kind," I replied. I was glad of the little interlude. "I caught him listening at the keyhole the last evening I was here."

"The Yank" was very angry, but what's the use? Sam will be Sam to the end of time. He had made sundry ineffectual attempts to get in to our little conferences. He had several times knocked at the door, with the query: —

"Did you ring, Sir?"

A few times he suggested: —

"Do you want any hot water, Sir?"

which I resented, as an imputation.

And a few times he charitably and solicitously reminded "The Yank" that "this was the toime for his midicine."

But I nearly stumbled over him the last evening I was going out. He was on his knees on the door-mat, his ear glued to the keyhole, but he jumped up in an instant, and began demonstrating with the medicine bottle and glass, which he had taken the precaution to bring with him.

I looked at him severely, but he was unperturbed, and merely wiped the wine-glass with the napkin. I was genuinely angry.

"Sam?" said I.

"Yes, yer Reverence," he said.

"Sam," said I, "you are a good young man, and a pious young man, and fairly sober, except when you take that 'liminade' which is bad for you."

"The Docthor said, yer Reverence, —" he replied, but I shut him up.

"I know, I know all that," I said, "you have a 'wake stomach,' etc., etc.; but what I'm coming to is this. The Catechism says, 'we ought always to pray,' and I perceive you are trying to carry out the recommendation. But, in future, when the pious fit comes on you, I would recommend you to seek any other place in the hotel, except this door-mat ——"

"'Pon me sowkens, I was only shtoopin' down ——"

"That'll do," I said. "But remember, one word from me to the American gentleman ——"

"You wouldn't harrum a poor bye like that, yer Reverence," he pleaded. "God knows ——"

"'Sh," I said. "I want no more asseverations. But less prayers, Sam, and a quiet tongue, will do you no harm."

For I heard he had circulated the report around the parish that "The Yank" was making a "gineral confession," and that he must have been the "divil's own bhoy," because he had already been at it three weeks, and would probably continue for three weeks longer.

But I must come back to the narrative, which had now become very fascinating to me.

CHAPTER XXI

"But there were two friendships, that, without casting any light on the history of the past for me, brightened considerably my young years. The one was with the living, the other with the dead. Donal Connors was the intimate and particular friend of our little family. Unlike other strollers, who came into the forge for a chat, or on business, he rarely spent much time in the forge, but he often visited the cottage, where he was always thrice welcome. I could see, even without any information on the subject, that there was some secret tie from the past binding him to our family, for he always assumed an attitude of familiarity which every one else avoided. He came in and out of the kitchen like a member of the family, and I noticed that, on all grave occasions, he was the only person ever consulted by my father or mother. I had heard, in a dim way, as of a far-off legend, of the tragedy that had taken place at Glenanaar twenty years before. But my mother's connection with it was carefully concealed from me, and I was too proud or shy to inquire. But neither my father, my mother, nor I, ever visited that lonely cottage up there in the deep saddle of the hills. Of course, I knew Donal's

wife by appearance, and it was not attractive. But
she never spoke to us, nor we to her. Now, Donal
was the only person who showed his deep friendship
for me by warning me against my too demonstrative
patriotism. Sometimes, in a half laughing way, he
would meet all my passionate speeches about Ireland
and England, by a joke or a smothered rebuke: —

"'If you don't keep yourself quiet, young man,
believe me, you'll get a hempen cravat some of these
days, or make the acquaintance of Botany Bay.'

"To which I would reply with flashing eyes:

> Far dearer the grave or the prison,
>   Illumed by one patriot name,
> Than the trophies of all who've arisen
>   On Liberty's ruins to Fame.

"'I never trusted a man yet who could quote po-
ethry,' Donal would reply. 'You can't dhrive a pike
wid yere tongue.'

"'Then what about the speech of Emmet or the
speech of Meagher?' I would answer. 'Isn't it these
burning words that have kindled the fire of patriotism
in the breasts of young Irishmen?'

"'Yes! But thin, Emmet and Meagher did something theirselves before they thought they had a right
to tache others to folly them.'

"And as I had done nothing beyond sharpening a
pike-end, I had to be silent.

"He must have spoken to my mother, too, to restrain
me. For she, in her own gentle way, gave me sundry
warnings to be cautious in my language, and to re-

member that loud talkers are always more or less suspect.

"'Suspect?' I cried. 'Who could suspect me? Isn't me life before the world, and who can point to a blot or stain on any one of us?'

"Then the hot blood would mount up to her pale face; but, of course, I never understood the reason. So blind are the young, so fortunately blind. It is an ill hand that pulls the veil from their eyes.

"The other friendship was with the dead. Every Sunday, on returning from Mass, we had to pass by the old graveyard at Templeroan. How well I remember it, as, holding my mother's hand, we passed from the road through the iron gate, and got in under the shadow of the trees. Many a time I called up the picture from memory, when I was far away — the old ruined Abbey, festooned with ivy, the moss-covered gravestones, leaning hither and thither, the great brown lichens on the walls, — all things so ancient and time-worn and venerable. You might remember a single grave, Father, right in the centre of the aisle of the old Abbey? The stone is now falling aside, and the inscription is hardly legible, but in my childhood and boyhood it was a fresh modern slab, inscribed: '*Sacred to the memory of Edmond Connors*,' with date of death and age. Well, this was the shrine where every Sunday, as long as I remember, my mother and I worshipped and prayed. Here I had to repeat the Litany for the Dead, word by word, after my mother, and then I had to kiss the grass that feathered the grave, and the name on the tombstone. Then we went home together. I never asked questions until I grew to manhood. Then I learned that this old man had given his life for my mother, and I sought to know no more until the whole revelation came.

"Meanwhile, I was rushing on, every day gaining strength and agility. I never knew the taste of fresh meat, or 'butcher's mate,' as it was called. On Sundays we had a bit of bacon and at Christmas and Easter a fowl. But our daily diet, unless we had a visitor, was milk, home-made bread, and potatoes, and on these I developed the thews of Anak.

"After a little time the excitement about the Fenian rising had died away, and with it a good deal of our boyish enthusiasm. Then came the Gaelic Athletics and here I easily took the lead, until I became captain of our team in football and hurling and I became known over half the country."

"So you did," I exclaimed. "When ballads are written about a man, his fame is universal and secure."

"Yes! if it's worth anything," he replied. "I'm not sure that it would not have been better for me to have lain low then, as I desire to do now."

"I don't think that's a manly sentiment," I replied. "Everyone must give the world the best that's in him, without fear or hope of reward."

"I never could understand that," he replied. "I can never see why a man should not keep to himself, or for himself, whatever of great or good he possesses."

"Because," I replied, "the reward of genius is labour, and none other has it a right to seek after."

He was silent, brooding over this strange proposition. At length he said: —

"I don't understand it. All I know is, that I flung myself into the thick of the fight and there I met the revelation of the past and the one great disappointment of my life."

He paused, recalling the historic incidents of his life, and summoning up the ghostly details from the past. Then he went on: —

"Of course, you cannot understand it," he said, "but like all other young fellows I fell head over ears in love. I cannot remember now how or where we met, but I think it was coming home from a great hurling match, where I was the laurelled conqueror. These things attract the notice of girls, and I suppose it was then I first met her, whose face has been haunting me for a quarter of a century, and whom I have travelled three thousand miles by land and three thousand miles by water to see once more and be forevermore blessed or disappointed. But, wherever we met for the first time, we met again and again afterwards, and our trysting-place was a great wide whitethorn tree that grows down there by the road where the plantation of firs cuts off the bare heather from the land that has been reclaimed. I have gone out a few times to see it since I returned home. It seems to have been blasted by lightning or cut away, for it is not half the size of the tree I knew so well.

"Our little affair was frowned upon, of course. That is inevitable. I was but a blacksmith, and she was a daughter of a purse-proud, independent father, who expected to see his child married, as he used to say, to 'her own aiquals.' But she, poor girl, was true as steel. When I heard of her father's objection I offered to release her, but she refused to be released. Then I faced him. I met him coming home from Mass one Sunday morning. We had never spoken before. If I had had experience I would not have spoken to him then.

"'I beg your pardon,' I said. 'I understand you have an objection to my meeting Nora?'

"He looked me all over.

"'Who the divil are you?' he said.

"'I am Terence Casey,' I said, 'the son of Redmond Casey, the smith at Glenanaar, and as good a man as you any day.'

"He was speechless with rage.

"When he recovered himself he said with some show of deliberation:—

"'I don't know you, boy, but this I know. If any child of mine has had hand, act, or part with any of your breed, she has my curse forever and ever.'

"'Tis true I'm only a tradesman,' I said, 'but I can give her as good a life as a broken-down farmer any day.'

"This went home, for though he had the name of being rich, some people said he was stretching himself too much, and had to borrow money.

"'A dacent tradesman,' he replied, 'is as good as anny other man. 'Tisn't to your trade I object, but to yourself. I'd as soon my daughter would marry the divil as wan of your breed.'

"'That's your last word?' I asked, full of wonder at the objection to my family.

"'The last word,' he replied, 'but not my last deed, as you'll have raison to remimber if you go anny further in that matther.'

"I met Nora that evening.

"''Tis to my family your father objects,' I said, 'not to meself. What fault has he to find with me family, I don't know. We held our heads as high as anny of our nabors. At laste, I never hard a word agen us till now, did you?'

"She hung down her head and said nothing.

"'If you share your father's opinions, Nora,' I said, 'let us part. If you think you lower or demane yerself by marrying me, in God's name, let there be an ind to the matther. We'll part good friends.'

"She held out her hand. Ah! 'tis well I remimber it. There never yet was a truer woman made by God.

"'Ted,' she said, 'I've promised to be yours. Until you throw me off, no power on earth shall separate us.'

"And I registered the same promise in my mind, but with the addition of a great oath. Ah, Father, don't wonder that I've crossed the ocean to see her once more. That night, and another night, I could

never forget. Alas! I didn't know then how swift
would be the revelation, and how terrible the separation
that we deemed impossible.

"Of course, I never spoke a word of this at home.
Young men are shy about these things, and then, I
really didn't know how it would be taken. My own
idea was to leave my father's home, if I were married,
and open a forge down there near Wallstown or the
vicinity, where I was sure, as I thought, of plenty of
customers, without interfering with my father's business. I dare say my father and mother heard of it,
but they never alluded to it. My father had an Irish
temper, and so had I, and I think he deemed it wiser
not to open up matters of crossness before their time.
And he was quite right. But sometimes my mother
would watch me in a strange, curious way, and then
turn away with a sigh.

CHAPTER XXII

REVELATIONS

"ALTHOUGH popular enthusiasm had more or less died out after the '67 rising, my own feelings seemed to be rather intensified. And, with all the thoughtlessness of youth, I was not slow to express myself freely on those political matters which are best consulted for by silence. But no! I had read up Irish history, especially Mitchell's, and my blood ran flame.

"It was Ireland, and Ireland, and Ireland, ever present to waking thought and sleep's dreams. How I raged against her persecutors, and how I yearned for revenge! But all my fury was reserved for her traitors, from MacMurrough downwards through all her black history, and the words 'traitor,' 'informer,' 'approver,' seemed to hold me by a kind of obsession. But people only smiled. At home, they had long since ceased to remonstrate with me.

"One Sunday evening we had a pitched battle, a great supreme trial of strength at hurling between the parishes of Glenroe and Ardpatrick in the County Limerick, and Kildorrery in the County Cork. I belonged to neither parish, but I was asked by the latter to go with them, and no objection was made by the other side. It was a glorious evening; the whole country-side was there, our blood was up, and we fought like demons for victory. So intense was the feeling on both sides that a big faction-fight was expected, and we were near it, and I was the innocent cause. After several unsuccessful tries, I had managed to get the ball within reach of the goal, and swung my hurley round my head for the final stroke. I made it successfully, and won the match, but the back swing had struck an opponent, a young lad, on the mouth, and had smashed in his front teeth. I was so excited that I never thought of looking around until I saw the black ball sailing out between the poles. Then I turned. The boy had spat out his bloody teeth, and there was a crowd around him. I was instantly accused of having done it deliberately, and you know how the passions of an Irish crowd rise. I denied it, and expressed my sorrow. But between their rage at defeat, and the boy's sufferings, they could not be satisfied. Their anger rose every moment, until at last an ill-disposed fellow came near me, and relying on the help around him, he struck me, and said:

"'You did, you Sir! I saw you hit him, you b—— son of an informer!'

"The hurley fell from my hand, as if I were paralyzed. The Kildorrery men, who had been grouping around me with the conviction that they were bound to support their champion, slunk away, one by one. I put on my coat without a word, and left the field. Father," he continued, "there are certain times in men's lives when all things seem to be rushing together,

and night and day, life and death, heaven and hell,
seem all alike. That moment was one. It was a
sudden flash that lit up all the past, and darkened all
the future of my life."

He paused and gulped down his emotion, and my
sympathies began to increase towards him at every
pause in his narration.

"I had crossed two fields towards home, when my
humiliation gave way to a sudden paroxysm of passion
that literally lifted me off my feet. I had taken for
granted that there was some foundation for the ruf-
fianly taunt. Then the thought swept back upon me:
what if the fellow is a liar? I ran back. The crowd
had partly dispersed, but groups of young men, seeing
me return in such an excited state, began to gather
together again, and they had formed a knot around
the wounded boy (who was still spitting blood) and
his champion. I strode up, and my face must have
been a fright, for the crowd gave way. I burst into
the midst of them and said to the fellow that had
struck me:—

"'Grogan, you struck me a coward's blow a few
minutes ago. I didn't mind that. But you said something at the same time that I do mind. Can you
prove it?'

"'Go home, Casey, with your friends,' he said, 'and
let's hear no more of it now.'

"'By the living God,' I cried, in a fearful fury, 'you'll
prove here and now what you said, or I'll ram the
lie down your throat.'

"'I tell you, go home,' said he, somewhat frightened. 'You have done mischief enough already.'

"''Tis a coward and a blackguard,' I exclaimed, who won't take back his words, or prove them. Now, confess that what you said was a lie!'

"'I tell you, Casey, let well alone,' he said. 'Don't mind a hasty word said in a passion.'

"'I wouldn't,' I replied. 'But that was more than a hasty word. Come, quick, I'll stand no humbugging now! Say you told a lie, when you said I was the breed of an informer.'

"'I can't say it,' he said, holding down his head.

"'Then 'twas the truth?' I asked.

"He was silent.

"'Come, you ruffian,' I said, now losing all control of myself, and seizing him by the collar. 'Deny what you have said in a lie, or, by Heavens, I'll make you eat your words.'

"He tried to swing himself free, but I held him with a grip of iron. One or two fellows came forward to help him. I kicked them aside. Then he was badly frightened, and blurted out:

"'Bear witness, boys, that he is forcing me to do what I don't want to do.'

"'I only want you to tell the truth, and shame the devil!' I cried.

"'Then the shame be yours, Terence Casey,' he replied. 'You know as well as I do, that your mother is the daughter of Cloumper Daly, the informer.'

"''Tis an infernal lie, you scoundrel,' I said, with

clenched teeth. 'Take back the word, or I'll smash your face so that your mother won't know you.'

"'Unhand him, Casey,' said an old man. 'Sure the boy has only said what every man in the counthry knows.'

"'Do you know it?' I said.

"'I do,' said he, 'an' everybody else.'

"'Then,' I said, lifting my face to heaven, 'may God help me, for that's the first time it was ever told me!'

"As I left the field, the crowd, understanding my feelings, gave way with a certain kind of pity and respect. They found it difficult to understand how the knowledge of the terrible secret could have been so long kept from me. But they evidently believed in my sincerity, and pitied me under the awful revelation.

"As for myself, a whole crowd of horrible thoughts, recollections, forebodings, sensations, swept every vestige of reason and common sense away. I was a sheer madman, if madness is the inability to control one's imagination or feelings. I did not return home that night; I quietly made up my mind never to sleep a night under that roof again. I went up among the hills, seeking out one particularly desert and savage spot, which seemed to have been never trodden except by the feet of goats. There I wandered round and round all that terrible night, a prey to every kind of humiliating and shameful thoughts. If I rested even for a moment on a red boulder, or a clump of heather, I was up in a moment again. There was no sitting or standing still under such a fever of thought as was stinging my brain to madness. The worst and most painful recollection was, that I had been actually courting shame and humiliation all these years, by my fierce denunciations of the class whose blood ran in my own veins. I now recalled with untold agony the smile that ran around a whole circle of auditors when I was unusually vehement in my patriotism. How these men, who held my secret, must have despised me! What a hypocrite they must have deemed me! But this was not the worst. The worst was that I, who so loved my gentle mother that I almost worshipped her, began to loathe and hate her. I struggled against the hellish feeling a long time. I tried to recall every little incident of affection and love that had surrounded my childhood and my youth, all the little marks of maternal solicitude that had knit my own affections so closely to her that I would gladly have died to show my loyalty and love. But the words, 'Cloumper Daly's daughter,' 'Cloumper Daly's daughter,' and all they meant, would come up with all their loathsome associations, and do what I would, I could not conquer an indefinable contempt and dislike for one who had sprung from the lowest and most degraded of the species. All this seemed to me then and seems to me now the purest extravagance; but you know how we were brought up, and how fiercely traditions of this kind take hold of Irish imaginations. Tainted blood, inherited shame, is a terrible heritage amongst a people who attach supreme importance to these things. And the words I heard nearly a quarter of a century ago in that field near Kildorrery, 'the breed of an informer,' have haunted me all my life, and will haunt me to my dying day."

He stopped again, and I didn't interrupt him. I perfectly understood all that this meant. A loss of caste amongst the Orientals would be nothing to the entailed shame of which he was so painfully conscious.

"You remember my anxiety about concealing my identity here," he continued. "You thought it unreasonable: I don't."

"I think," I said, "that the people now, under more enlightened circumstances, and better education, are freeing themselves from many of these old prejudices. At least, you don't hear any references to them in ordinary life."

"And I," he replied, "had grown to the age of manhood before I ever heard of my mother's shame. Then it broke on me like a flash of lightning."

"That's quite true," I said, "but at least it argues a more rational and a more Christian frame of thought, that the wretched business was never flung in your face for so many years."

"That's quite true," he replied. "But would you believe, it followed me across the ocean, and embittered my whole life?"

"Impossible," I said.

"'Tis true," he answered. "I have never yet met but one, and you, Father, who did not shrink from me

at the moment of revelation. And how can anyone
wonder that I have sought her across sea and land,
and shall find no rest till I find her, if haply she is
yet living?"

"That was the young girl you spoke of, whose
father objected to your marriage with her?"

"Yes! And his words were not the least bitter that
came back to me that night beneath the stars, when
I remembered them, and recognized their meaning.
But I must go on to the end, if I am not tiring you."

"By no manner of means, my dear fellow," I replied.
"I am deeply interested in the narrative. I never
thought this quiet little place could have produced
such a romance and such a tragedy."

"Well," he continued, "I came down the following
morning from the hills and entered the forge, and,
without a word, flung off my coat, and put on my
apron. My father and myself worked steadily on,
without exchanging a word, until just about dinner
time, when Donal Connor came in. He said: 'I heard
ye were near having a big row at the match yesterday,
Ted. Who won?'

"'We won,' I said, laconically, and went on with
my work.

"After a few minutes, my father said:—

"'What was the row about that Donal spakes of?'

"I said nothing, but went on working.

"After a few more seconds, he again asked:—

"'It must be a mighty sacret whin you can't answer
a civil question of your father.'

"I flung the sledge aside, and confronting him, I said, with very ill-concealed fury:—

"'Lave me ask you another question. What the divil possessed you to marry the daughter of an informer?'

CHAPTER XXIII

PARTED

"My father did not answer, although I saw his face draw down and whiten, and I expected a burst of fury; but a voice just behind me, which I knew to be that of Donal Connors, said with a hoarse savageness:

"'Because he was a better and a braver man than you, you contemptible cur!'

"I turned swiftly and saw, — and, oh, my God! the vision will never leave my brain, — neither Donal Connors, although he was within a yard of me, nor anything else in God's universe, but the pale face and the staring eyes of my mother. She had come out with Donal to call us in to dinner, and had heard my insulting question. She said nothing, only looked at me with speechless sorrow, and I could have gone down into hell with shame. And yet, standing there in all my self-loathing I could not forgive her for the shame she wrought on me; I could not forgive her for the blameless disgrace she had inherited. Mark you! If she had been a fallen woman morally, and had been raised by the consecration of marriage to a new and honourable life, I could easily have forgotten it. But here it was blood that was tainted, and I hated her, as well as myself.

"'Come in to the dinner,' she said, and turned back into the house.

"I went straight to my bedroom and commenced to pack up every little thing I possessed in this world. Even then, my good angel whispered to me: Go down, and clasp your mother's knees and beg her forgiveness, and get her kiss of peace. But the devil whispered: *Cloumper Daly's daughter! Cloumper Daly's daughter!* and I listened to him. I took up my wretched bundle and came to the door. I could see by a glance the two men sitting at dinner, the white table, the big pile of potatoes, the red salt meat, the cabbage, and the porringers. My mother stood at the door. She said quietly:—

"'Ted, where are you going? Aren't you comin' to your dinner?'

"I said nothing, but tried to pass her. My father cried out:—

"'Come in, Nodlag, an' let that fellow go to the divil, where he'll be welcome!'

"My mother stood aside and I passed out. About a hundred yards down the road I turned to get a last look at the old place. She was standing in the doorway again, and when she saw me, she stretched out her hands towards me. I turned away."

Here the poor fellow was simply choked with emotion and was silent for several minutes. He resumed, as soon as he could steady his voice:—

"They may say as much as they like about drink, and 'tis bad enough, God knows! And there are

other things worse! But far and away the worst devil
that can occupy the heart of man is pride! And yet,
see how things work. That last look at my mother,
and my own sin, were also my salvation. You know,
Father, that when you go abroad you hear lots of
queer things you never heard of in Ireland. Well,
many and many a time in miners' camps in Nevada,
in drinking saloons in California, in rough huts in
some cañon of the Rockies, I had to listen to many
and many a word against God and religion from men
who had no belief in either. And these things make
an impression. But the thought of my sin, and my
mother's patient face, banished the temptation, and I
prayed God to leave me my belief in Him and His
great world beyond the grave, if only that I might
have the chance of going down on my knees and begging
forgiveness for my one great sin. I never saw her
face again. I heard far away in the Rockies that she
died soon after my departure, and that she was buried
side by side with the old man who had been her lifelong
friend. There I made my first pilgrimage on my
return to Ireland. There I knelt and prayed as I had
never prayed before. And so terrible was the flood
of anguish that came down upon my soul that I tore
up the grass above her grave, and cried aloud in my
agony. You'd hardly believe it of a cool, calculating
Yankee. But there are hot springs in the human heart
that never leap to the surface till they are bored through
by sorrow and remorse.

"Well, that afternoon, as I turned my back upon my

own home forever, I felt without a friend in the world.
I knew from what had occurred the day before at the
hurling match, and from what had been revealed at
home, that my secret was the world's secret, and that
there was no question of my facing the acquaintances
of my youth and manhood again. I made up my
mind to change my name; then I saw that my father's
name was unsoiled, and I thought I would cling to it.
and go out to the New World, to make my fortune or
fail, like so many more of my countrymen.

"One face only I should see before I went, one hand
I should grasp, and then liberate forever, as I couldn't
offer her mine. I sent her word, and she came to me
at our old trysting place beneath the aged whitethorn.
It was one of those lovely spring or early summer
evenings, that haunt you forever, especially if associated
with some tragic or pathetic event in your life. She
saw at once, with a woman's swift insight, that something serious had occurred. My bundle of clothes and
heavy stick indicated this. But she said nothing. She
allowed me to speak. I said simply: —

"'I have come, Nora, to say good-bye! and forever!'

"Her eyes filled with tears. She said: —

"'You have heard something?'

"I answered yes. Then I said: —

"'It was not kind of you, Nora, never to tell me this
all these years.'

"She looked up and said: —

"'Unkind? I though I was doing enough when I

was prepared to take you, for good or ill, in the face of the world!'

"My brave girl!

"'Then,' I said, 'you always knew the horrible taint in my blood?'

"'I knew about your parents,' she replied. 'I knew nothing of yourself, except ——'

"'That with all you knew, and in spite of the opposition of your parents and friends, and in face of the world that would despise you, you were still prepared to take me?'

"'Yes,' she replied, modestly, but firmly.

"'Then, Nora,' I exclaimed, 'I should be the meanest man on the face of the earth, if I took advantage of your love and loyalty to bring you to shame and sorrow.'

"'That means you are giving me up, Terence Casey?' she said.

"'It does,' I replied. 'Don't ask me to repeat what you know already, that I think more of you than of any one else on the face of the earth, and if I were a free man, I should marry you, and no one else, though she was Queen of England. But how can I take advantage of you, and bring you to shame before the world?'

"'You are going away?' she said, simply.

"'Yes,' I answered.

"'Where are you going?' she asked.

"'To America,' I replied.

"'What can they know of you or me in America?'

she asked. 'Let us go abroad, as man and wife, in the face of the world. And who cares, or will care, about our history, in America?'

"She looked up at me as she spoke. It was the hardest temptation of my life. There was truth in what she said, but there was also the stinging truth that no one, least of all an Irishman, entirely cuts the cords that bind him to his motherland. And if there were no shame for her or me, there would be the reflected and keener disgrace on those she left behind. I made up my mind at once.

"''Twould never do, Nora,' I said. 'Your people would suppose that I acted shamefully towards them and you. They would never forgive me and they would never forgive you.'

"'I'm prepared to bear that, if you are prepared to bear the same,' she replied.

"'I don't mind my own shame,' I replied, 'but I mustn't ask you or your family to share it.'

"'There!' she replied. 'I mustn't be throwing meself at you any longer. Good-bye, Terence Casey!'

"'Good-bye, Nora! I leave you free, as there was a hand and word between us. But will you promise me one thing?'

"'What is it?'

"' I want you to go and see my mother some time and think of me when I am far away. Perhaps, but — there's no use of thinking of those things! See her sometimes, Nora, and tell her, will you tell her from me, Nora? Will you tell her ——?'

"'What?' she said.

"'I want you to tell her,' I said, sobbing, 'to tell her from me ——'

"There I stopped. I couldn't go further if I had an offer of half the world.

"'There, good-bye, and God bless you!'

"I turned away my head, took her hand in mine, and dropped it instantly and strode away. I had gone a few yards, when she cried after me: —

"'Ted!'

"I turned round and looked. The full sunset was on her face and hair, as she stood in her Sunday dress there beneath the blossoming thorn. She held her hands clasped and fallen down before her. I dared not look further, or I would have gone back and dared the world and the devil with her. I waved my hand in a parting farewell; it was the last I saw of the face that has been haunting me all these years, — the face of Nora Curtin."

"Thunder and turf!" I exclaimed, and it wasn't that I said either, but something more expressive; "what did you say, man?"

I had jumped from the chair and was confronting him.

"Nora Curtin!" he said, almost alarmed at my excitement.

"Of where?" I said, forgetting grammar and everything else.

"Of Glenanaar, or if you like, Ballinslea," he

replied. "Don't you remember how reluctant I was about your widow-nurse from Glenanaar?"

"But, my dear fellow, that *was* Nora Curtin, and she's not twenty yards in a bee line from you this moment."

"Then," he said, rising up, "I go straight to seek her."

"Oh, you won't," I cried, pushing him back into the chair. "Do you want to give the little woman a fit?"

He became quite excited.

"Father," he said, steadying his voice, "just listen to me for a minute."

I let him talk on whilst I was making up my mind what to do. I knew he had a certain vision before him, the vision beneath the whitethorn in the sunset, and all the et ceteras of youth and beauty. I knew also that time and sorrow had wrought changes, and that age with *its* et ceteras might not seem even to so faithful a soul so attractive as he had dreamed. Yet, it was a magnificent chance for that good little woman, in whom now I felt an increased interest, and for her two dear children whose future looked so difficult and uncertain. It was a chance not to be thrown away. There were, I knew, great probabilities of disappointment, but the fear of them faded as I listened to him.

He moistened his lips, and went on · —

"You see, Father, it is this way. I carried with me in my exile a vision of two women — one whom I loved and had wronged, the other, whom I loved, but could not sacrifice, even for my own welfare. These two haunted me for the quarter of a century I have spent abroad; and when I say haunted me, I mean that they were ever present to my mind, — always in my waking moments, and sometimes in my sleep. In the beginning, the excitement of looking for work and failing to obtain it sometimes blurred that vision. But then, when I began to reach some certain degree of success, they came back more vivid than ever. If I lay awake at night, as often I did, too tired even to sleep, I saw them on my right hand and on my left — my mother always in the old listening attitude, as if she were hearkening for some far-away voice, and I knew it was mine she desired to hear; and on my left, Nora, always as I saw her in her blue serge dress there beneath the thorn in the sunset. Then when I began to gather gold and the yellow dross soiled my hands and my dress, I said, I do not value it but for them. For them I shall hoard it, and keep it, and go back some day and — there I left the future and dare not lift the veil. Then one day it came to my knowledge that my mother was dead, and only one part of the vision remained, but it came more vividly just because it was now isolated and alone. And it saved me from rough men, from a vicious life, from the thousand and one temptations that beset a young man in a place where men's passions are let loose, and no law of man or fear of God can restrain them."

"The moment your mother was dead," I interrupted,

"you should have sent straight for Nora, and taken her out and married her."

"I would have done so," he replied, "but for one thing. You know, you can understand, how the horror of being known and pursued by the phantom of my shame did gradually disappear under the excitement of my new life; so much so, that I had almost forgotten it, and had begun to reason that Nora was right, and that I should have listened to her suggestion, when an appalling incident occurred that brought back the whole thing again, and made me fly farther from civilization than ever. It shows how small is the world, and how I must despair of ever getting rid of this horrid thing that will pursue me to my grave."

CHAPTER XXIV

THE PHANTOM AGAIN

"It happened in this way. Life is still pretty rough out West, but nothing like what it was when I went out there first, a raw, inexperienced fellow, used to hardship, but a stranger to violence. It's very different giving a fellow a shoulder, and sending him sprawling on the soft grass, and putting the cold iron to his forehead with your finger on the trigger. Yet that's what it all comes to out there where there was no law, no trial, no jury, no judge. You simply heard that you were looked for, and the next thing was to find a lasso round your neck, or the revolver at your head. I did not relish that kind of thing much nohow, so I kept away from these rough fellows as much as I could, and worked my own way in silence. But do what I could, I should knock up against them from time to time in a saloon, in the diggings, across the prairies, up amid the snows. They were rough fellows, each of whom had a pretty bad record in his past; but there was a singular code of honour between them. Your claim once opened was respected, until you sold it, or abandoned it. Your little heap was as safe as in the Bank of England. You had only to say: —

"'Bill, or Jake, there's three thousand there in dust and solid. Keep it for me till I return.'

"And you might not return for six months or a year, and it would be safe in his hands. He would give his life to defend it. The one that would break that code of honour answered with his life.

"Well, it happened one night up in Nevada, where the silver mines had been opened up, and rapid fortunes were being made, I found myself sitting round a camp fire with a lot of desperadoes. It was a cold night and we clustered close around an immense fire of blazing logs, before we sought the shelter of our huts. The bottle went round, and many of the fellows were noisy enough. But one great, burly fellow, who sat on my right, smoked leisurely, and only at rare intervals drank, and then moderately. Many of the fellows, half drunk, had got back to their rude bunks, and still we two smoked and smoked, and, strangely enough, in absolute silence. I was mute, because I knew my man. He was called Big Din, from which, and from the strange dialect he spoke, half brogue, half miner, I concluded that he was an Irishman, but well acclimatized. I knew him to be a desperado, ever anxious to pick a quarrel, which ever ended but in one way. At last, when nearly all had gone away, and the blazing logs were now smouldering into red embers and white wood ashes, I rose stiffly and said: —

"'I guess we had better cut this now!'

"He said, gruffly: —

"'Sit down, youngster. I wants to hev a chat with you.'

"'You wasted a deuced lot of time in making up

your mind,' I said, gaily. 'I guessed you wos a Quaker
or a statoo.'

"But I sat down.

"'You're from the ould dart, I guess?' he said at
length. 'So am I. Now what part might you have
kem from?'

"He had turned around, and putting his face close
to mine, so that I could smell his breath, he screwed
his eyes into mine, as if he would read my soul.

"In an instant, I realized the importance of the
question, and said: —

"'From the borders of the County Limerick. Now,
where do you hail from?'

"He flung the ashes from his pipe, and rose up.

"It don't make no matther, youngster. Tell me,
have you ever kem across in these here counthries a
fellow called Dailey, a hell's fire of a darned cuss!'

"Dailey! Dailey!' I repeated. 'No, I can't say I
have.'

"'If iver you meet him,' continued Big Din, 'tell
him there's some wan on his thrack, and the sooner he
gives hisself up to justice the betther!'

"'I will,' I said. 'But I guess that's not likely.
'Tis a big counthry out here.'

"'Tis smaller than you think,' he said. 'And the
whole wurruld is smaller than you think. That is,'
he added, meaningly, 'whin revenge is on your thrack.'

"'But,' he continued after a short pause, which I
thought would never end, 'ye niver hard of the Doneraile conspiracy in your part of the counthry?'

"'Never,' I answered, promptly. 'What was it about? It must have been a long time ago.'

"'It was, and it wasn't,' he said. 'Not long enough to be disremembered yet, specially whin it comes home to yerself. There's an ould sayin', an' a thrue wan: "what's bred in the blood is got in the bone." Eh?'

"'I heard it,' I said, as calmly as I could.

"'Wal, there it is as plain as a pike staff. Dailey, the —— cus, gev good men an' thrue into the hangman's hands over there in the ould dart thirty years agone, and Dailey gev my mate into the Sheriff's hands here in Sacramento. *Thiggin thu?* Good-night, youngster, an' be an hones' man ef you can!'

"The night was cold, but I was frozen and flushed alternately there in the snows of Nevada. It was fortunate for me that the fire had burned low, and threw but a few red and black shadows on our faces, for otherwise my agitation would have betrayed me. I got away as fast as I could, but spent that night, and many others, pondering on these strange sayings, and wondering how would they ultimately affect me. What puzzled me mostly was, who this Dailey was of whom Big Din spoke. It surely could not be my grandfather, unless he had lived to a very advanced age. And then, how did his secret history transpire? I saw at once that he had effectually concealed his name under the new pronunciation[1] more effectually than if he had changed it altogether, because even I, when I heard the name Dailey, never connected it

---

[1] Daly is generally pronounced Dawley in Ireland

with the family. But the whole affair made me feel nervous about myself and my future. I determined to leave there at once, and strike north, further away from civilization, but further away also from a great and possible danger. I went to the north of the Great Salt Lake City, passed through Idaho, got through a pass in the mountains right under Fremont Peak, and at last settled down, and bought a ranch near Shoshone Lake, in the extreme north of the State of Wyoming. That is my home now, and there I will take Nora, if she will have me. Say, Father, when may I see her? My time is up here, and I must be going back. I had one hope coming here, and that is now near being realized; and one fear, but that is vanishing."

"You know, my dear fellow," I said, "I would take you to her this moment, but it means a shock. Give me a day or so to prepare her."

"Wal, then, Father," he said, "let us say Sunday night."

"Be it so," I replied. "But you said you had one fear. What fear?"

"The fear that this dreadful thing would follow me here. Or rather, that it would crop up here, where it can never have entirely died away."

"Your alarm is quite unfounded, my dear fellow," I said, and I fully believed it. "The Doneraile Conspiracy is as forgotten here as the famine. We're living now under new conditions of life. What would be the talk of the country firesides for months and years, when you were a boy, is now forgotten in a week.

You should get that dread off your nerves as soon as possible."

"I've tried," he said, "but I can't say I have succeeded.   When you once get a bad shock — but I did not finish my story."

"No," I said. "I left you comfortably settled at Shoshone Lake, wherever it is, on your ranch, and amidst your fishing and your cattle."

"Wal," he said, "there's not much more. I lived there some years, working hard, but very happy. I was well off, and many an offer of marriage was made me, that would have doubled my means. But no! That was not to be. I had a great deal of time on hands; there the winters are long and terrible, and I had to while away the loneliness by reading. You know I had but little education at home. Wal, there I had to read. I bought every book I could find, and read the whole winter through. Then, from time to time, a French Canadian trapper would cross the border, or a German settler would come along prospecting, and I picked up a smattering of their languages from them. So that I have altogether read a good deal, though I cannot call myself an educated man. Wal, one summer I left my little diggings and went up to Buttes. It is now a big city, and promises to be a capital yet. Then, it was but a rising town, and had an evil reputation for the classes that congregated there. Probably I would have avoided it; but I wanted a few winter necessaries, and especially books. I was very careful to avoid saloons, and the

public halls; but fate would have it, that I struck across
an old chum, and, as usual, we had a drink together.
As we entered the back parlour of the saloon, a young
man, not more than twenty-five or twenty-six years of
age, rose up, and, after glancing stealthily at us, passed
out. He had been smoking and reading a newspaper,
which he flung aside the moment he saw us.

"'On the run, I guess,' said my old mate, and we
thought no more of it. Late in the evening, and just
as the full moon was coming up the valley and making
its way slowly through the gorges, I had my team
tackled and ready to start. I was passing the saloon
at a trot, when again this old chum of mine, now
much the worse for liquor, again accosted me. He
was surrounded by a number of men grouped here
and there at the door of the saloon. I was very angry
for the delay and the danger, but I had no alternative
but to dismount, hitch my wagon to the rail outside
the saloon, and go in. I was not long detained. One
of these awful tragedies that happen swift and sudden
as a tornado in these lawless places liberated me.
We had gone into the inner parlour of the saloon.
Four men were playing poker with a grimy pack of
cards. I recognized two — Big Din, now gray and
grizzled, but apparently as dangerous as ever. Sitting
quite close to him was the young man who had left
the saloon as we entered that morning. I could see
he was ill at ease. His hands shook as he dealt out
the cards. I concluded it was drink. It was deadly
fear. Several dangerous-looking fellows lounged about,

and occasionally looked at the players. Suddenly, I heard a voice saying in a quiet, passionless tone: —

"'You're chating, mate!'

"There was an oath from the young man and a nervous declaration of innocence.

"'See here, you Pete, and you Abe, just watch this youngster, and see if I'm right.'

"It was the closing in of the wolves around the doomed man, and I hastened to go.

"'Stop!' cried my friend. 'There's goin' to be some fun, I reckon. You may never see this 'ere circus again!'

"The play went on silently. Then again Big Din said: —

"'Now, was I right, mates? You seen the darned cuss yersels.'

"In an instant there was the crack of a revolver, and Big Din's hand hung helpless at his side. The young man had arisen, the smoking weapon in his hand. He saw that he was doomed, and determined to anticipate. His hand was seized in a moment and one of the roughs said: —

"'Allow me, youngster; 'tis too dangerous a toy for a child.'

"He took the revolver from him and drew all the charges, save one.

"'Five paces,' said Big Din, whilst they were binding his wounded arm, 'and his face to the lamp.'

"In a second the two men were face to face. I crouched low, fearing the miscarriage of a bullet.

"'Stand up,' said a voice; 'there is no danger here. Big Din never missed his game yet.'

"The word was given. The two reports rang out simultaneously. I heard the crash of glass behind Big Din's head and knew he was safe. When the smoke cleared, the young man was at my feet, and I saw the tiny stream trickling from his forehead. Big Din came over and turned over with his foot his dead antagonist.

"'I knew we'd meet,' he said. 'Lie there, you sneak-thief; you —— son of an informer!'

"I gathered my wits together, and with the dreadful words pursuing me, like demons, I loosed my team, and sped fast into the night.

"For days and days the dreadful words haunted me. They seemed an echo of what I had heard that evening in the field at Kildorrery, and I could not help asking myself would they pursue me all my life long, and even to my grave. I knew they had an intimate connection with myself; for putting all Big Din's questions together, it was quite clear that these Daileys were my own people, and that probably my mother's father had married again, and that that young lad was my uncle It seemed too terrible, and yet stranger things have happened. For the world is small and one never knows whom you may knock up against in the vicissitudes of life.

"However, time and occupation more or less dimmed my recollection of these things, but the old horror came back when I finally determined to visit this old land again. I argued if such things can be carried across the ocean, and confront you away from civilization, surely the same, or worse, may occur on the very spot where these things happened. However, Father, you have reassured me somewhat. It only now remains to see Nora, learn my fate, and leave Ireland forever."

I little dreamed that the old phantom would crop up, and in the most unexpected place. But it was soon exorcised and forever.

CHAPTER XXV

AFTER MANY YEARS

THE next few days I was at my wits' ends to discover some way of breaking the eventful news to Mrs. Leonard, and securing her consent to a proposal that would lift her and her children out of poverty forever. And I had also to suggest some little changes that would make the ravages of time and trouble less visible to the eyes of him who had kept his dream so faithfully all these years. This was no easy task, for if always extremely clean and neat, Nora Leonard had bidden farewell to all human vanities forevermore. I threw out a few little hints that she might have unexpected visitors, that her cousin, Father Curtin, might call, and that really she should tidy up things, etc. I saw my words fall on unheeding ears, and I simply determined to let matters take their course. I told the "Yank" this, and that he should be his own cicerone on the important occasion. He told me all afterwards.

He had dressed himself with unusual care that Sunday evening, and when the night fell he went forth to reconnoitre. He had no difficulty about finding the wretched shop. It was unmistakable. The empty package papers in the windows, the dim, par-

260

affin lamp swinging from the low ceiling, the strings of onions and red herrings, the tea-chests, alas! without tea, — all indicated the wretchedness and poverty of the place. As he sauntered up and down in apparent carelessness and listlessness, although his heart was beating wildly, and he had never been so nervous in his life, he caught a glimpse through the window-packages of a great, glowing mass of auburn hair. He couldn't see the face, but his heart stood still. It was the same he had seen twenty years back beneath the hawthorn tree, with the setting sun glinting upon it. That settled matters. He gulped down something, pulled nervously at the cigar between his teeth, and stepped into the dingy shop. A tall, girlish figure arose and confronted him. Carried away by the extraordinary likeness to the young girl he had parted from so many years ago, he could not help exclaiming: —

"Nora!"

Then in an instant reason came to his aid, and he coughed, and said: —

"Can you let me have some cigarettes?"

The girl flushed crimson, and then turned pale, as she stared at this unexpected customer. She went over to a little glass door and tapped. The door opened gently as the girl said: —

"Mother, a gentleman wants some cigarettes. Have we any?"

And Nora Leonard, the girl who had bade him good-bye so many years ago beneath the hawthorn, and in the light of the setting sun, now came forward wearily into the dingy, dusky shop, beneath the blurred and smoking lamp. His heart gave a great sob, as he saw at once the terrible change; but he said he would go through it to the end. "And if she is changed so much to me," he thought, "I must be equally changed to her. She can never recognize me."

"I'm afraid, sir," she said, looking vacantly around the wretched shop, "that we cannot oblige you. What we have are worthless. If you would call up at ——'s, or at the hotel, you could get what you require."

"Wal," he said, "I guess I ain't particular. There just behind you is a package of 'Egyptians.'"

She turned to look. He saw how the crease in her hair had widened, and how gray was the knot she had looped up and tied behind. She put the package on the counter, and said: —

"I fear they're mouldy and must be thrown away."

"Wal, never mind, never mind," he said. "How much shall I pay?"

Something in his attitude or manner struck the mind of the poor woman, for she got nervous and trembled. But she said: —

"Would you consider sixpence too much?"

The wretched price she asked, denoting extreme poverty, and her attitude of beseeching humiliation, touched the strong man deeply. He placed a half-crown on the counter, and she said: —

"I fear we haven't got the change, sir. Take it back, and you can pay when you call again."

She pushed back the coin towards him. He took it and at the same time grasped her hand firmly, and said: —

"Nora!"

The colour left her cheeks instantly, and her eyes opened in affright, as she said, without disengaging her hand: —

"Who? What is it?" and then, as the recognition flashed suddenly upon her: —

"Ted!"

"Yes!" he said. "I'm glad you know me. I thought I should be too much changed."

For some seconds these two, so long parted, stared at one another in silence, the strong man's hand resting softly upon hers. The quick recognition gratified him exceedingly, as he looked and looked, and tried to reconcile the changed figure and features with what he had known. At last she said: —

"It is just as if you came back from the grave!"

"I'm glad you had not entirely forgotten me," he said.

"How could I?" she replied, almost unconsciously. Then the possible meaning of her words flashed back upon her and she blushed. In the sudden transformation he thought he saw the Nora of his dreams again. But this vanished and it was only a broken, almost aged widow that confronted him.

"And this is your daughter, I suppose?" he said, disengaging his hand and stretching it out to Tessie. "She is so extremely like what you — like you, I mean," he stammered, "I actually called her 'Nora' when I came in."

"An' how long have you been home?" Nora inquired.

"A couple of months," he replied.

"An' you never called before?" she said, reproachfully.

"I was laid up at the hotel," he said. "I received a hurt."

"Then," she said, as a new light dawned upon her, "you're the 'Yank' all the town was talking about?"

"I suppose so," he said, smiling. "I was never made so much of before, I think."

"And it was you, I suppose, the parish priest wanted me to go and nurse?"

"I believe so," he said. "I'm sorry you didn't accept his Reverence's offer. You'd have spared me some suffering."

"Then," she replied, as the light of great solicitude dawned in her eyes, "you were bad?"

"Wal," he replied, "I wasn't exactly bad. But you can guess how lonely and miserable a fellow would feel in a strange place and not a human being to exchange a word with for weeks."

She felt a curious kind of remorse as if she were to blame for all that dreary time he had spent, and her face showed it.

"If you had known it was I," he said, noticing her look, "you'd have come? Say you would."

She shook her head.

"No, Ted," she replied. "I would not, though I

am sorry for you, and all you went through. Let bygones be bygones!"

"You're changed, Nora," he said, sadly. "And I suppose so am I. But I wanted to ask you a few questions about them that are gone."

"Won't you come into the parlour?" she said, he thought, reluctantly. "There's no one here but Kathleen. The place is very small and narrow," she added, apologetically.

It was — very small and narrow and ill-furnished. A few shaky, old chairs, the cretonne covering them faded and soiled, a dark cupboard in one corner, a few prints on the mantelpiece flanked by some paper flowers, and the table at which Kathleen sat — that was all. A wretched hand-lamp, smoky and bleared, such as would hang from a stable wall, gave poor light, and must have strained the sight of the girl, whose long hair swept the pages of the book she was reading. He thought of his own comfortable cottage by the lake and beneath the Sierras, of the rich furniture brought all the way from New York, of the veranda, hidden under wild, luxuriant creepers, of the easy chairs and lounges, the books and pictures; and once again his heart gave a great sob. Kathleen looked up from her book, Joyce's "Child History of Ireland," and stood up to go as the stranger entered. She gave him a long, deep, searching look, and held out her hand in a cold, curt greeting. Her mother said:—

"You needn't go, Kathleen. This is an old friend."

The girl sat down, and without taking further heed bent her head over her book again.

He took the proffered chair and said:—

"Would you mind my smoking, Nora?"

He didn't care about smoking just then, but his nerves were trembling and he was making great mental attempts to control himself.

"No!" she said, simply.

He smoked in silence for a few seconds. There was no sound in the room. Kathleen was bent down over her book, yet somehow he felt her keen, gray eyes searching him again and again. At last, with some hesitation, he said:—

"I heard that mother died soon after I left for America?"

"Not very soon," said Nora, rising to kindle the wretched fire, which served for cooking, heating, and every other domestic purpose. "I think you were gone about six months when she sickened. Then she lingered on and on for twelve months more. And then she died."

"What was her ailment?" he asked.

"Some said one thing, and some said another," replied Nora. "The doctors said it was a decline, but she herself always said it was a broken heart."

It was the blunt truth, but then Nora always was blunt and he liked her not the less for it.

"You kept your promise, Nora," he said. "I know you did."

"What promise?" she asked.

"That you would go see her often, and that you would tell her all that I told you."

He spoke as of events that occurred yesterday. Twenty-five years had rolled back and left no trace to obliterate the anguish and passion of that time.

"Yes!" she replied, simply. "There was hardly a day some of us didn't go to see her. Donal Connors was a great friend in the time of trouble."

"He was a good man. Is he alive still?"

"He is, indeed, and as strong as ever. He has a houseful of children about him now."

"But the other part of your promise! Did you give my mother my message?"

"I did," she said, simply. "But one deed is worth more than many declarations," she added.

Again it was the bitter truth she was speaking. He felt it deeply. He knew that the deadly blow he had given his mother was not to be healed by empty protestations of sorrow.

"Looking back upon it all now," he said, in self-defence, "I do not think I could have done anything else. I think I was right in getting away. I could never undo the injury. I could never get back that one word."

"I'm sorry to hear you say so," said Nora. "It wasn't the word you said that killed your mother, but your backing up that word by abandoning her forever."

"But how could I go back and face her and father again?" he argued. "I faced the world, the sea, the mountains, the prairies, wild beasts, wilder men, rather than look upon her sad eyes reproaching me."

He had flung his cigar into the grate, and rubbed his hands across his eyes. These he kept shaded now. Kathleen had closed her book, and was watching him intently.

After some moments he stood up to go. Nora said: —

"Are you going back soon?"

"Yes!" he replied, blinking at the bleared lamp. "What should I do in this unhappy country?"

"I hope things have gone well with you over the water?" she said.

"Yes," he replied, "everything has prospered with me. So far as worldly goods are concerned, I have no reason to be dissatisfied.

This implied some exception to his general happiness which his listeners were not slow to perceive.

"Yet one cannot help feeling an exile and a hankering after old ties!" Nora said.

"True! But it wears away. Especially," he added, "after you have once come back and seen all your dreams flung to the winds."

Nora flushed up and stooped down to the fire to conceal her confusion, although the Yank had not a thought of what was in her mind.

"You dream over there," he continued, "of the blue mountains, the silver river, the white thorn in the May-time, the dance, the hurling-match, the boys and girls you knew. You feel that you must see it all again, or die. You come back. All is desolation and loneliness and ruin. The mountains are there, and the rivers, and the blossoms, and the wild flowers, and the leaves; but it is a land of the past — no present, no future! Do you know that I walked four miles to Templeruadhan on last Thursday, and never saw a human being — not a living thing but a couple of donkeys and a goat!"

"And who's to blame for that?" said Kathleen, with flashing eyes, now for the first time breaking silence. "I'll tell you. 'Tis you, Irish-Americans, who fly from your country, and then try to make everyone else fly also."

"Thank God!" he said, smiling sarcastically. "I feared you were dumb!"

"No, nor deaf, nor blind," she said, angrily. "'Tis ye, the recruiting-sergeants of England, that are sweeping the people away with your letters: 'Come! Come! For God's sake, leave your cabins, and come out to wealth and comfort.' And ye are patriots!"

She spoke with intense sarcasm, her gray eyes glowing with passion.

"I'm almost tempted to say, in your own words," he replied, smiling, "Come! Come!"

"No!" she said, stamping her little foot. "If you were to give me all the gold in California, and all the silver in the Rockies, I wouldn't leave my own country."

"There, Ted, don't mind her," said her mother. "She has picked up all this nonsense from Thade

Murphy. I suppose you'll come to see us before you go?"

He lingered behind. The momentous question that had been on his lips for twenty-five years remained unsaid. He could not say how he was defeated. Everything was against him. He said good-night, lingered for a few moments, talking to Tessie in the wretched shop, and went back to his hotel to fight with his conscience and sense of honour.

"What more can I do?" he reasoned. "I have had the best intentions and see how they are frustrated. Evidently, Nora regards such a thing as out of the question. And yet ——"

The truth was, the old figure and face had glimmered away into that dream of the past of which he had spoken. He had seen, and been undeceived. Time, which he thought had stood still, had been marching ever onward and leaving his footprints everywhere.

"I'll bluntly put the question some day this week," he said. "And then ——"

He stood undecided. He was afraid to say what he thought. A new dream had come into his life, and the old dream was fading as a second rainbow melts beneath the brightness of the first. He was ashamed to admit it. Nevertheless, he sat down and wrote the agent of the line he travelled by to give him a month's grace.

CHAPTER XXVI

AN ANCIENT REBEL

"WELL," I said to him a few days later, "all's well? And you're 'off to Philadelphy in the mornin''?"

"No," he said, but not too sadly, I thought. "All went wrong, and I blame a young spitfire for it. If that's the class of young girls that are being reared in Ireland now, you'll have another Rising before twenty years."

"Kathleen?" I asked.

"Yes!" he said. "She hadn't the good manners to leave the room, and it struck me that Nora didn't wish it either."

"But you'd have said all you wanted to say," I suggested, "if Kathleen had not been there?"

"Ye-e-es!" he said, I thought, dubiously. "I'd have ended the matter then and there forever."

"Then you saw no great change?" I asked.

"Ah, there is, Father," he replied, candidly. "I could never believe that time could work such havoc."

"And still you are determined?"

"Yes!" he said. "But I think 'tis useless. I saw that Nora was as nervous as myself, and I think she was relieved when I left. But, now, if Tessie had been there instead of that young rebel — by the way

271

where lid she pick up these revolutionary ideas? Do they teach these things in the convents now?"

Then he mentioned all the details of his visit.

I was not much surprised at these developments of my young friend, Kathleen. With all kinds of tendencies to tomboyism, she showed occasionally indication of a character self-willed and stubborn, yet generous and enthusiastic. She was the plague and the darling of her own class. She got more premiums and stripes than any other girl. But she never got a prize for what is called "ladylike deportment." It was difficult to get an act of contrition from her for her misdemeanours, but it was very genuine when it came. Many a time I had to lift her, when an infant, in my arms off the stool of repentance, where she had been placed, face to the wall, and shamefully covered with her pinafore. Her little frame would be rigid as iron under the stress of strong passion, and then would melt away into limpness when the soft spot in her heart was touched. It was clear that this young, strong character would take its decided bias from circumstances; and the circumstance was near at hand that made her a bigoted little rebel, and in her own imagination, and that of her teacher, an Irish Joan of Arc.

Just across the street was another huxter's shop, with somewhat greater pretensions than Mrs. Leonard's, because there pigs' heads were sold, and I know Mrs. Leonard never ventured beyond red herrings. It was owned by a Mrs. Murphy, a good, kindly,

grauver Irish matron, who was proprietress and facto-
tum in the establishment. Her husband, Thade
Murphy, was blind, and never ventured abroad but
to Mass on Sundays. In the long summer evenings
he would come out and sit and smoke on the stone
bench outside the shop window, and roll his poor
sightless eyes around, and welcome every one who
stopped for a little *seanchus*. But during the long
winter evenings he never appeared, but smoked by
the kitchen fire, and dreamed of the past. It was
eventful enough. He, too, had been a '67 man; and,
if all the young fellows who went out that bitter night
in March, thirty-five years ago, were not pronounced
rebels, not one man came back from the short-lived
revolution who was not the sworn foe of foreign domi-
nation in Ireland. For a few years Thade Murphy
pursued his usual avocation of carrier between the
village and the railway; then the ophthalmia contracted
on the mountain snows became aggravated by constant
exposure to the weather, until it terminated finally in
total blindness. I often urged him to go to Cork and
put himself under surgical treatment. No! It was
the will of God, and there was no gainsaying it. He
tried all local remedies — hypothetical and infallible,
but they failed him. Even the "fasting-spit," three
times each morning, did not succeed. And then with
the resignation, the fatalism of the race, he gave up
remedies and calmly accepted his fate.

Kathleen Leonard, like all children, was in and out
of the shop at all times. When she was in the sixth

standard, and able to read fluently, she would often spend half an hour with the blind man in the kitchen, reciting scraps of poetry, or reading little passages from her school-books to while away the lonely hours for the poor, stricken fellow. By degrees, she ascertained his predilections in reading, and adapted herself to them. And so A. M. Sullivan's "Story of Ireland," "The Penny Readings from the 'Nation,'" etc., became favourite books, until at last the pupil went beyond her master, and caught the sacred fire to create a conflagration. No wonder! A calm Englishman said once to the present writer, speaking of England's treatment of Ireland: "'Twas appalling!" A very conservative Irishman declared: "It turns my blood into molten fire." It was no great surprise, then, that a young, ardent, impetuous nature, like Kathleen's, should have flamed into rebellious sentiments which, though we smiled them down, were very real and pronounced. It was only by degrees the truth dawned upon us; and, strange enough, it was sufficiently singular to cause some comment.

"I don't know where she got it, I'm sure," said her mother. "'Twasn't from me, I have had something else to think about; and surely 'twasn't from her father. It must be that old Thade Murphy has turned her head!"

"The children now don't trouble much about Ireland and her nationhood and her welfare," I remarked. "Whilst the 'American fever' is on them they care little for the motherland. It is some consolation at least that one child has righteous sentiments towards her country."

"You always stand up for her, through thick and thin," said Mrs. Leonard. "You and Thade are her sponsors. The only thing where he differs from your Reverence is, that you'll make a nun of her, and he says she'll be married to some fellow who has been in jail three or four times, and she'll be the mother of another Robert Emmet."

"Not a bad thing, either," I said. "She'll be the happy woman, if that's the choice that's left her."

Soon, however, Kathleen's fervour became a troublesome element in our little, quiet, village lives. She became openly insubordinate in school. Part of the programme for inspection was the recitation of certain poetical extracts in the school-books. And these had not only to be carefully committed to memory, but delivered with right intonation and emphasis. It happened that Macaulay's "Horatius" was one of the pieces selected, and in this the sixth standard was drilled and drilled every day. On the very eve almost of the inspection, the class was marshalled as usual, and the monitress, full of zeal, was demanding a full and scientific rendering of the noble lines. Each child had a stanza to herself, and when it came to Kathleen's turn, the monitress said: —

"Go on, Katty Leonard!"

Kathleen hesitated.

"Go on, miss! 'Then out spake brave Horatius.'"

Kathleen's hands hung rigid by her side, her little

fists clenched tightly, as, to the utter consternation of the monitress, she said in a firm, passionate tone: —

After Aughrim's great disaster —

"No, no, no," cried the monitress. "What ails you, child? 'Then out spake brave Horatius, the Captain of the gate.'"

Then the storm burst. With blazing eyes, the girl went on, without stopping, whilst the monitress sat paralyzed: —

> After Aughrim's great disaster,
> When our foe, in sooth, was master,
> It was you that first plunged in and swam
>   The Shannon's boiling flood;
> And through Slieve Bloom's dark passes,
> You led our Gallowglasses,
> Altho' the hungry Saxon wolves
>   Were howling for our blood.
> And as we crossed Tipperary,
> We rieved the clan O'Leary,
> And drove a *creacht* before us,
>   As our horsemen southward came.
> With our spears and swords we gored them,
> As through flood and flight we bore them,
> Still, Shaun O'Dwyer *achorra*,
>   We're worsted in the game.

There was consternation in the class. Some of the girls tittered, some turned pale at the awful audacity. The monitress bit her lips and said: —

"Go on, Miss Leonard, go on. Perhaps there is more of this kind."

There was dead silence now in the school. Those who were reading stopped suddenly, pencils ceased to rattle on slates, and pens were held suspended over the ink-wells. The sudden notoriety and the monitress's sarcasm touched the girl's pride, and she continued with ever-growing emphasis: —

> Long, long we kept the hillside,
> Our couch hard by the rill-side;
> The sturdy knotted oaken boughs
>   Our curtains overhead;
> The summer's blaze we laughed at,
> The winter's snow we scoffed at,
> And trusted to our long steel swords
>   To win us daily bread;
> Till the Dutchman's troops came round us,
> In fire and steel they bound us;
> They blazed the woods and mountains
>   Till the very clouds were flame;
> Yet our sharpened swords cut through them,
> In their very heart we hewed them —
> Oh! Shaun O'Dwyer *achorra*,
>   We're worsted in the game.

"Perhaps you are not quite finished yet, Miss Leonard," said the monitress. "Go on. You had better end, as you've begun."

Nothing loth, Kathleen continued: —

> Here's a health to your and my King,
> The Sovereign of our liking;
> And to Sarsfield, underneath whose flag
>   We cast once more a chance;
> For the morning's dawn will wing us
> Across the seas, and bring us
> To take our stand, and wield a brand
>   Among the sons of France.
> And though we part in sorrow,
> Still, Shaun O'Dwyer *achorra*,

> Our prayer is: ' God save Ireland!
>   And pour blessings on her name!'
> May her sons be true when needed —
> May they never feel as we did.
> For, Shaun O'Dwyer *aglanna*,
>   We're worsted in the game.

The monitress was crying with vexation when the mistress of the school came to inquire what it was all about. Kathleen was pale with excitement, but defiant, as the matter was solemnly reported.

It was a bad breach of discipline, and could not be overlooked. And my services were requisitioned. Now, although of fairly equable temperament in ordinary life, Rhadamanthus on his sooty throne could not hold a candle to me where law and order are concerned. The following day I called over the delinquent to the seat of judgment. She came, alarmed, but defiant.

"This is a nice condition of things, young lady," I said. "Let me see! Insubordination, disobedience, contumacy, contempt, rebellion, and revolution, — all in one act!"

"I couldn't help it," she said, her lower lip trembling.

"You couldn't help it," I repeated, sarcastically. "Then you didn't know your poetry?"

"I did, but ——" as a great big tear gathered and fell.

"But what?" I exclaimed, not a bit softened.

"But (*sob*) — I thought (*sob*) that (*sob*) we shouldn't (*sob*) be praising (*sob*) these old Romans (*sob*) for what (*sob*) our own countrymen (*sob*) did as well (*sob*)."

"That's all right," I said, unrelenting. "But do you think it right for a little girl, I beg your pardon, a young lady, like you, to take the law into your own hands?"

There was no answer to this but a good deal of weeping behind a pinafore.

"Now do you know what will become of you, if you go on in this way?"

"I (*sob*) don't!"

"Well, let me first tell you the consequences to others. If that unruly recitation of rebel poetry was reported to Dublin, one or two Commissioners would get sudden and awful deaths. And if it reached the Treasury in London, do you know what would happen?"

"I do-don't."

"Well, I'll tell you. They'd send the Channel Fleet to Queenstown, and perhaps they might go so far as to call up the North Cork Militia."

She looked at me dubiously.

"That would mean," I continued, relentlessly, "placing two or three millions more of taxation on the broken backs of Irishmen, and all because a little girl won't have the sense to keep her patriotism within bounds."

"But, sure you often said yourself ——"

"Never mind what I said. But, now coming back to yourself, do you know what will happen to you? Well, you'll be transported to Botany Bay, or Pentonville, or Mountjoy; you'll have to sleep on a plank bed — do you know what a plank bed is?"

"I heard (*sob*) of it, but I never saw (*sob*) it."

"Well, don't fret! You will, and the experience won't be pleasant. A plank bed is a medium between a feather tick and a flagged floor. And you'll have to eat skilly out of a rusty iron spoon, and dress these luxuriant tresses of yours, if they're not cut off, with a dirty comb, with no teeth in it, and which has been used by every virago and drunkard for the last twenty years."

She gave a little shudder here.

"And you'll have to wear a thick, bulky dress of frieze, with the Queen's arrow marked all over it, and white worsted socks and boots that never saw the colour of blacking. But it will be all right. I'll go to see you sometimes, and I'll recite for you through the keyhole of your dark cell: —

> Ah, Kathaleen *achorra*,
> Sure, you're worsted in the game."

This sarcasm made her mad, so she dried her tears defiantly. I had then to speak to the school and explain the nature of her penance.

"I've told this young lady already the nature of her offence, which is a gross breach of school discipline. She may be right or she may be wrong in preferring 'Shaun O'Dwyer a Glanna' to 'Horatius.' That's a matter of taste. But no child has a right to take the law into her own hands. That would mean a subversion of all discipline. You have a right to constitutional agitation for the redress of wrongs or the assertion of rights. But whilst the regulations are there in black and white, they must be respected. Now there is an amiable custom in the great public schools of England to compel misdemeanants both to contrition and reformation of character. That is, boys are punished for mistakes in their class-lessons by being compelled to write out fifty or a hundred lines of Virgil or Homer. They are thus taught that it is easier to say one line well than to write fifty. And so, Miss Kathleen Leonard will bring me to-morrow, written out in her own well-known Civil Service style, and the Civil Service is that of England, whose caligraphy she is so proud in copying, the whole and entire of that famous Lay by Lord Macaulay, called 'Horatius.'"

There was a great sigh, I don't know whether it was relief or consternation, when the dread sentence was passed and the business of the school resumed.

Next day, just at twelve o'clock, I called up the delinquent. She came forward, shamefacedly, with bent head, and handed me her copy-book, wrapped in brown paper, and tied with red tape.

"All right!" I said. "I'll take it home and study it at my leisure. But mind you, if there is one line missing, or one word misspelt, you'll have to write it all over again."

I took it home and forgot all about it till after tea-time. Then I took it up, having first placed the "Lays of Ancient Rome" open on my desk. What I saw was this, written in the firm, upright hand I knew so well: —

ONE WILD HURRAH!

(*A Lay of Modern Ireland.*)

I

I'm growing old, my hair is white,
　　My pulse is dull;
I know no more the fierce delight
　　Of life, when full.

II

The frail bark of my life sweeps on
　　To that dark sea,
Whence murmurs the dread monotone —
　　Eternity.

III

And nothing stirs the withered leaf,
　　Wrinkled and sere.
I smile not; and the keenest grief
　　Declines a tear.

IV

I'm dead; but for this fluttering breath
　　My marble smiles
Down the long lines of conquering Death
　　In twilight aisles.

V

And yet, dear God! if still the day
　　Would dawn for me,
When I could catch the first, faint ray
　　Of Liberty;

VI

If 'thwart mine eyes the light did flash
　　From Freedom's flags,
Borne in the wild tempestuous dash
　　That downward drags

VII

That banner, black with blood — the thirst
 Of alien hosts;
If once mine ear could hear the burst
 That drowns their boasts,

VIII

And I could list the thrilling tramp
 Of marshalled men,
Borne from serried camp to camp
 In dell and glen;

IX

And if the emblazoned bannerets
 Of Freedom shone
Above the snowy minarets
 Of Slieve-na-mon, —

X

I'd gaze into my gaping tomb
 Without a sigh;
I'd bless amid the gathering gloom
 My God on high.

XI

Then, catch one gasp of fading breath
 From Time's grim claw;
And speed along the gulf of Death
 One wild Hurrah!

I rubbed my eyes. Then my spectacles. There was no mistake. I turned over every other page of the copy-book. They were blank. It was a spick-span new copy-book. There was no other mark, but a pen-and-ink sketch of a round tower, a wolf-dog, and Erin, represented by a young lady, probably Kathleen herself, with great flashing eyes, helmeted head, hair

coiled up in a Grecian knot, a flashing sword in her
right hand, and the broken links of a chain at her
feet. In a corner were the words: —

KATHLEEN LEONARD, for
THADE MURPHY, REBEL and PATRIOT.

"What did you do?" Well, never mind. You
may be sure I did the right thing. I always do. I
only introduce the circumstance here to show how
Kathleen became chief actor in the *dénouement* which
was now rapidly approaching. And it dawned on my
slow imagination at the same time, that this was no
longer a child, but a woman. The mighty emotion
that had been stirred within her soul had transformed
her suddenly, and though I still treated her as a school-
girl, I felt that she was altogether a different being
from the little hoyden who used to sing to vex her
mother:

> I won't be a nun,
> And I shan't be a nun,
> And my parents often told me
> That I won't be a nun;
> There's an officer on guard,
> And 'tis with him I will run
> And my heart is full of pleasure
> And I won't be a nun!

CHAPTER XXVII

A FEW evenings later the Yank got his opportunity, and seized upon it. He had called every night, but something always occurred to put aside his final declaration, and its result. Sometimes there was a strange visitor, whom the Yank regarded, of course, as an intruder. Sometimes Nora was at the church and would not return till rather late, and he had to while away the time by talking to Tessie in the shop and telling her of the strange land beyond the seas. She was an attentive listener and was eager for all manner of information about America, its citizens, its nationalities, races, institutions. Somehow the time used to pass quickly, and when Nora would return at half-past nine or ten o'clock he would tear out his great gold repeater with surprise and declare that he never suspected it could be so late.

But this evening Nora was at home, the girls were at a small party given in the neighbourhood, and the Yank felt his time had come.

"I suppose, Ted," she said, as they sat in the miserable, stuffy parlour together, "you'll be going back soon?"

"I suppose so," he said, laconically.

"And you'll be going alone. You're not taking with you what everyone said you came for?"

"What was that?" he cried, suddenly interested. "The people know my business better than I know it myself."

"Perhaps," said Nora, smiling, "you have a wife in America already, and you could not take back a second?"

"I might have had," he said, in a tone of sadness, "over and over again, but for one thing."

"And what was that?" she asked. "Surely, you haven't been such a fool as to let the old fancy and fear pursue you across the water?"

"It did," he cried, "and I haven't got rid of it yet. I have brought it with me. But it wasn't that!"

They were both silent, looking at the fire. At last he said: —

"Nora, do you remember that evening twenty-five years ago, when we parted, under the hawthorn?"

"I do, well," she said, without the least emotion.

"You offered yourself to me," he continued, "in spite of my folly. You offered to brave the world with me and to break with parents and kith and kin forever, to follow me, an exile, and under a horrid ban of ignominy and shame."

She continued looking steadily at the fire as if calling up the past.

"Well," he said, "I was fool enough to reject your love and — your protection, for such it would have been — then. If I make the offer now, will you reject me?"

He felt as if the fate of his life were hanging in the balance. Did he wish for a Yes, or a No? He could not tell. There were two pictures forever gliding before him, one forever obliterating the other, blending, fading, restored again, and ever again to be blotted out. Which should it be? Here, on the one hand, was an old love revived, the sense of honour, the memories of a quarter of a century, in which the picture of that faded woman before him rose sainted and beautiful to his fancy; there was the great pity for her present wretchedness, and the poverty of her children; there was the dream of what might yet be under new skies and changed environments. And on the other hand, there was the other picture of youth, and freshness, and loveliness, and he saw his future wife a young queen away in that lovely and beautiful home amidst the snows. Which was it to be?

"And tell me, Ted," said the faded woman, in her old, blunt, matter-of-fact way, "was it that brought you back to Ireland after all these years?"

"Yes," he said, firmly. "As I told you, I had many and many an offer of marriage from millionaires in Montana and Nevada. I could have married the daughters of men who owned as much land as there is in all Ireland; I could have paved my floors with silver, and roofed my ceilings with gold. But no! That evening, there in the sunset, over in Ballinslea, was always before me. It came up before me many a night as I lay awake beneath the stars; I saw it facing me when I was tempted to evil in the saloons of 'Frisco and Mexico; it kept my faith alive, because I wanted to be able to meet my mother in the other world and to be able to ask you to be my wife in this; and now my time has come. My heart bleeds for you, Nora, and your little children. I can't bear to think of you, struggling along in such awful poverty, and I, who was never good enough for you, having everything that man's heart can covet in this world. If I go back without you I shall always be ashamed of my wealth. The picture of you and your children struggling against misery and poverty will be always coming up before me. Come with me, bring Tessie and Kathleen, and we'll be happier than even we could have been before!"

The second and more beautiful picture had now faded away.

Nora Leonard sat with hands folded tight in her lap. She was moved, deeply moved by the poor fellow's fidelity, but she was not a bit shaken in her determination.

"Do you remember, Ted," she said, firmly, "the reason you gave for not taking me with you twenty-five years ago?"

"I do," he said, "and though it broke my heart, I don't think I was wrong. I refused to take you with me because I could not ask you to share my shame and sorrow, or to reflect that shame and sorrow upon your family."

"And for much the same reason," she said, "I can't accept your offer now. I'd only be a burthen to you, and perhaps a shame, in these strange lands, and amongst strange people. I'm an old woman, worn out and faded from the trials of life, and I'm not fit to take the position you offer me. In a year or two you would tire of me ——"

"No! no!" he cried. "You don't know me. If I waited for you so long, how could I tire of you so soon?"

"It wasn't me you were waiting for," she said, "but some one whom you thought was me. It wasn't an old, broken-down woman that appeared to you in the camps and saloons of America, but the girl you left standing under the hawthorn the evening you left home forever!"

It was so humble, so candid, and so true, that he found himself admitting it, almost against his wish. And with the acknowledgment there sprang up such a sudden feeling of admiration for this brave woman, that he mentally resolved to blot out the other and brighter picture forever.

"As for our poverty," she said, "we have borne it now for so many years, it has become easy. Thank God! we want for nothing. We have enough to eat and drink, and if our clothes are not in the fashion, they are at least good and serviceable enough. And in a few months Tessie will be of age and we shall be able to claim the few pounds her father left."

"Tessie will be such an heiress then," said the Yank, "it will be hard to please her in a husband. Nora, she's so like you — like what you were long ago, that I went near saying to her, that first night I came into the shop what I have now said to you."

"Yes!" said the mother, musingly, "it was Tessie, whom you never saw, and not I, who has been haunting you all these years."

"She's a noble girl," he said, with a sigh. "Happy is the man who'll get her."

"She's but a child," said Nora.

"Well," he said, rising up and speaking with some bitterness, "there's one good done. The breed of the informer will die out, and forever!"

One evening soon after, as the summer days were closing in, Kathleen sat in a *sugan* chair in Mrs. Murphy's back parlour. Thade Murphy sat over against her, calmly smoking and occasionally taking the pipe from his mouth to utter some comment on what she was reading. After one such observation, he suddenly said:—

"Close that book, Katty, and listen to what I'm goin' to say to you this blessed night!"

He had always something so important to divulge, and he always spoke in so oracular a manner, that Kathleen was not too much surprised. But she closed her book and listened.

"There was wan class of Irishmen that you never hard me spake of," said Thade, "partly because I wouldn't dirty my mouth wid them, and partly because no dacent writer iver mintions them; but I must spake of 'em now. Can you guess what I mane?"

Kathleen guessed MacMorrogh, and O'Brien of the Burnings, and the clan that met the Munstermen returning from Clontarf, and would have annihilated them. She also guessed at the shadowy Danaan, and then came down to every barrister who took place and power from Ireland's enemies.

"No!" said Thade. "You have mintioned a bad lot enough. But you haven't sthruck on the worst a-yet."

"Apostates!" shouted Kathleen. "They who have abandoned their country and their God!"

"You're near it," he said, "but you haven't hit it yet."

There was deep silence, Katty pondering over the fire and trying to conjecture what lower depth of infamy there could be.

The old man rose up, and he was very tall on his feet, and stooping over to where the voice of the girl directed him, he said, or rather hissed, in a tragic voice: —

"In-form-ers!"

Then resuming his seat, he said more calmly, but still oracularly: —

"There may be a hope for these misfortunate, mis-guided min, who have dirtied their hands with English gold; and I am not the wan to say that even a Souper may not have a chance. Some people are now getting so tindher-hearted that they'll sind Turk, Jew, and Atheist, to heaven. But no wan ever in his right sinses could forgive an informer. We have forgot Keogh, and Scorpion Sullivan, and the rest of their dirty thribe, but we haven't forgot, though we never mintion their names, a Corydon, a Nagle, or a Carey!"

After this burst, the old man, whose white, sightless eyes seemed starting from their sockets, subsided into momentary silence. But it was but the pause between the thunderclaps. Standing up again, and leaning over towards the girl, who was drinking in his fierce spirit, he said: —

"To quote the words of a man who didn't know what he was talking about at the time: 'Hell isn't hot enough nor eternity long enough' for thim!"

Kathleen was almost frightened, but she shared these sentiments so fully that her indignation conquered her terror.

After another long spell the old man said again: —

"Do you think that you understhand all that I mane by thim words, a *girsha ?*"

"I — I think I do," said, or rather stammered, Kathleen.

"Thin," said the old man, reaching the grand climax of his revelations, "you must know that you have wan of thim reptiles benathe your own roof."

If he had told the girl that Satan was in her house, under the disguise of a wildcat, or that there was a familiar ghost haunting the garret under the roof, she could not have been more surprised and shocked. She sat speechless, not knowing what to think, and awaiting further revelations. The old man, rightly interpreting her silence, said at length: —

"Is there a returned American, called Casey, frayquentin' yer house these nights?"

She was obliged to say "Yes!"

"What brings him there, d'ye think?"

Kathleen couldn't conjecture, but thought from appearances that mother and he appeared to be old friends.

"They were," he said, significantly. "But he wants to be closer than frinds now."

Kathleen couldn't understand.

"No wandher," he said; "you're young an' innicent, and don't know the shlippery ways of the wurruld. Had you anny conversation wid him yerself?"

"Not much," she said. "But I pitched into him and all his old Irish-Americans for dragging away the people from their own motherland, just when she wants them most."

"Put the hand there," he said, stretching out his hard first. "You'll save yer counthry a-yet. Good God! a hundred girls like you would do what we failed to do."

"I did," said Kathleen, now quite excited with the flattery, "and I told him they were all over there only recruiting sergeants for England!"

"Good again!" said the old man. "Now listen. About eighty years ago, in the time of the Whiteboys, twinty-wan as dacent min as this parish ever produced were arrested by the yeomen (Hell's fire to them, with their pitch-caps and thriangles) and carried up to Cork Gaol to be tried for their lives. They wor as innicent as you are this moment, but their innimies wanted blood, blood, an' they should have it. There was no case agin them, but the Crown never yet in

Ireland wanted matayriels for a case, so long as they could get ruffians to swear black was white fur their dirty gold. And there wor plinty of them. O'Connell saved the lives of the misfortunate min. I never thought much of O'Connell. He got his chance for Ireland and he threw it away. If that day at Clontarf he had only said the wurrd! But he thought, bad-cess to him, that the whole counthry's freedom wasn't worth a drop of blood. He was a thrator, but he didn't know it, and we must give the divil his due. He saved the lives of these min. But no thanks to the Judges, the Juries, the Prosecutors, laste of all the Informers, who swore up to the mark, wurrd by wurrd, what they were taught, and for which they got their divil's airnings, the blood-money of dacent min."

He paused for breath before the grand revelation.

"They left their counthry and wandhered like Cain, wagabones, over the face of the airth. But they left their spawn, the spawn of reptiles, behind them. Wan of thim, the chief wan, the ringlayder, the spokes-man, was called Cloumper Daly, and Cloumper Daly's grandson is the Terence Casey who is now frayquenting your house and wants to marry your mother!"

The thing seemed so horrible that the girl could not speak. She looked curiously at the old man to see were his wits wandering, for he often said he was getting into his second childhood. But she had never found him tripping hitherto. He had day and date for everything. Even when he communicated to her, under awful vows of secrecy, the exact place in Old-

court graveyard where they had buried, with many
rites and prayers, a coffin full of rifle-barrels and
cartridges, well greased and protected against the damp
with oiled silk, she found she could trust him, although
it nearly cost her her life to keep closed lips on the
secret. But this revelation was so unutterable and
unthinkable that she could not speak. He misunder-
stood her silence.

"I dare say," he said, in that old cutting, ironical
way with which he always spoke of his enemies, "ye'll
all get a rise in the world now. They say he has
plinty of goold dollars, an' as much land as you couldn't
walk in a mont'. An' sure, 'tisn't I that should be
sorry for yere uprise. Ye have suffered poverty
enough, God knows! But thin, ye always kept a
dacent name. At laste, I never hard of a Curtin of a
Linnard brought to shame a-yet. And shure, afther
all, a dacent name with poverty is better than a dirthy
name wit' all the goold of Californy. But that's
nayther here or there! The ould times are gone, an'
the ould dacency wid thim. There's nothin' now but
munny, munny; and shure it would be well becomin'
of me to begrudge it to ye!"

Every word cut like a knife into the mind of the
sensitive and passionate girl. She began to see before
her nothing but ignominy and disgrace. At last, in a
paroxysm of anger and shame she said:—

"What shall I do? Tell me, oh, what shall I do?
We can never lift our heads again!"

"You'll get used to it," said the old man, with savage

irony, "when ye're over there in yere grand house, or rowlin' about in yer carridge and pair, ye'll forget all the ould honour and repittation of yere race and family. But ye'll have to change yere name. You'll be Miss Casey, *inagh*, or perhaps they'll call ye afther yere grandfather, Daly, the informer. Miss Kathleen Daly! Well sure, nobody will know ye at all. But," he added with a sudden thrust, "yere father will turrun in his grave!"

CHAPTER XXVIII

ACCEPTED

"Look here," I said, a few days after to the Yank, "you won't mind my saying a little word to you?"

"Not in the least, Father," he said, looking surprised.

"Well, I'd advise you to bring that matter to an issue, one way or the other. There's a good deal of talk in the town. You have been noticed visiting that house and there are tongues wagging, I can tell you!"

"People will talk," he said, standing on the defensive. "And for real, downright gossips, commend me to an Irish village. One would suppose that Nora Curtin would escape if anyone could."

"It isn't Nora," I exclaimed. "You forget there is a younger and more attractive figure than Nora there, and, to tell you the truth, and to be very candid, I don't like to hear Tessie Leonard's name in the people's mouths. I baptized her, I gave her her first Communion, I know she is the best and holiest child in the Universe, and I assure you, my dear friend, that I am awfully grieved to hear her name mentioned with yours, especially as there can be nothing in it."

"The old objection?" he said, sadly. "I knew it would follow me to my grave!"

"No," I replied, "I cannot say that it is. At least,

I am not aware of anyone that knows, or has spoken of that matter. As I told you, the thing is dead and buried. But why don't you speak to Nora and settle matters, once and forever?"

"I have spoken," he said, dejectedly.

"Well, 'tis all right, I hope?"

"No, 'tis all wrong," he replied. "My journey of six thousand miles is gone for nothing. She refused me!"

And he told me all that had occurred.

"Well, there's no accounting for tastes," I replied. "But I am genuinely sorry for you and more sorry for her. What in the world possessed her to refuse such an offer, and from so old a friend?"

"The very same pride that made me refuse her," he replied. "She's afraid she would bring shame on me away in the back-woods of America, and that I would tire of her."

"But you did see a great change?" I repeated.

"Yes, a great change! But that didn't make one hand's-breath of a difference. I came to make her my wife, and that I would have done, and never repented of it, if she had only consented."

"God help her now!" I murmured. "But your duty, my dear Terence, is plain. You have acted a brave, manly part. You can do no more. But for the reasons I have alleged, I would go back to Wyoming as soon as possible, if I were you!"

"I'll take your advice, Father," he said, humbly. "But it is hard to have waited all these years for nothing. I'll call and say good-bye to-night and leave to-morrow for Cork or Queenstown."

Just as it was dark, Terence Casey issued from the door of his hotel, and turned the corner to Mrs. Leonard's. His heart was heavy. The dream of his life was over forever. He would return to America a lonely man, and he would have the mortification of seeing all his wealth lying around him with no one to enjoy it or inherit it after him. The pursuit of wealth is hard, the enjoyment of it bitter, he thought. Would it not be better for him a thousand times to have been a poor day labourer with some place he could call a home, and all the tender associations connected with that word? He was half angry, too, with Nora. She was unreasonable, proud, sensitive. He thought he had only to say the word, fling his gold at her feet, and she was his forever. But no! A cold refusal was all he got. These Irish are as proud as the devil, he thought. Well, thank God, one thing is settled and done with forever. Not a whisper has been breathed of his parentage or descent. He has been disappointed where he was most certain of success. What he most feared is exorcised forever. The people have changed a good deal, he thought. They are getting short memories, and so much the better. Nevertheless, his heart was heavy as he stepped on to the earthen floor of the little shop.

He was arrested on the very threshold by the sound of voices in angry altercation in the parlour. There was no one in the wretched shop, and the parlour door was partly opened, but the white muslin screen effectually cut off all view both from within and without. He listened for a moment. Then, thinking it was some neighbouring scold who had come in to exercise her vocabulary about a frightened hen, or a whipped child, he was about to retire into the street and wait, when he heard his own name mentioned and in not too complimentary a manner. The speaker was Kathleen.

"I was never disobedient or disrespectful to you, mother," she was saying. "But it was a bitter day for us when this man came to disturb us. I never liked him from the moment I put my eyes upon him. And now here's the whole town talking about us."

"And what have they to say against us?" said Tessie, with an unusual tone of determination. "If a gentleman ——"

"A — what?" said Kathleen, contemptuously.

"A gentleman, I said," retorted Tessie.

"Then, as usual, you don't know what you're talking about," said Kathleen.

"'Sh, girls," said the mother, anxiously. "You're both young and you know nothing of the world. You'd better leave these things alone."

"I didn't start the conversation, mother," said Tessie. "But Katty thinks the whole world is watching her and is growing interested in her."

"I think nothing of the kind, Miss," said Kathleen. "I'm not speaking of myself at all, at all. I'm only telling what the whole town is talking about."

"And let them talk," said her mother. "What have they to say?"

"Enough to bring shame and sorrow upon us forever," replied Kathleen. "I'd rather beg my bread from door to door than to see that Casey come in here."

"Come in here?" said Tessie. "What are you talking about, Katty? You're taking leave of your senses."

"I'm not taking leave of my senses," said Kathleen. "I say the whole town is talking of that man coming around here, and, — if I must say it, I must, but ye have dragged it out of me, — of marrying you, mother!"

"Shame, Kathleen," said Tessie, reprovingly. "You ought to make that a cause of confession. You have insulted your mother shamefully."

"Let her alone, Tessie," said her mother, resignedly. "She means no harm. But it may be a comfort for you to know, Katty, that I have no notion of ever marrying Terence Casey, or anybody else."

"I knew it!" said Kathleen, exultingly. "But I'd rather see you dead, mother, than marry him."

"Why?" said her mother, coldly. "What do you know about Terence Casey?"

"What do I know, mother? What everybody knows — that he is the son of an informer!"

"Who told you that?" said her mother. "I suppose that old blind lunatic over the way, who is filling your head with all these notions! But he's wrong this time. Terence Casey is not the son of an informer. He's the son of Redmond Casey, of Ballinslea, as decent a man as ever lived."

"Then he's a grandson," said Kathleen, feeling herself defeated.

"That's ancient history," said her mother. "All I know is that he came here, across the whole of America, and across the Atlantic, to lift us out of poverty and misery and to give us a comfortable home forever."

"Then I'm glad you didn't take it, mother," said Kathleen. "Better poverty and hunger than shame and disgrace."

"You're so full of conceit that you don't know what you're talking about," said Tessie, angrily. "For my part, I think it a noble and honourable thing that Mr. Casey should have remembered mother so long and tried to befriend her in the end. That covers up every family failing, which, thank God, no one minds now. We haven't so much to boast of ourselves."

"That's a reflection on my father," said Kathleen, bridling up. "No one heard of a Leonard disgracing himself."

"And where has Terence Casey disgraced himself?" Tessie asked. "Is it a disgrace for a man to build up a fortune in America and then come back to ask the friend of his youth to share it?"

"You're so hot over the matter one would think you were wishing to share it yourself!" said Kathleen.

"What if I were? I see no shame in that."

"Do you mean to say that you'd accept as a husband the son, or grandson, of an informer?"

"I'd think of the man himself, not of his ancestors," said Tessie.

"And you'd accept him with all the ignominy and disgrace in the eyes of the people?"

"There is no ignominy or disgrace except in what we do ourselves," said Tessie. "Almighty God will never ask us what our grandfathers did or didn't. If I knew Terence Casey to be otherwise a decent man, and a good, practical Catholic, what his grandfather or great-grandfather was wouldn't stand in my way. And there must be something unusual about a man who remembered his early affection for mother after so many years."

"I'm saying nothing against the man himself. But if his grandfather swore away the lives of honest men ——"

"Even so," said Tessie, impatiently. "There, let us end the subject. It doesn't concern us."

"Whatever you like. I didn't start it," said Kathleen.

"Not yet!" said Terence Casey, opening wide the little glass door and standing in the room. "I overheard, very unwillingly, every word, or nearly every word, you have said, Nora, and you, Tessie, and you, Kathleen. I knocked several times and could get no answer. I came to say good-bye to you all, but I little suspected that I should hear in your house, Nora, and from your child, that same dreadful charge that drove me to America a quarter of a century ago, and has been haunting me like a spectre since. I was assured it was dead and forgotten here, but we can never know ——"

"I meant nothing against you, Mr. Casey," said Kathleen, "but listeners seldom hear good of themselves."

"But they may hear the truth sometimes," he said in a broken way, "even though it be not pleasant. It is quite true that my grandfather was — well, an informer," he gulped down the word, "but God knows! I and my poor mother have more than atoned for his crime, if banishment, and sorrow, and all men's hands against us, can be thought sufficient punishment. Twenty-five years ago I refused your mother's generous offer to share my shame and go with me to the world's end. 'Twas a foolish sentiment that made me part with what would have been the greatest blessing of my life. And many and many a time, when I heard of her trials and struggles here, I bitterly reproached myself for having brought such sorrow on a woman who loved me and whom I loved. May God forgive our pride! It is the worst inheritance we have got. It is the cause of all the heart-breakings and desolation of the world. Well, I leave town to-morrow, and Ireland in about four weeks. I would have remained longer, but I am informed that the gossips here at home have been coupling my name with the family in a way I never could dream of, nor hope for ——"

"Don't say that, Ted," said Mrs. Leonard. "It is what you were dreaming of all your life."

"You don't understand me, Nora," he said. "It

was you were the dream of my life, but the people think otherwise."

"And the people are right," said Nora. "What you were dreaming about is the girl you left on that Monday evening under the hawthorn at Ballinslea."

"And that was you," said Casey, in bewilderment.

"It was not," said Mrs. Leonard. "Look at me and look at Tessie there, and say are the people right or wrong?"

"Mother!" cried Tessie, rising up, her face red with blushes at the sudden revelation.

Terence Casey stood transfixed. He had to admit that this was the picture that was ever overshadowing the old, faded one, and that now looked so perfect and beautiful a contrast. He felt that all along he had been a traitor to his old ideal, but he argued that he had done nothing but what was honourable and just. Could it be, that just as he heard what he least expected here in this humble home — the reproach and shame of his long life, he should also hear the words that were to make his happiness forever? Something whispered: This is your life's chance, seize it! And he did.

"Tessie," he said, with great gentleness and deference, "your mother has said something I could never bring myself to utter. I will not say whether she is right or wrong. Neither shall I take an unfair advantage of your words, which I overheard at the door. But this is truth, God's truth! All my life long I have been anxious to link myself with your family.

One disappointment has arisen after another to prevent it. If now my hope, my ambition, the dearest desire of my heart is to be fulfilled, and if you, who are so far above me, are to be the link, I should think all my sad life crowned by a supreme beatitude. But I shall not deny what your mother says, neither shall I take an unworthy advantage of your generous defence and still more generous determination. But if, on consideration, you will not recall your words, then I shall have reaped, after all these years, almost more than I expected or desired. In a word, I ask you to be my wife. Will you?"

Tessie was silently weeping. Kathleen was studying her closely and critically.

"Mother, what shall I say?" said the weeping girl.

"Whatever you please, child," said the mother.

"I'll do what you wish, mother, and nothing else," said Tessie.

Mrs. Leonard rose up and said, not without emotion:—

"As I said, I leave you perfectly free, Tessie; but there is no man in the world I'd rather see you married to than Terence Casey. But she is very young, Ted, and will not be of age till twelve months more or so. Can you wait?"

"Yes, and longer, if I have her promise!"

"Speak, Tessie!" said her mother.

"Yes, mother, since you wish it," said the girl.

Quite gay from the sudden revulsion from despair and gloom, Terence Casey turned to Kathleen.

"Will you forbid the banns?" he said.

"No! but I wouldn't marry you," she said, with flashing eyes.

"It makes no matter now," he said, gaily. "I live near Salt Lake City, but I am not a Mormon! And now good-bye! This day twelve months I return to claim the fulfilment of your promise!"

CHAPTER XXIX

FROM LAKE SHOSHONE

THERE was a good deal of variety of opinion amongst the neighbours about the propriety of this engagement and the risks and possibilities that might accrue from it. And the opinions, as indeed all human thought and action, were formed and coloured and biassed by vanity, or jealousy, or hope, or charity.

"He's ould enough to be her grandfather," said one.

"People will do anything for money," said another.

"Wisha, wasn't it quare," said a third, "that a man who was coortin' the mother should marry the daughter?"

"She's as good a girl as ever walked in shoe leather," said a fourth. "She deserves the best husband that God could give her."

"Yes, to be sure," echoed another. "But how do we know but he has three or four wives in America? They do quare things over there, whin they're away from the eyes of the people."

"Oh, the priest will see to that," said a neighbour. "The Yank will have to make an Affidavy, or somethin', besides presintin' letters from every parish-priest he ever lived under."

"Yerra, whisht, 'uman, sure there are no parish-priests over there. They're all cojutors. And, sure, that same would be the big job for wan who was here, there, and everywhere, as the fit took him."

"They say he has lashins of money. He don't know what to do with it."

"Well, they deserve their uprise, as hones' and dacent a family as ever was raised in the parish."

So human opinion ranges, and sometimes it was pleasant to hear and sometimes the reverse.

Tessie herself, poor child, had to pass through a severe ordeal. Between congratulations, warnings, hopes for the future, doubts, speculations, she didn't know what to think.

"Sure, we're all glad of your uprise, Miss Tessie! You always had the kind word for the poor, and — the kind deed, if God gave it to you!"

"Wisha, sure we hope, Miss, that you're not goin' away altogether. Sure, 'tis a wild place out and out, wid snow on the ground nine months of the year, and wind that would blow you to the back of God-speed. Can't he lave you here wid us, and come to see you sometimes?"

"We're glad to hear the good news, Miss Tessie, but look before you a bit, agragal. I wanse knew a Yankee fellow, like Casey, who came over here, and inticed a poor, raw, innicent girl like yourself to go wid him. Sure, whin she wint over, he lef' her, standin' wid her fingers in her mout', on the sthreets of New York. An' she soon found that he had a wife or two in every State in America."

"I hope you won't forget us, Miss, whin you go over

there. There's my little Ellie now. She'd be the fine maid for you! You could train her yourself, for she's apt to larn, and a claner or a betther little girl there isn't in Ireland."

"Wisha, I wandher, Miss, would your husband lind us a few pounds? If I could buy the little pig now, she'd be fit to kill about Aysther, and 'tis a pity, out and out, to see all the pratie-skins and cabbage thrown out for nothin'."

Not a word was ever whispered about Terence Casey's parentage. The old had forgotten it, the young were indifferent to it, in their enthusiasm about the great athlete of the ballad and the song. It was only in the dark recesses of Thade Murphy's kitchen that terrible things were said, and dark forebodings about the future were oracularly uttered.

"I nivver thought that a Linnard would sell herself, body and soul, for goold," Thade would say. "But the wurruld is changing every day. What was it that you said to him, Katty? Repate it for me, wurrd by wurrd!"

"I told him," Kathleen would say with pride, "that I wouldn't marry him, not if he had all the gold in California, nor all the diamonds in the Queen's crown. There's something better than either in the world, and with that we won't part."

"I never doubted you, *m'ainim me shtig*," the old man would reply. "And, believe you me, and believe you me agin, your poor sisther will have raison to repint her bargain. You can't get blood out of a turnip, nor dacency from an informer. But what do the people be sayin', achorra?"

"Some one thing, and some another," Katty would reply. "No one thinks that any good will come of it."

"And how does she feel herself?" he asked.

"I think she's sorry enough for her bargain already," Kathleen would answer, anxious to justify herself to her own conscience. "She'd get out of it now if she could."

This was not strictly true, but it had some little foundation, for the poor girl was so harassed by questions, forebodings, prophecies, omens, and requests. that she grew paler and thinner than she had been And at last she came to me to write and say all was at an end and to get Terence to break his engagement.

"I shall do nothing of the kind," I said, "for any old women's gossip that may be floating around. People will talk, must talk, or they'll burst, and that would be a catastrophe. But unless you yourself are sorry, or that you dislike him, or that some other more serious impediment arises, you'll take the good fortune that God sent you and be grateful for it. Is that your mother's opinion?"

"It is," she said, drying her tears. "She ridicules all this gossip. But ——"

"But what?"

"How are we to know that he is not deceiving us? People change so much when they go abroad!"

"If you mean that he has, or may have, other ties abroad," I replied, "you may leave all that in my hands. I'm bound to see after all that before I put the ring on your finger. But do you think that a man would come over twice three thousand miles to marry an old, faded woman, whom he loved long ago, if he weren't a good man?"

"N — no!" she said. "And I know 'tis wrong to harbour such suspicions, but when people are dinning them into your ears morning, noon, and night, they make an impression."

"They're certainly making an impression on you," I said. "If you go on fretting as you are, and pulling yourself down, you'll be as gray as myself, when Terence comes back, and maybe he'll he thinking of a good excuse to get rid of a white-haired, lanthorn-jawed, oldish-young lady!"

There's nothing like touching people on the quick, that is, appealing to the weak point, where they are most sensitive, to bring them to their senses. There's a certain luxury in allowing ourselves to be argued into doing what our inclinations suggest. We like to be persuaded, not against, but according to our will. But that little appeal to human vanity put an end to argument. I heard no more of these scruples.

The wheel of time dipped into the depths of winter and rose up into spring and summer, almost with a rush, so swift is the revolution, so rapid the cycle of seasons and times. The eventful day was at hand. I had settled all scruples, removed all impediments, and there remained only the academical question, would they be married in Cork or at home, and would

Kathleen act as bridesmaid to her sister? On the first question I put down my foot firmly. They should be married in the church of their baptism, their first confession and Communion and confirmation, and nowhere else. I was not going to give in to these new-fangled notions of city weddings with cold, icy déjeuners at hotels, etc. On the second point there was trouble enough until we arranged that the young Joan of Arc would not be asked to take hand, act, or part in an unpatriotic marriage; and after a while, when the young lady found that the world would go around as usual and that even the marriage would take place with a certain amount of éclat, even though not graced with her presence, she was glad enough to be asked. And so at last the eventful day came round.

We'd have beaten Ballypooreen hollow, only that Tessie implored, with tears in her eyes, that, as we insisted on her being married at home, it should be at least as quiet as possible. Terence had given *carte blanche* to the hotel proprietor to make the material jollification as profuse and perfect as possible. And like a sensible fellow, our host took the ball at the hop. That long table, running the entire length of the coffee-room, was simply dazzling. Such cold meats, garnished with all kinds of frills and fandangoes, such translucent jellies, such pies and puddings and tarts and confectionery, such gorgeous pyramids of fruit, great pineapples, and purple and green grapes, and bananas, and yellow oranges; and, loading the sideboard, such gold-necked bottles of the "foaming wine of Eastern France," as I took care to mention in my speech, were never seen before.

Sam was in his element. He brought in every farmer and every farmer's wife whom he saw passing the hotel windows, and who were to be the guests, to exhibit his great triumph. Nay, even the labourers' wives and daughters, who came in to town in their little donkey-carts to make their cheap and humble purchases, were all brought in to admire this magnificent display of culinary and other sciences. And I am afraid many poor mouths, accustomed to plainer fare, watered at the sight of such tremendous and appetizing viands. I gave him all credit for his industry and skill. He modestly disclaimed the honour, and placed it all to the credit of Terence Casey.

"Look here, yer Reverence," he said, flicking off invisible crumbs from the spotless tablecloth, "I ought to know a gintleman by this time. And Misther Casey *is* a gintleman. They comes here, all kinds and sorts of people, commercial thravellers, ginthry for the fishin', agents gethering rints, bad — to thim, but I tell you what, yer Reverence," he flung the napkin on his arm and struck an attitude, "*tisn't everywan that wears yallow boots that's a gintleman.*"

"How do you distinguish them, Sam?" I asked. "I ask for information because every time I see the tanned boots, especially if there are yellow gaiters above them, I feel an inclination to take off my hat."

"Lord bless yer Reverence," said Sam, compassionately, "if you knew all I know. Thim's the fellahs that 'ud split a sixpence to giv' me a thruppenny bit; an' thim's the same fellahs that giv' all the throuble. 'Here, you sir! There, you sir! Waitah, this chap's underdone! Waitah, this stake is burned! Hot wather in me room at six o'clock in the mornin'! Hot wather in me room an' a hot bawth before dinner!' They'd make a saint curse, begobs, an' I'm not much in that way ——"

"No matter, Sam," I said, "you will be yet, if you have patience and eschew lemonade ——"

"But as I was sayin', yer Reverence," said Sam, unheeding the interruption, "Misther Casey is different from all that. He's as quiet about the house as a child. He washes himself wance a day, which is as much as any Christian wants; and he sez, as soft as a woman, an' softer than a good many av them, as I know to me sorra, 'Sam, wud you be kind enough to do this?' 'Sam, wud it be too much throuble to do that?' and *he* won't be hairsplitting. 'Keep that change, Sam, and buy tobaccy!' or 'Take that home to the ould 'uman, Sam!' Ah, yer Reverence, I knows a gintleman whin I sees him, and Misther Casey *is* a gintleman!"

"Well, he's getting his reward," I said, tentatively, "he's getting as good a wife as there is between the four seas of Ireland."

"She is indeed, yer Reverence," replied Sam, somewhat dubiously, I thought. "Av coorse he could do betther for himself, and get as much munny as he cared to ask for. But she's a nice, clane girl, an' sure she's wan of oursel's."

"Sam!" said I.

"Yes, yer Reverence!" said Sam.

"This wedding is an important matter; the whole parish, I am told, will be asked here. I hope that you will do yourself credit ——"

"Is it me, yer Reverence?" said Sam, as if this innocent remark implied something.

"I know," I said, unheeding, "that you are an awfully good fellow, but this will be a day of great temptation. And Mr. Casey will be extremely anxious to have everything correct and respectable. And wouldn't it be a pity," I continued, looking around admiringly, "if with such a magnificent and superb display anything should occur to mar the honour and glory of the parish, and even of the country?"

"Begobs, it would, yer Reverence," said Sam, humbly. "Here! I'll take the pledge for life, in the name o' God!"

He knelt down and I gave him the pledge till the day after the wedding.

Terence Casey duly arrived, examined all these details, approved of them, and looked the happy man he felt. Tessie wanted to walk to the church in her own simple, modest way, like every other girl in the parish. He wouldn't listen to it. He had a gorgeous equipage with two horses over from Mallow, and two outriders. I think it was these last that made Tessie faint. At least, she had a little weakness just before they started for the church, but swiftly recovered, and never looked better. What did she wear? Well, I give that up. I draw the line there. The French would bother me entirely. But I know she had a ring that looked as if it would light the firmament of heaven if all the stars were quenched. And, tell it not in Gath! The fierce, uncompromising little rebel, who did condescend to act as bridesmaid to her sister, did wear and exhibit without a pang of shame — well, no! I must not tell it. Thade Murphy is alive yet. Swiftly the ceremony concluded, silently and swiftly the holy Mass, that binds all Catholic hearts together from the "rising of the sun to the going down of the same," was celebrated; swiftly the registers were signed, and then, Kathleen — shall I tell it? Yes, I will, to her credit — did kiss her brother-in-law; and in that little act of condescension did blot out the painful memory of that unhappy heritage of shame that had haunted the lives of Nodlag and her child.

Who was at the wedding? Everybody. And everybody was not only in excellent humour, but felt a share of the exuberant happiness of the bridegroom and the bride. 'Tis a little way of our own we have in Ireland, to try and kick the ladder from under a fellow-countryman who wants to get to the pinnacle of things, careless whether we kill him or maim him for life. But when he comes out safe overhead we all wave our hats and say Huzza! And so, on this day, there were none but good wishes for the happy pair; the memories of the past were all subdued and hallowed and the forecasts

of the future were sunny and golden. Why will poor
human nature be always manifesting its worst and
darkest features, when the bright, kindly, loving side
can be turned out as easily?"

To crown it all we had our traditional Irish bard
in a glorious ballad-singer, who, just outside the hotel
window, not only revived the great epic of the past,
but adapted it to the present. At least, I presumed
so from the first verse which is all I am privileged to
remember: —

> Come, all ye lads and lasses,
> And ye bould, brave gallowglasses
> Come, listen to the sthory,
> That I'm going to tell to ye.
>
> 'Tis all about the rover,
> The gay and gallant lover,
> Terence Casey, the great hurler
> From the hills of Ballinslea.

I have a dim recollection, broken, however, by the
clinking of glasses and the rattle of knives and forks
and the tumultuous jokes and laughter of happy
people, that Tessie was compared to Vaynus and
Nicodaymus, and was pronounced to be the most
gifted young lady, so far as personal attractions were
concerned, to be found in the Green Isle — and that
is a big word! And so the fun waxed fast and furious,
and speeches were made and songs were sung, until
the inevitable and inexorable hand pointed to the hour,
and the young, happy couple had to drive to meet the
Mail at Mallow, *en route* to Paris, if you please. Yes,

nothing else would satisfy Terence. Tessie suggested Killarney, but he put it aside contemptuously. It should be the gay capital and nothing else.

There was just one figure wanting from all the gaiety — the little, faded figure that had once shone so bright to Terence's eyes there on that summer evening beneath the hawthorn at Ballinslea. She stayed at home with her beads, praying for her child. And when people chaffed her about all the good things she was losing, she said that she preferred her little brown teapot to all the luxuries they could provide. There was a swift, brief, loving parting, when Tessie came back to change her dress. I am afraid Kathleen forswore all her principles, won over by the goodness and kindness of her brother-in-law. At least, the hated words, "son of an informer," never again crossed her lips and never again smote on his heart.

A few weeks more and Terence and his bride were settled down in his beautiful home near Lake Shoshone. He used every entreaty to induce Nora and Kathleen to come with them. But Nora, clinging to old customs, preferred the little shop, the little parlour, the quiet spot in the church, and her little brown teapot to all the splendours of brownstone mansions by picturesque lakes. Besides, there is a probability that Tessie's exile will be a brief one. The glamour and charm of Ireland, the witchery of her scenery, the old links and associations so pleasantly revived, the home feeling, the kindly hearts and willing hands, have made

an impression on Terence Casey. The *heimweh* is
upon him, and I have got a notion that he is yearning
for a spirited game in the old fields, where he might
use the silver-mounted hurley, or caman, presented to
him by the local skirmishers on the occasion of his
marriage. Some day, if chance arises, he will sell out
his ranch and mansion and buy some little cosey nest,
down near some storied, singing river in the old land.
That's what we want. The old order changeth! The
land of Ireland is passing into Irish hands once more.
And the many deserted mansions here and there
throughout Ireland, and the many ruined castles, stare
from their gaping windows across the sea, and seem
to say to the exiled Gaels: —

"Come back! Come back! Back to the land of
your fathers! Let us hear once more the sound of the
soft Gaelic in our halls; the laughter of your children
beneath our roofs, the skirl of the bagpipe and the
tinkle of the harp in our courts, the shout of our young
men in the meadows by the river, the old, heart-break-
ing songs from the fields, the *seanchus* here where our
broken windows stare upon weed-covered lawns. Come
back! Come back! The days are dark and short
since ye went; there is no sunshine on Ireland, and the
nights are long and dismal! And there in the moonlit
Abbey by the river rest the bones of your kindred!
Their unquiet spirits haunt every mansion and cottage
and the wail of their Banshee is over the fields and up
along the hills! They shall never rest in peace till
your shadows sweep across their tombs and your
prayers, like the night winds, stir the ivy on the crum-
bling walls!"

Other books from The O'Brien Press

Pictorial Ireland
Yearbook and Appointments Diary
Superb full colour photographs of Ireland's wonderful
landscapes, towns, people. Each year a new diary, available
every summer in advance. *Wiro bound £6.95.*

Irish Life and Traditions
Ed. Sharon Gmelch
Visions of contemporary Ireland from some of its most
well-known commentators — Maeve Binchy, Nell McCaf-
ferty, Seán Mac Réamoinn, Seán MacBride. Deals with nature, cities, prehistory, growing up in Ireland (from the
1890s in Clare to the 1960s in Derry), sports, fairs, festivals,
words spoken and sung. 256 pages, 200 photos.
£6.95 paperback.

Old Days Old Ways
Olive Sharkey
Entertaining and informative illustrated folk history, re-
counting the old way of life in the home and on the land.
Full of charm. *£5.95 paperback.*

Kerry
Des Lavelle and Richard Haughton
The landscape, legends, history and people of a beautiful
county. Stunning full colour photographs. *£5.95 paperback.*

Sligo
Land of Yeats' Desire
John Cowell
An evocative account of the history, literature, folklore and
landscapes, with eight guided tours of the city and county,
from one who spent his childhood days in the Yeats
country in the early years of this century. Illustrated. *£14.95
hardback.*

A Valley of Kings
THE BOYNE
Henry Boylan
An inspired guide to the myths, magic and literature of this beautiful valley with its mysterious 5000-year-old monuments at Newgrange. Illustrated. *£7.95 paperback.*

Traditional Irish Recipes
George L. Thomson
Handwritten in beautiful calligraphy, a collection of favourite recipes from the Irish tradition. *£3.95 paperback.*

Consumer Choice Guide to Restaurants in Ireland
With the Consumer Association of Ireland
About 300 restaurants assessed by consumers from all over the country. An essential guide for the traveller.
£4.95 paperback.

THE BLASKET ISLANDS — Next Parish America
Joan and Ray Stagles
The history, characters, social organisation, nature - all aspects of this most fascinating and historical of islands. Illustrated. *£7.95 paperback.*

SKELLIG — Island outpost of Europe
Des Lavelle
Probably Europe's strangest monument from the Early Christian era, this island, several miles out to sea, was the home of an early monastic settlement. Illustrated.
£7.95 paperback.

DUBLIN — One Thousand Years
Stephen Conlin
A short history of Dublin with unique full colour reconstruction drawings based on the latest research.
Hardback £9.95, paperback £5.95.

**Exploring the
BOOK OF KELLS**
George Otto Simms
For adult and child, this beautiful book tells when, how
and why the famous Book of Kells was made, and gives a
simple guide to its contents. Illustrated in colour and black
and white. *£6.95 hardback.*

Celtic Way of Life
The social and political life of the Celts of early Ireland. A
simple and popular history. Illustrated. *£3.95 paperback.*

**The Boyne Valley Book and Tape of
IRISH LEGENDS**
More than an hour of the very best stories from Irish myth-
ology read by some of Ireland's most famous names: Gay
Byrne, Cyril Cusack, Maureen Potter, John B. Keane, Rosa-
leen Linehan, Twink. Illustrated in full colour.
£6.95 (book and tape).

The Lucky Bag — Classic Irish Children's Stories
'Long stories, short stories - all good stories' - *The Irish
Times*. 204 pages of the best for children from Irish literature, with sensitive pencil drawings by Martin Gale.
£4.95 paperback.

*The above is a short selection from the O'Brien Press list. A full
list is available at bookshops throughout Ireland. All our books
can be purchased at bookshops countrywide. Prices are correct at
time of printing, but may change. If you require any information
or have difficulty in getting our books, contact us.*

THE O'BRIEN PRESS
20 Victoria Road, Rathgar, Dublin 6.
Tel. (01) 979598
Fax. (01) 979274